HEART AND STOMACH

OF A

QUEEN

Like time-travel?

Check out the Turning Points series
at jodielane.com

The Siege of Masada
Transylvanian Knight
To Kill An Emperor
Renaissance Woman
Heart and Stomach of a Queen

Turning Points Short Stories:

Siege of the Heart
The Time-Traveller's Date
A Soldier's Love

Like portal-travel?

Check out the Wanderer of Worlds series
at deliastrange.com

Axiom
Untethered
Transition
Genome
Husk
Façade
Backlash
Promises

HEART AND STOMACH OF A QUEEN

JODIE LANE

Heart and Stomach of a Queen
Copyright © 2019 Jodie Lane
Cover Design © 2019 1231 Publishing

The characters and events portrayed in this book are fictitious or are used fictitiously. Any similarity to real persons, living or dead, is purely coincidental and unintentional.

ISBN: 978-0-9946498-8-1

Published by Jodie Lane
www.jodielane.com

To Joey.

ACKNOWLEDGMENTS

Six years ago, I was embarrassed into becoming a writer, and I have never been so grateful for someone teasing me about my vague aspirations. Here I stand at the end of a five book series, and there are many people to thank for supporting me on this journey.

Carolyn, Rebecca, Alicia and Jess—your proofreading has been invaluable and I am so grateful. I'm so fortunate and grateful to have such a terrific group of critically-minded writers and readers upon which to draw. Scott and Alan from the North Lakes Writers Group—always appreciate your feedback, especially since you don't always get the full story!

Thank you Dee for editing and cover design for this book and the ones before, and of course Barb for proofreading. It so gratifying to hear you say how my writing has improved!

My friends and family—this series would not have been finished without your encouragement and support. I cannot thank you enough.

CHARACTERS

From modern-day Earth:

Gwyn Turner – accidental time-traveller from the twenty-first century
Stephen and Danielle Turner – Gwyn's parents
Naomi and Justin Turner – Gwyn's twin siblings

From the future:

Agent Michelle – Time-Space Agent from the twenty-seventh century
Brrrys – A Time-Space security officer, good friends with Michelle

From fifteenth century Spain:

Queen Isabella* – ruler of Castile and Leon
King Ferdinand* – ruler of Aragon, Valencia and Catalonia, disputed claim over the Kingdom of Naples in Italy
Princess Juana* – "the Mad." Second daughter of Isabella and Ferdinand
Princess Katherine* – third daughter of Isabella and Ferdinand (married Arthur Tudor, then Henry Tudor (King Henry VIII)

Isabel – a fifteenth century healer from a Basque village – daughter of a converted Jew
Rafael – a Castilian soldier, owes a lot of money
Diego – a Castilian soldier, helping Rafael pay back his debt

From elsewhere in Europe:

Prince Philip of Flanders* – "the Handsome." First son of Maximilian of Austria and the Holy Roman Empire and Margaret of Burgundy.
Cesare Borgia* – son of Pope Alexander VI, Duke of Valentinois
Meric – a friend of Gwyn and Michelle's, murdered by Cesare Borgia
King Charles I of Spain* – son of Juana and Philip
King Philip II* – son of Charles

*denotes real historical person

MAP OF SPAIN
under the reign of Isabella and Ferdinand, most Catholic Kings

One

2623 AD

The Shift is here. Owen shivered despite the warmth in the lab. He couldn't really call it a cell—it was larger than his last apartment—but the data displayed on the screen in front of him chilled him more surely than any prison could.

"Ah, Owen." Jaysen Fitz strolled into the lab. "We are in the process of making history, or unmaking it, as it were." He chuckled at his joke. Owen gave a wan smile.

"What… what happens now?" he asked.

Fitz hooked a stool with his foot and dragged it closer. The screech grated on Owen's nerves. Fitz sat, still smiling, his good mood a contrast to Owen's sense of dread. "Now? Nothing just yet. I don't understand all the particulars but my associates assure me that there are a number of turning points in the fifteenth and sixteenth centuries. Once the nexus on those closes on them history will be forever changed and *this* reality will fade away. Thanks to your own projections we have seeded people at appropriate times to… *guide* the future of humanity to a much more fitting destiny."

"Oh." What could Owen say to that? Trapped by these Earth First fanatics, he was dependent on their goodwill to live. Would they kill him now as they had threatened?

Fitz noticed Owen's discomfort and leant forward, clapping the smaller man on the shoulder. "Never fear, Owen! We still have use for you. My scientists are good but they aren't the best. Not like you. You must explain to me sometime how it all works—how the Shift doesn't change things immediately even though it's all in the past to us now."

"Um," Owen mumbled. *Even if I dumbed it down for you, your head would explode, you dirt-grubber.* He didn't dare say that. "It's to do with temporal displacement." Owen's gaze drifted back to his computer, the display of lights overlaid by a multi-coloured wave representing four dimensions. The lights represented turning points—they lay in a channel of blue light. He'd watched one light explode like a tiny sun going nova, shifting the course of the channel, but somehow it had shifted back. He had theorised during his time at the Agency that it would take several turning points to shift the course of history, particularly when they were relatively close to each other, as these were.

In the background, Fitz prattled on about humanity taking its rightful place as lords of the galaxy, with Earth at the centre of this glorious empire.

Owen stared glumly at the lights. Before the Agency had been enmeshed in scandal and all operations suspended, they had multiple Agents dealing with single turning points. This scatter was a temporal and geographical nightmare. How could anyone hope to fix all that?

As he watched, one of the lights winked out. Owen frowned. He checked another screen. His calculations showed the turning point had been there. Had it spontaneously resolved itself? It was possible.

"I'll leave you to it!" Fitz clapped him on the shoulder again. Owen nodded and tried not to look confused, swinging his eyes back to the computer as soon as the lab door locked.

Another turning point winked out. Owen dragged data from one screen to another, speaking algorithms into his self-designed program. He checked the result twice.

It wasn't an anomaly. Somewhere, in the fifteenth century, someone was repairing history.

* * *

1496 AD

"So that's the queen," Gwyn whispered, peering past the velvet curtain at the figure on the throne. "She looks… pissed off."

Michelle *tsked.* "She looks serious; something a queen ought to be. While I don't agree with her religious policies, she certainly is a formidable monarch. She's been at war for most of her adult life."

"Mm. Fair enough."

Michelle bit off her retort. A squabble would attract attention—they were disguised as men, pretending to be attachés with the Habsburg delegation from Emperor Maximilian of Austria and the Holy Roman Empire. Their mission was to ensure that betrothal between Juana of Castile and Philip of Flanders would take place. The firstborn son of Maximilian and Margaret of Burgundy, who had brought the Low Countries into her marriage as part of her dowry, Philip was set to inherit a significant portion of Europe. These negotiations allied the Houses of Castile and Aragon in Spain with the Habsburgs of Austria, and would form the basis for a worldwide Spanish empire.

Gwyn's lack of focus frustrated Michelle. This was not their first mission in Spain. In Tordesillas, whispers in the right ears had caused the Spanish and Portuguese ambassadors to agree on the division of the so-called "new world." Gwyn and Michelle had also intervened in the forcible expulsion of several Jewish families, diverting the attention of soldiers so the unfortunate exiles could leave intact.

This was their third turning point.

Queen Isabella continued speaking. "And in the event of my daughter's ascension to the throne of Castile?" She sat at the head of a long table, resting her hands on the carved lion heads that graced the armrests of her elegant wooden throne. An unfurled scroll lay before her, held open by jewelled weights.

"Her husband will become king *jure uxoris,* by right of his wife," the Hapsburg ambassador replied, his Dutch accent clipping the Latin vowels. Both queen and ambassador spoke Latin in order to dispense with interpreters. Michelle was ever-grateful for translation features of the chronokinetors that she and Gwyn wore.

"Not king consort," the queen said.

"No, majesty. The precedent of your own marriage is clear. Seeing that the Infanta is third in line, with God's blessing it won't be an issue."

At the mention of her marriage, Queen Isabella's lips grew taut. It was the source of quiet gossip that King Ferdinand hardly saw his wife anymore, preferring to campaign around the country and, it was whispered, grace the beds of various noblewomen.

"Very well. Speaking of my first heir, I am happy with all the details of his betrothal to Princess Margaret of Austria."

Gwyn swayed and clutched her head.

"Gwyn?" Michelle hissed. "Was that it?"

"Mmm." Gwyn staggered back from the curtain shielding them from the rest of the room. She lurched for the low servants' door and pushed past the guard out into the hall. Michelle hurriedly followed.

The guard caught her arm and steadied her. "Are you not well, señor?"

"My friend is feeling a little faint." Michelle switched to Castilian Spanish.

The guard nodded sagely. "The heat, it is too much for you northerners." He waited until Gwyn straightened before letting her go.

"Thanks," she gasped. "That was it, Michelle—the turning point. We're good now."

Michelle caught the look the guard gave Gwyn—a puzzled frown tinged with dawning comprehension—and she guessed Gwyn's nausea had rattled the girl's concentration and her disguise as a man was slipping. "We have to go. Thank you for your help!" She grabbed Gwyn by the arm and towed her down the hall.

"Keep it together," she muttered in Gwyn's ear.

"Yeah, yeah." Gwyn's face was pale but the sheen of sweat had faded. Once they reached the inner ward of the castle, they shared a sigh of relief.

"Good work." Michelle clapped Gwyn on the back. "That one hit you hard."

Gwyn nodded. "I know, right? I don't know if it was because we helped negotiate two marriages, not just one. It was a big one."

"Fascinating," Michelle murmured, shaking her head wistfully. "One day I'll find out how you do it."

They shared a moment of silence. A hawk wheeled above them in the cloudless sky, dark brown wings outstretched against the endless blue. Warm air drifted over stone walls, and Michelle breathed in the smell of the pomegranate flowers from the trees in the courtyard.

She glanced sideways at a frowning Gwyn. They had not spoken of what happened in Italy several months ago, but Michelle knew it haunted the girl. They worked well together now, but with none of the humour and camaraderie Gwyn had shared with Meric. "I miss him, too," Michelle said, bumping Gwyn's elbow with her own.

Gwyn's eyes lost their faraway look and she gave a brief smile. "I know. Alright, what's next? Back to town?"

Michelle nodded. "Yes." They left the castle and made their way down the road on foot. The walled town of Segovia clung to a hilltop surrounded by the plains of Castile. Michelle admired the view even as they discussed plans for their next mission.

"La Infanta Juana will enter her marriage by proxy this August in the city of Valladolid," Michelle told Gwyn. "We have to make sure she gets to the Netherlands safely to meet her husband, Philip. The data I have on the turning point is that bad weather, illness and a horse-riding accident all lead to her death."

"Bad weather?" Gwyn raised an eyebrow. "Don't tell me a storm is going to sink her ship."

"Lightning strike, actually."

"What? That's ridiculous!" Gwyn's exclamation drew a stare from a passing merchant.

"Keep your voice down," Michelle admonished. "Check the timeline yourself. I'm just going from the data I had from the Agency before I came back to this time."

Gwyn sighed. "I will. Should we get supplies from the market first? I'm assuming we'll need horses to ride to Valladolid."

"Affirmative, but we'll jump several months ahead before we ride. We have to give the Habsburg delegation time to return the contract to the Holy Roman Emperor. Once we are in Valladolid we will work our way into Princess Juana's household as ladies of the court and await whoever they send as a proxy to perform the marriage."

Gwyn pulled a face. "That's going to take some work. Wouldn't it be better to disguise ourselves as servants?"

"How about one lady and one maid? We should be able to pull that off. Then it's only one letter of introduction to forge."

They argued genially back and forth about who would play lady and who would play maid as they explored Segovia's marketplace. Still dressed as a clerk, Gwyn was able to purchase parchment and ink without comment. "I ran through our supplies writing notes to the Habsburg ambassador," she told Michelle as they stopped to snack on roasted almonds. "Bloody quills kept snapping." She munched on a handful of nuts. "I suppose if I'm a maid I won't be expected to have nice handwriting."

"Hah—nice try." Michelle stopped at the next stall to buy oranges. The stallholder offered a slice to taste. "Mmm, try this, Gwyn." The aroma of citrus clung to her fingers even after she paid. "You're a similar age to Princess Juana—if you become friends you can stay close to her and keep her safe."

"Who's going to keep *me* safe?" Gwyn muttered darkly, and Michelle's stomach clenched with guilt.

"You'll be safer as a lady," she insisted. "I can do the running around as a servant, we'll exchange gossip and notes—it's the perfect plan. It won't be easy—you'll have to practise your haughty lady attitude, and we definitely will have to brush up on correct deportment, but you blend in well."

She didn't miss the slight straightening in Gwyn's back, and smiled.

At the inn that evening they enjoyed a quiet dinner and shared a carafe of local wine in celebration. Michelle kept a watchful eye on the common room. It was early, and the clientele wasn't rowdy. Some guardsmen strolled in and ordered drinks. They started a game of dice and a few locals joined in. Michelle noticed Gwyn watching them too and approved. Of all the times they'd had trouble in inns and taverns, it was usually from soldiers wanting to start a fight. *She's wising up.*

One guard rose and disappeared, presumably to the privy. When he returned he cast an appraising eye over the light crowd. He spotted Michelle and Gwyn and came over. It was the guard from the castle— the one who had helped Gwyn.

"Enjoying Segovia?" he asked.

"It's a nice town," Gwyn replied warily.

The guard ran his eyes up and down Gwyn. His puzzlement was evident at first, then a broad smile spread over his face. He hooked a chair with his foot and sat down at their table. "You're a woman," he said quietly, grinning. "I knew there was something odd about you at the castle. It's only spring, and even a Dutchman wouldn't faint in this weather."

Gwyn smiled and shrugged. "I've stood by and watched plenty of men faint from things other than heat. You lot aren't as tough as you think you are," she mocked, but Michelle could hear the edge in her voice.

"Gwyn, shut up," Michelle ordered. *That's not keeping a low profile. Way to ruin the evening—I'll have to bloody fight our way out of here!*

"Michelle, it's fine," Gwyn drawled, examining her ink-stained fingers. "This guy isn't going to make a fuss."

The conviction in her tone amused the guardsman. "You're both women?" he asked incredulously. "What can I say? My queen is every bit her husband's equal but she is royalty—you're just clerks!" His voice rose, but cheers from the dicing circle drowned him out.

"No need to get excited." Gwyn rolled her eyes to Michelle, who was incensed. *Don't draw me into this!*

Gwyn beckoned the guard to lean closer. "It's like this—you're loyal to the queen, right?"

"How dare you?" The guard grabbed his sword hilt.

"I *said*, don't get excited." Gwyn beckoned again. "I'll take that as a yes. Well, on your honour, don't say anything, because we are loyal to the queen too and if you reveal us as women, you'll expose the queen to slander and maybe even ruin the alliance she has just forged with the Habsburgs."

"What?" the guard breathed, leaning in.

Michelle decided to chime in. "We can't tell you the details, but you mustn't give us away. Can we trust you?"

The guard looked at them. "How about I forget I ever saw you. I don't want to mix with spies." He stood and made his way back to the dice game, shaking his head.

Gwyn placed her hands on the table and stretched her fingers flat. They were shaking.

"Come on," Michelle said. "I've had enough for one night."

Two

1496 AD

Snapping awake, Gwyn sat up and looked around. Michelle was already crouched, hand on her crossbow. Hoofbeats rumbled on the nearby road. A large company, Gwyn judged by the sound.

The trees and bushes outside the forcefield dome were hazy, but she could see the road farther up the slope from where they were camped. As she watched, dozens of soldiers trotted into view. The early morning sunlight glinted on their armour as they rode north.

An idea struck Gwyn. "Michelle," she whispered. "We should go after them!"

The frown she received was unfair, in her opinion. "Why in all the stars would we do that?"

Gwyn kicked off her blanket and rummaged through her saddlebag. "Find your servant dress. Help me get into this." She yanked her brocaded blue and silver dress from the bag. Full of distasteful memories but too valuable to waste, they had brought it with them from Italy. Gwyn quashed the memory of Cesare Borgia's gritty touch on her skin, concentrating fiercely on dragging off her tunic and breeches and stepping into the dress.

"What? Why?" Michelle wasn't moving, which infuriated Gwyn. *She expects me to jump at her command yet she questions every idea I have!*

"Credibility!" she hissed. "Our guards were killed by bandits or something. We join those soldiers as distraught lady and maid, gets us an escort into Valladolid, then it looks more official when we present ourselves to Princess Juana."

Michelle considered this. Gwyn ground her teeth in exasperation. "Alright," said Michelle. "Our horses don't have side-saddles, though."

"The bandits took our horses. We were stopped for the night. One guard fought while the other threw me on his horse and then died fighting. Come on!" Gwyn shook out her hair and hastily twisted it into loops, shoving in pins from her purse to secure it. Michelle laced her bodice and donned her own dress. They quickly saddled the horses and kicked them into a gallop.

"We're going to break our bloody necks!" Michelle yelled as Gwyn took the lead. They hurtled down the road and within minutes caught sight of the soldier's column. Gwyn slowed to a canter, waving a hand and calling out in Castilian.

"Help! Please help!" *Okay, Gwyn, you've always wanted to play a noble lady, this is your chance.*

The soldiers bringing up the rear turned and shouted, drawing their swords and taking a defensive position. Gwyn reined in her horse and ignored Michelle's muffled swearing. "Please help us," she pleaded. "Bandits attacked us and murdered my guards. We've spent the night in the forest—it was awful!"

"Stay where you are," one soldier ordered. Another man rode up the line and returned with a captain.

"Señoras, state your business here."

Gwyn repeated her story, loading her tone with conviction and appealing to the honour of the captain and his men to escort them to Valladolid where, she said, "La Infanta Juana is waiting for me to join her ladies. I have a letter of introduction here!" She gestured imperiously to Michelle without turning, hoping that the other woman was playing her part and looking suitably servile.

The hard-faced captain grimaced. "Esteban, you and your squad will guide and protect the Señora and her maid. We'll ride ahead and take a message to La Infanta. Your letter of introduction will be best. May I have it?" He held out an expectant gloved hand.

Gwyn hesitated. They had been counting on using the power of the chronokinetors as well as the letter to convince Princess Juana of their legitimacy. The forgery alone might raise suspicion.

The captain cleared his throat.

"Of course!" Gwyn exclaimed. She turned to Michelle with a frantic look.

Michelle sighed and drew the elegantly addressed parchment from her skirt pocket. "My lady," she murmured, passing the letter over.

Gwyn proffered it with a brittle smile. "We are indebted to you."

"Hmm. Corporal Esteban here will see you safely to Valladolid." His nod was respectful but perfunctory, and he wheeled his horse to return to the front of the line.

Gwyn looked at Corporal Esteban, then Michelle, and did her best to shrug elegantly. Michelle sighed and the corporal looked bemused. "Shall we?" Gwyn said.

* * *

They maintained an easy pace in deference to the ladies' supposed inexperience riding astride. As they approached the fortified city in the late afternoon, Gwyn entertained thoughts of a bath and hot food.

"Shall I see if there is a place you can freshen up before attending on La Infanta, my lady?" Michelle's dry tone broke into Gwyn's contemplation of dinner as they entered the outer ward of the castle.

"Huh? I mean, yes, of course." *Stay in role, Gwyn.* "Corporal, would you be so kind as to see if your captain delivered our message?" Her stomach rumbled, and the corporal's lips twitched.

Before he could move, an imperious noble lady swept out into the courtyard, a disdainful eye cast over Gwyn and Michelle's rumpled attire. "Follow me, Lady Gwynia," the noblewoman ordered, her tone as steely as her tightly coifed hair. "La Infanta is expecting you." She turned and led the way into an airy stone hall.

"Ah, we were hoping we could make ourselves somewhat more presentable." Gwyn hastened to keep up with the older woman. A glance back at Michelle's calm face and Gwyn took courage. She did her best to match the noblewoman's imperious tone. "I have had an arduous journey and would like to freshen up before attending on La Infanta." Was that a slight huff of amusement from Michelle behind her? She didn't want to break character and look again.

The noblewoman stopped and raked Gwyn over with an unimpressed gaze. "La Infanta is expecting you *now*. One does not keep royalty waiting."

A brief battle of wills was silently locked. Gwyn's resolve ebbed as quickly as a snowflake on a summer's day. "Er, of course, lady…?" She wanted to shrink into her boots.

An arched nose lifted as the lady replied, "I am Lady Valentina de Zamora, mistress of La Infanta's wardrobe. And I, like Princess Juana, am very curious as to how *you* come to be recommended as a lady of La Infanta's court."

Uh oh. Bluff it out, Gwyn. You knew this was going to happen, you just expected to be on the front foot. She regained some of her poise despite the heat that flamed her cheeks. "An honour to meet you, Lady Valentina." She dipped a curtsey with a straight back. "Please, lead on."

Lady Valentina sniffed and resumed her onward sweep. Gwyn risked a peek back. The tiniest smile played around Michelle's lips, and Gwyn gave a reassuring nod. *I got this.*

She needed every ounce of confidence once they passed through the heavy carved wooden doors.

Princess Juana of Castile, La Infanta of Spain, favoured her famous mother, with pale skin and strawberry blonde hair. Her expression was less controlled than the militant queen, however. Haughty shoulders thrown back. Hazel eyes demanding answers. Juana clutched Gwyn's letter of introduction in her heavily jewelled hand. Gwyn swallowed.

"I received your letter, *Lady* Gwynia," Princess Juana declared. "It purports you to be the niece of my mother's dear friends, Lady Maria of Salamanca. I know of no niece, and I know all the nobility of Castile. Who are you?"

Gwyn hadn't expected the confrontation to be so blatant. She needed to think fast. "I'm not surprised you don't know of me, your highness." She smiled ingratiatingly.

It didn't work. Juana frowned and narrowed her eyes. Gwyn tried again.

"Ward is perhaps the better term." She focussed on Juana. *She doesn't have to like you, she just has to believe you.* "I was in a convent in Naples for many years, but never took my vows. Lady Maria patronised the abbey where I lived, in memory of her dear, departed sister, my mother." Gwyn dropped her voice a fraction. Despite herself, Juana leant in to listen. Gwyn continued, a hint of a sob quelled by stoicism. "My mother was noble; my father a mere squire. They married in secret, much like our honoured queen, and she died giving birth to me. I was sent away and the family never spoke of it. My mother's memory has been eradicated from all polite company—it all happened before you were born, your highness." Gwyn wiped an imaginary tear away and cleared her throat. "I am not ashamed of the love my parents bore each other. I have lived my life in the service of God, but my aunt was pleased to suggest to her majesty that my pious upbringing would better serve as a lady of your court. I sailed from Naples and join you here before you left for Burgundy to marry Prince Philip."

Consideration ticked over in Juana's eyes. The rest of the ladies—dressed in square cut heavy brocade despite the warmth—sighed in pity at Gwyn's tale while maintaining a sneer of superiority. Lady Valentina frowned heavily but forbore to comment, waiting instead for Juana to respond.

They didn't have to wait long. Rapid decision making seemed to be part of the princess' personality. She turned to one of her ladies-in-waiting. "Your prayer has been answered, Lady Antonella. You did not wish to follow me to Burgundy and my mother has sent a pious little nun to replace you. You may go."

Gwyn almost reeled in shock. The animosity in Princess Juana's tone was unmistakeable. Lady Antonella—a dark-haired young woman—flushed bright red and curtseyed. "As your highness commands." She studiously ignored the suddenly blank gazes of the other ladies and set down her embroidery, walking to the door before curtseying again.

The guard outside shut the double doors behind her.

Juana revelled in the shock. She smiled triumphantly and swept her arm out dramatically. "Welcome to my household, Lady Gwynia. Valentina, see that Lady Gwynia is roomed with my other ladies—she may have Antonella's old dresses, as Antonella won't be needing them anymore. They were gifts from my royal self anyway."

With that pronouncement, the princess stuck out her hand. Gwyn realised she was meant to kiss it, and almost tripped on her skirt stepping forward. Titters of laughter came from the other ladies. Gwyn fought rising heat in her face and made a passable curtsey, brushing her lips against Juana's soft skin. When she looked up the princess' eyes were fierce. "Don't think you can mince in here and show me up with your Hail Mary's and your fasting and praying. My mother and father might be the most Catholic monarchs, but that doesn't make me the Whore of Babylon just because I don't confess and flagellate myself ten times a day. I will be a married woman soon, and not submissive to my mother's will."

Quelled by the intensity and the threat, Gwyn murmured acquiescence and curtseyed again.

As Lady Valentina escorted her from the chamber, Gwyn exchanged glances with Michelle, not daring to speak. *And I've got to look after that presumptuous little cow for the next few months? Man, I wish I was playing the servant!*

Three

1496 AD

"Hold still, I can't lace this up properly if you keep jerking!" Michelle yanked the strings on Gwyn's stomacher, ignoring the grunts of protest.

"Stupid fashion," Gwyn muttered between grunts. "You don't have to make it so bloody tight!" She frowned down at the gold and cream skirts of the dress as she clutched the bedpost for balance.

"I agree, it's restrictive and impractical. Unfortunately you have to dress the part." Michelle finished lacing and retrieved the overskirt from the bed. Gwyn sighed and put her arms up, letting Michelle drag it over her head and down onto her hips.

"Yeah, I know. Good little convent girl thrust into noble life for the first time." Gwyn asked, grabbing the brush and attacking her hair before Michelle could. The humidity sent the brown waves into curls—luckily Lady Antonella had left a supply of bone pins.

"That seems our best bet. She is intimidated by her mother, and the queen is extremely religious."

Gwyn jammed another pin into her hair. "She seemed pretty defiant to me."

"Yes," Michelle said slowly, "but she's afraid too. That kind of defiance in a culture which demands unquestioning obedience to one's parents, let alone one's king and queen, is unusual. It's probably only because she knows she's leaving Spain soon that she dares to speak like that."

"I suppose you're right. Still, doesn't make her less of a cow—don't know what that Antonella chick did to piss her off, but that was pretty abrupt! And making a snap decision about me. She called me a liar then decided to take me on anyway—I mean, I know I'm persuasive but she seemed to decide more 'cause it was convenient, not because I'd convinced her."

Michelle handed Gwyn the hood to cover her hair. It matched the dress; cream with gold edging. "She'll learn to trust you. I know you can do it."

Gwyn tucked a stray wisp of hair behind her ear, looking down. "Thanks. Hey—thanks for not giving me hell about the soldiers and all. I thought it was a good idea at the time."

Michelle gave a wry smile. "It was a good idea—often you have to improvise. Next time we'll think of contingencies so we're better prepared. You pulled it off."

"Only through luck though."

Michelle shrugged. "At this point we're all running on luck. This is beyond anything covered in my training." *And I couldn't do it without you.* She couldn't quite say the words. She held a bubble of resentment deep inside, that Gwyn could do things she couldn't. The way she could see and feel timelines, not to mention her instinctual finding of the turning points. Thus far they had all matched Gwyn's visions to the data held on Michelle's tiny wrist computer. If the timeline broke…

If the timeline broke Michelle would be helpless, dependant on Gwyn to feel their way back to true history. Just like she had been in Italy—and looked how that had turned out. They had fixed the timeline, but Cesare Borgia had raped Gwyn and murdered Meric. Michelle itched to hunt the bastard down and make him pay.

It would never happen. She had to let it go.

"Hey." Gwyn quirked a smile at her. "Let's go do this thing."

Pious lady and obedient maid, they set off to join Princess Juana's court.

* * *

They attended morning Mass. Gwyn tried to stay focussed, envious that Michelle could sit at the back with the other servants. She found her attention drifting, the sonorous liturgy combined with heavy incense made her sleepy. She stared absently up at the stained glass, brilliantly lit in a myriad of colours. *Ugh, it's sunny outside, wish we could go riding.*

The priest intoned a blessing. Gwyn dragged her attention back to the altar. Princess Juana was looking at her, a frown on her face. Gwyn ducked her head and pretended to pray, resenting the hypocrisy. Without meaning to, she thought back to the last night in Segovia, with the guard from the castle. *Should I tell Michelle? No—she'll think I took a stupid risk.*

The rest of the day was dull. Dress fittings—the princess' wedding gown had tiny pearls sewn into the cuffs and hem, and the seamstresses adjusted Antonella's best gown for Gwyn. The proxy wedding would take place in the city cathedral, so they went there for Juana to rehearse her vows in Latin and her ladies practised carrying her long train.

Back at the castle, the afternoon was filled with embroidery, court gossip and listening to a lute player. The other ladies ignored Gwyn and Juana was content to make snide comments about Gwyn's fictional upbringing. "Did bandits steal your rosary too, Lady Gwynia? Surely you need to say some Hail Mary's?" or "I'm afraid we don't attend Matins, Lady Gwynia, but you can see my confessor if you like."

Gwyn complained to Michelle at night. "What is her problem? I thought the convent story would sell."

Michelle helped Gwyn out of her dress, then handed it to her to hang over the change screen. "It sells—she believes that her mother recommended you, or it suits her to believe you. The historical records I have, and the rumour amongst the servants though, is that she isn't the devout Catholic daughter the Queen wants her to be. She questions her tutors, reads books that are forbidden by the Inquisition. Apparently her mother ordered her whipped once."

Gwyn gaped. "She's a princess!"

Michelle shrugged. "And her mother is a queen; the most devout Catholic queen of the age. She and Ferdinand have driven out the Muslims and the Jews or forced them to convert. The Inquisition is burning heretics. You remember those Jews we helped escape from soldiers?"

"Oh yeah, those jerks. The soldiers, that is."

"That's happening all over Spain."

Gwyn flopped onto the four-poster bed. "I remember reading it wasn't as bad as some history makes out. That only a few thousand Jews and Muslims were forced to leave."

"That's still a few thousand people whose lives were thrown into disarray, especially because they were forbidden to take anything of value. And think of all the ones who stayed and converted but kept practising their religions in secret. They are persecuted horrendously and spied on by their neighbours."

Gwyn sighed. "People suck. So Juana is a bully because her mum is."

Michelle changed out of her servant dress and into breeches, and began a stretching routine. Gwyn dragged herself up to join her.

"Regardless of whether she is a bully or not, you had better work harder to get into her good graces. You can't save her life if you're not close to her."

Gwyn groaned. Michelle shot her a look. "Focus, Gwyn. The survival of the Allied Planets depends on us."

Like I could forget! Gwyn bit back her retort and hung her head. "I know," she said in a low voice. "But if I think about it too much I want to be sick. How are you not terrified? Every turning point we fix should be a relief, but it just makes me more scared that we won't be so lucky next time."

Michelle clasped her hands together and pressed her forefingers to her lips. At last she said, "Maybe a change of tactics is in order."

* * *

Mass again. Gwyn used the time to sink into her timepiece and examine the turning point that was fast approaching. A horse-riding accident where Princess Juana would be thrown and killed. No marriage to Philip of Burgundy, and no inheritance of the Castilian throne following the demise of her brother, elder sister and nephew. The Habsburgs would never rule Spain; the shape of European history would be quite different.

She opened her eyes. Princess Juana was staring at her again, frowning. Gwyn rolled her eyes and was darkly satisfied at the look of shock on the petulant princess' face.

"Were you bored in Mass, Lady Gwynia?" Juana demanded once they were out of church and walking in the gardens. Michelle and the other maids followed a discreet distance behind. Gwyn ducked a curtsey at the sudden attention, eyeing the other ladies cynically as they shuffled elegantly away from the target of their mistress' disapproval.

"I'm afraid so, your highness," Gwyn remarked. "I've heard the gospel of John preached many times before. I'm afraid my attention wandered."

Juana drew herself up as the other ladies-in-waiting gasped discreetly. "I am shocked that you should be so blasé about the worship of our Lord."

Gwyn waved a hand at the garden with its orange trees and bougainvillaea. The riot of fuchsia and orange, coupled with the scent of flowers made it a paradise. "Is God not present here too, your highness? In the flowers and the trees? I am not a theologian, but surely sitting in a stuffy cathedral is not the only way to worship the Lord?"

The only sound was the hum of bees that busied themselves amongst the subject of Gwyn's discussion. Gwyn wished she knew what Juana was thinking.

"Hmph." Juana made a most un-princesslike noise and stared Gwyn down. "You may be right. Perhaps we should ask Father Orlando."

Gwyn curtseyed again. "An excellent idea, your highness."

They walked on.

* * *

Father Orlando, the princess' private confessor, was not impressed with Gwyn's theory. He admonished Juana severely for entertaining such heretical observations and recommended fasting and prayer for all the princess' ladies to encourage a more pure focus on God. Juana appeared chastened and complied.

The other ladies, Sofia, Marietta and the imperious Valentina, treated Gwyn with even more disdain than before. Gwyn was just grateful Michelle snuck food in for her at night—being hungry made her cranky. After a week they received word that the Habsburg count who would represent Prince Philip in the proxy marriage was due to reach Valladolid before the end of summer. Juana ordered the fasting to finish and they celebrated with a feast that night.

"So you are not the perfect little nun, Lady Gwynia," Juana commented, cheerful with wine.

"Perhaps the convent I lived in was too liberal," Gwyn replied, smiling with downcast eyes.

"We have heard of the corruption in Rome," Lady Valentina chimed in disapprovingly. "The Pope has a mistress! And flaunts his children openly!"

"It *is* terrible." Gwyn agreed seriously. "Naples is just as bad, I've heard. It's one reason I was glad to leave my convent and come to Castile."

"And do you think Burgundy will be better or worse?" Princess Juana wanted to know.

Gwyn considered. She wanted to keep Juana off-guard and intrigued, but not enough to prompt a letter to the queen to investigate Gwyn's story. Michelle had been sneaking into the other ladies rooms and searching their correspondence, making sure no one else thought to write and ask questions. "I imagine it will be less restrictive than Castile but less corrupt than Rome and Naples," she said cautiously, as if the thought had just occurred to her. "After all, there are scholars there who are critical of the Church, and they are permitted. I have heard the lands of Flanders and the Germanies are more… austere than here in Spain, however."

"And how do you know what is and isn't permitted in the lands to the north?" Valentina demanded.

Juana narrowed her eyes at Gwyn. "True—you are a contradiction, Lady Gwynia. We thought you a modest nun, now it seems you are widely read and far more outspoken than is proper."

Gwyn thought Juana was as contrary as the wind but didn't let it unsettle her like it had before. *She's a rebellious teenager, bored yet afraid. I'm exciting to her now, and not just as a target to bully.* She bowed her head then looked Princess Juana in the eye. "There is a lot more to me than appearances suggest, your highness, just as there is to everyone." That truth was easy, and the conviction in Gwyn's voice ended the conversation for the moment.

"She doesn't know what to make of me, but she's curious," Gwyn reported to Michelle later that night. "I hope that'll be enough to move up in the pecking order. Ugh, I hate these games—it's so high school."

Michelle shrugged. "You hate it because you're genuine with people. It doesn't bother me."

Gwyn raised an eyebrow. "Are you really an android? That would explain a lot about you. I imagine you have humanoid robots in your time."

She could have laughed at the shock on Michelle's face. The other woman glared and clenched her fists. Gwyn's lips quirked. Michelle's shoulders relaxed and she shook her head. "You're a clown, Gwyn."

When Gwyn's face broke into a smile, Michelle grinned back.

Four

1496 AD

The turning point loomed. Michelle's data and Gwyn's ability to see into the timeline confirmed that a horse-riding accident would kill Princess Juana days before her proxy-marriage was to take place, but Gwyn was no closer to being a favourite with the princess. Juana called on Gwyn for her opinion now and then, despite Lady Valentina and the others blocking every attempt Gwyn made to get closer to the princess. Michelle's efforts with the servants provided no clues either. General gossip confirmed Princess Juana to be intelligent and wilful yet cautious when it came to upsetting the status quo.

"It's today, Michelle, and I don't even know if she'll invite me out riding!" Gwyn paced. The sun's first light crept over the window sill. The day would be hot—August baked the plains of Castile and leeched the moisture from the air. Flowers that had bloomed in weeks past now browned, grass yellowed and crunched underfoot.

"If she doesn't, get to the stables anyway," Michelle ordered. "I've prepped one of the grooms—told him you were an ace rider who could ride astride."

"Was he shocked?" Gwyn asked dryly.

Michelle grinned. "Perversely so. Good thing we'll be leaving soon or you'll get a reputation."

"Ugh."

That reminded Michelle. "Gwyn, I wanted to talk to you about something. You know the last night we were in Segovia?"

"Yes…"

Michelle ploughed on. "I saw you by the well after you went to the privy that night. I saw you with the guard." Michelle wondered at herself focussing on Gwyn's personal issues when the mission was critical, but it had been brewing in her mind.

"Ye-es…" Gwyn replied slowly. "Are you going to tell me that was stupid? That I'll get a reputation as a whore? I kissed him, that was all." Her jaw set mulishly.

Michelle chose her words carefully. "I know your time has different rules and standards when it comes to sexual engagement. Different even from my time, where no stigma is attached to any kind of sexual choices as long as it is between consenting adults." This next bit was uncomfortable. "Rape is unheard of. What Cesare Borgia did to you would be virtually impossible in my society, so I don't know how best to support you."

Gwyn's mouth quivered. Michelle rushed on. "What I'm trying to say is, if casual liaisons help you feel more in control emotionally and mentally, then I'm all for it. Just keep me in the loop, so you can be safe."

She waited for Gwyn's response. "Sure, thanks," Gwyn said gruffly. "Come on, we'll be late for Mass."

They weren't late—Princess Juana wasn't even there so Gwyn hovered at the back of the church, Michelle at her side. When Lady Valentina came in alone, Michelle nudged Gwyn, who frowned.

"Where is her highness?" Gwyn stepped forward to intercept Lady Valentina.

Valentina looked down her nose at Gwyn. "She has ridden out to meet Count Heinrich, who will stand proxy for Prince Philip at her wedding. Were you not told?" A smug smile played across her haughty face.

Michelle saw panic in Gwyn's face and interrupted. "Are you still feeling unwell, my lady?" she asked, raising her eyebrows meaningfully. Gwyn shot her a look of confusion. Michelle sighed internally. "Shall I prepare a warm compress and brew willow bark tea?" She placed her hand on her own stomach, looking sympathetic.

Gwyn clicked. "Oh! Yes, please, Michelle. Forgive me, Lady Valentina—the moon. I may have to pray in my rooms this morning." She waved her hands vaguely and clutched her abdomen. Michelle took her arm and hustled her out.

"Stables, now," Michelle instructed.

"I don't know which way they've gone! And I'm not bloody dressed for riding!"

"Leave that to me." Michelle hauled Gwyn into an alcove and dragged breeches off from under her skirts. She swapped her boots for Gwyn's satin slippers. "Hurry."

They hastened down corridors, smiling at puzzled passersby. Most of the nobles were attending Mass and no servant stopped them to ask what they were doing. The smell of hay and horse grew stronger as they emerged into the courtyard next to the stables.

"Matias!" Michelle shouted, catching the attention of a groom shovelling manure into a hand cart. He stopped, batting flies from his face.

"Er, yes? My lady." He caught sight of Gwyn and bowed.

"Matias, my lady Gwynia needs a horse. She has an urgent message to take to La Infanta, and I understand she's gone out riding." Michelle cursed the stupid slipper which was pinching her foot already.

Matias stuck the pitchfork into the manure pile. "I could take it, my lady." He bowed again to Gwyn.

Michelle overrode him, using the chronokinetor to convince him that her way was best. "The message is verbal and in Latin. Lady Gwynia must deliver it herself. Besides," she winked at the groom, "it'll be your only chance to see what a good rider she is." She grinned.

He grinned back, look around to make sure no one else was in earshot. "How fast a horse do you want, my lady," he asked Gwyn.

Gwyn glanced at Michelle, then raised her eyebrows at Matias. "The fastest one here," she declared.

Michelle and Gwyn huddled quickly while Matias raced to ready a steed. "If I reach them before they meet Count Heinrich we should be fine," Gwyn said, her eyes glassy. "The timeline that I can see shows that the Count's horse spooks at a bird and Juana's horse rears. She falls and breaks her neck."

"You'll have to slow them down or get between them." Michelle bent to lace Gwyn's boots.

Matias returned leading two horses wearing standard saddles. "I shall accompany you, my lady."

"They'll be on side-saddles," Michelle called as Gwyn mounted. "You should catch them."

Gwyn replied with a "Yah!" and kicked her horse into a trot. Matias swung up after her, a look of thrilled mischief on his young face. Michelle supposed it was a great adventure to him, seeing a noble lady ride like a man. *More exciting than shovelling shit, I'm sure.*

She tried to be calm, ignoring the helplessness that bubbled in her stomach as she watched them ride out. Gwyn had to do this alone.

* * *

Gwyn knew at once the horse was too strong for her. It was all she could do to hold on as they galloped out the gate, Matias whooping with excitement as he followed. *Bloody hell, I'm going to be the one with a broken neck!* She locked her knees and tried to keep her upper body loose, rolling with the motion. They settled into a canter as they hit the road out of Valladolid.

"You really can ride, my lady!" he yelled, grinning as he caught up and passed her.

Lucky this bloody horse is happy to follow. She thought too soon—her mount tried to take a chunk out of the other horse's rump. "Stop that!" Gwyn snarled, yanking its head back. The imminence of the turning made her feel sick.

"This way, my lady," Matias called. They approached a fork in the road and he swung to the right. They passed a farmer leading a mule and several peasants working in the fields, harvesting hay. Dry scrub grew along the roadside as they blasted past, and a group of riders grew larger up ahead.

Ah crap, what's my story for why I'm out here? Matias thinks I'm delivering a verbal message. Juana is going to think I'm crazy, galloping up like this. She hauled the reins low and hard. The horse fought, then decided that perhaps its rider could be right, that slowing down was a good idea.

Gwyn wasn't sure how many miles they'd covered since leaving the castle. It seemed to have been enough to let her mount work some restlessness out of its system.

At a jolting trot, then a walk, she reached the princess' party, Matias having fallen in behind. Lady Sofia turned to see who had joined them and frowning, alerted the princess. Juana turned, surprised. "What in our dear Lord's name are you doing here, Lady Gwynia? Did you have a hankering to meet Count Heinrich? He'll arrive soon enough; I'm just being courteous and welcoming him at the end of his long journey. There was no need for you to join us, and in such a..." she looked Gwyn over, "dishevelled state."

Gwyn flinched internally at the disapproving tone and tried to ignore her flushed cheeks and hair that felt like a bird had attacked it. "Forgive me for arriving so precipitously, your highness. I thought you might like my services as an interpreter if Count Heinrich's Latin is not as proficient as yours." It was a stretch, but it was all she had. She barrelled on before Juana could reply. "I speak Greek, German, French, English, Dutch and Flemish, so perhaps I can be useful in Burgundy too."

Gwyn caught Marietta pulling a disbelieving face to Sofia behind the princess' back. *Too bad, I don't have to be friends with you. I don't even have to be friends with Juana, though it would make getting close to her easier.* Part of her was glad—she didn't want to pretend friendship, or worse, really become friends with Juana and then just leave. *Probably better I don't like her.*

A shout from ahead snatched attention from Gwyn. Another group of riders were coming into view over a rise. Their dark tunics and fur-edged cloaks looked impressive but were ill-suited to the summer heat.

Juana shot a look at Gwyn. "Ride beside me, Lady Gwynia, and you may put your sudden interpreting skills to good use," she said tersely. "Though I will learn why you did not say something of this sooner."

Five

"Count Heinrich! Welcome to Castile." Juana nudged her horse forward and allowed the count, a stocky man with shoulder-length grey hair, to lean forward and kiss her hand.

"Thank you, your highness. I bring greetings from your esteemed betrothed, Prince Philip, and his father, Maximilian, Holy Roman Emperor," The count replied, also in Latin, though his accent was thickly Germanic.

"We would be most pleased if you permitted us to guide you to Valladolid." The flowery exchanges went on for several minutes before Juana turned her horse and led the party back towards the town. Count Heinrich rode beside her. Juana was irritated to see Gwynia nudge her mount to ride right behind. The horse huffed and fought the reins. Gwynia, dressed absurdly in breeches under her skirts and riding astride, pulled it under control. Juana turned back to the count, smiling to cover her confusion and annoyance.

"Pardon?" She didn't catch what he was saying.

He uttered something unintelligible, then raised his eyebrows expectantly.

Mother Mary, save me. His Latin really is terrible. He probably just rehearsed the greetings. "Lady Gwynia?" she called.

Her most peculiar lady-in-waiting rode forward and pushed between Juana and the count. "Count Heinrich asked if the trees are always so dry at the end of summer, your highness." She smiled at the count and said something in German, a bead of sweat trickling down her forehead. He replied in the same language, then Gwynia returned to Spanish. "I told him I was happy to interpret for you, your highness. He said he would be most grateful."

How did she know? Too much about Lady Gwynia did not make sense, but Juana had not been able to bring herself to interrogate her. "Very well." She kept a gracious look on her face, a gentle smile and attentive expression—she was a princess, and she represented her mother and the kingdom of Castile.

She mused that it was just as well Gwynia wasn't a princess—her lady in waiting was pale. Surely the heat wasn't worse here than in Naples?

Juana turned her practised smile on Count Heinrich again. "The castle is well-appointed for the breeze, and we have lovely shaded gardens where you can take your ease before the wedding. I shall order cool baths to be drawn for you and your party." *They smell like they could use them.*

The count did not get a chance to respond. A partridge launched itself from the bushes, startled by the passing horses. Count Heinrich shouted as the bird flew past his face, jerking the reins in alarm and cannoning his mount sideways into Lady Gwynia's. Her horse snapped and reared—Gwynia fought to bring the animal back under control. Juana's horse whinnied and skittered sideways but the princess was able to stay on despite the precariousness of her side-saddle. Sofia and Marietta twittered concern. Juana waved them back, hiding her fright and calling out, "Count! Are you alright?"

Heinrich spluttered in German—Juana used the excuse of needing translation to speak to Gwynia. She used Greek, thanking her tutors for a classical education. "Are *you* alright, Lady Gwynia? You almost fell!" She was rewarded with a look of surprise, then an exhilarated grin.

"Better me than you, your highness. I can stay on this horse." Her horse snorted as if to argue. Juana wondered what it must feel like to be so steady instead of perched like an egg on the edge of the nest. Gwynia listened to Count Heinrich. "He says he apologises for the fright he gave us all and wants to know if it is much farther."

Juana looked ahead and sighed in relief. The bell tower of the cathedral was in sight. She would be glad when this proxy wedding was over and she could be on her way to meet her husband. Castile stifled her and she wanted to be free.

* * *

Michelle paced. The guard on the northern wall ignored her and she was free to fret in peace as the sun beat down. After several minutes she realised the ridiculousness of her actions and retreated to the shade of one of the great square towers that interspersed the wall at regular intervals. "Meditate, you fool," she muttered and sat cross-legged, hoping no one would bother her.

She wished she could do what Gwyn did—connect with the chronokinetor on an intuitive level and 'see' the timelines. Michelle's access to the device was analytical, a skill born of years of training, though no doubt she had some natural, genetic advantage.

Never mind. There was little she could do right now except calm her mind and wait.

One thing she could do, and did, was use the geo-locative function of the timepiece to warn her when Gwyn neared. When the girl's proximity increased to less than a mile out, Michelle returned to the crenelated wall to look out across the fields.

One, two, three riders out in front. Riding steadily, which indicates no accident has taken place. Surely they would send a servant ahead if something dreadful happened? She squinted against the glare. *That's Gwyn in the middle, and Juana beside her. Thank the stars! Must be the Habsburg proxy on the other side.*

Jubilant, Michelle raced down the steep stairs which clung to the inside of the wall and hovered in the entrance courtyard. The clip-clop of horses soon rewarded her and she watched the princess' party return. Servants came forward and assisted the ladies to dismount, except for Matias, who wore an expression of admiration amidst the shocked expressions of the other castle staff as Gwyn swung off her horse and he steadied her. She nodded thanks and passed him the reins. Michelle ducked through the crowd to reach her.

"All good?" Michelle murmured. Gwyn was flushed—with exhaustion or excitement, Michelle couldn't tell.

"Yeah. Lucky I didn't land on my arse with that stupid horse. At least the princess is okay."

"Lady Gwynia." Juana's imperious tones cut through the short reunion. "Please clean yourself and select suitable attire to attend on me after my bath. I shall require your translation services with Count Heinrich."

"Yes, your highness." Gwyn wobbled a curtsey and Michelle caught her by the arm.

The Habsburg party disappeared into the depths of the castle with grateful expressions while the Princess and her other ladies swept off in the direction of her apartments. Gwyn and Michelle grinned. "She thinks I'm nuts," Gwyn said, "but useful. Fingers crossed that's enough to keep me close."

* * *

Close but not trusted. Gwyn watched the proxy wedding with interest from the back of the small crowd. Sofia and Marietta had pride of place, flocking behind Juana as she advanced to the altar and recited her vows in front of the bishop. She signed the contract that bound her person to Prince Philip of Burgundy, a man she had never met.

Ugh, I know it's the way things are done, but still, what a leap of faith. Or is it just out of duty? The ceremony was bizarre—she couldn't even pretend love was involved when the groom wasn't present, yet the princess seemed genuinely excited.

"We are joyous for you, your highness!" Sofia gushed delightedly afterwards, while Marietta wiped tears from her eyes, smiling. "May you be blessed with many children."

"My dear Sofia." Juana kissed her lady-in-waiting on the cheek. "I only pray you will be as fortunate in finding a noble, handsome husband."

Gwyn stood to the side, hearing the affection in the princess' voice, seeing the devotion in her ladies' faces. Were they naïve? Or just hopeful?

"Do you think she'll be happy?" Gwyn asked Michelle later as they packed. They were to leave in several days for Bilbao, where the princess would sail to the Low Countries to meet her husband.

"I thought you didn't like her?"

Gwyn shrugged. "I don't. I just feel sorry for anyone who has to get married to a stranger. Even if she does want to get out from under her mother's thumb."

Michelle glanced at her wrist computer. "By all accounts, she adores her husband and is devastated when he dies. All the stuff about her being mad seems put about by her father and son in order to wrest control from her. She was grieving, but tried to rule, and they locked her in a convent."

Gwyn's jaw dropped. "That's horrifying! I knew she was called Juana the Mad but I thought that's 'cause there was a history in the family. And I thought it was a lot later on, when she was old."

"It's ten years from now. Apparently she enjoys a happy marriage between now and then."

Gwyn grunted. "Well, that sucks."

A knock sounded at the door of the chamber. Michelle went to answer it. She paused, hand on the handle, and coughed pointedly.

"Oh!" Gwyn stopped helping Michelle pack and straightened. "Um." She grabbed the Bible from the table and flicked randomly, trying to look like a pious noblewoman.

"Lady Gwynia?" A maid bobbed a curtsey. "Her highness requests you join her at the stables. You are to go riding with her this morning. Please dress…" she blushed, "for riding like a man."

Gwyn raised her eyebrows. "Er… okay." The maid retreated. Michelle shut the doors.

"You appear to have an in," she said, smiling.

Six

1496 AD

Princess Juana awaited Gwyn in the stable yard, as promised. "I wish you to teach me to ride like you do, Lady Gwynia."

"Of course, your highness." Gwyn saw Matias the groom, reins in hand, leading a pair of horses out. She sighed in relief that it wasn't the mount she had ridden the other day. Matias grinned and cupped his hand as a step for Gwyn. She mounted, then watched—biting her tongue to hide her smile—as Juana's groom did the same for her, face red with embarrassment. The princess ignored him and mounted awkwardly, clearly unused to throwing her leg over the saddle.

Gwyn clicked to her horse, a beautiful bay mare, and nudged it over to Juana. "Feet in the stirrups, your highness, heels down, toes out."

"This is most indecent, your highness." Lady Valentina erupted into the yard, glaring at Gwyn. "Your mother will not approve."

Juana's lips tightened. "I am a married woman now, Valentina. I belong to my husband, and until he says I may not ride like this, I shall."

She's game. Gwyn wondered if the princess was using this weird limbo state of marriage to break a few rules. She couldn't blame her. "Keep your knees firm but your upper body relaxed, your highness," she instructed, leaning over to resettle Juana's white-knuckled grip on the reins. "Hands low, that way you've got the strength to guide your horse. That's good."

Juana straightened ever so slightly. "Let us go." She clicked her tongue, prompting her grey into an amble. Gwyn made to follow but was stopped by Valentina grabbing her bridle, eyes furious. "Your wicked ways shall not corrupt La Infanta. I have watched over her too long to see the devil's influence creep in right before she is delivered safely to her husband!"

Gwyn recoiled at the hate in the woman's voice. "Excuse me," she tugged her horse away from Lady Valentina, heart thumping.

The ride was pleasant, despite its tense start. Juana was either confident or so good at pretending to be that Gwyn found it hard to believe the princess had only ever ridden side-saddle. Their conversation did not venture beyond instructions for riding, and when they returned Juana said only, "Very good. We shall practise again tomorrow and the next day, and when we leave for Bilbao we shall ride thus." She barely waited for Gwyn to curtsey before disappearing into the castle.

"Your reins, my lady?" Matias politely held out his hand.

"Ah, yes, thank you." Gwyn's smile was returned by the groom, and she remained smiling as she joined the waiting Michelle.

"He's got eyes for you," Michelle murmured.

"What?" Gwyn stopped, startled.

"Come on, don't stop in the middle of the walkway." Michelle urged Gwyn on. "I just said our horsey friend there has eyes for you. Not proper, obviously, since he's a groom and you're supposedly a lady, but when did that ever stop people?"

"Oh." Gwyn felt heat in her face. Why was Michelle telling her this? Was she encouraging her to have a fling like she did back in Segovia with that guard? Not that one would call that a fling—just a kiss in the moonlight. She hadn't planned it.

Gwyn and Michelle retired to their room. With all the wine they had drunk Gwyn needed to use the chamber pot one last time before bed. Rather than leave it all night, she took it to the yard and threw the contents in the garden, scooping water from the well to rinse it and her hands. She paused, enjoying the quiet, the balmy air, and the stars shining above.

A burst of sound emerged from the tavern as customers left. A voice, "Go on ahead, I'll catch up." The guard. He saw her at the well and came over. "Cup of water to sober me up?"

Gwyn passed him the dipper. When he finished drinking, he sighed contentedly and let the dipper fall back on its string. It swung from the well post and Gwyn watched it, mesmerised. She felt relaxed and in control again, and wanted to know if she could banish the memories of Cesare, replace them with something less poisonous. Something to quash the lingering nightmares. She turned to the guard, putting a hand on his shoulder and drew him to her. She kissed him. Through his muffled noise of surprise, she tasted wine. Before he could do anything, she walked away swiftly, cutting in through the kitchens and up the stairs to the room where Michelle meditated. Gwyn peered out the window, seeing the guard still standing by the well. She couldn't see his face in the darkness. He scratched his head, shrugged, then walked out of the yard, following his companions.

Gwyn wondered what he made of it all. She didn't know what to make of it herself.

Michelle was still talking. "So your riding lesson with the princess went well?"

Gwyn dragged her attention back. "Yeah, she wants to do it again tomorrow. We didn't really talk, but I think she's starting to trust me."

"Good," replied Michelle. "You'll need that." She frowned and glanced behind. Gwyn followed her gaze. A maid carrying a basket of candles walked behind them. She stopped and fussed with a small candelabra fixed to the wall. Gwyn exchanged glances with Michelle and they walked on, speaking no more until they reached their rooms.

"Did you see the bracket of candles behind her?" Michelle asked. "Burnt down to stubs but she ignored them. I think she was eavesdropping on us."

Gwyn grimaced. "We should have spoken in Italian or something unsuspicious."

"Hmph, too late now. I wonder who she is spying for."

* * *

Juana's riding lessons progressed smoothly, which was well for Gwyn, who became distracted every time the groom, Matias, appeared. "This is stupid," she muttered to Michelle, who looked amused. "Why did you say anything? Aren't you always the one going on about the mission? We leave tomorrow for Bilbao! The next turning point is two days away!"

"Yes, but we agreed that trying too hard to gain Juana's friendship was no use, so it isn't terrible if she sees you as… as…" Michelle looked sheepish.

"Flighty? A slut?"

Michelle's eyes widened. "No! Firstly, you're not flighty, just inconsistent."

"Gee, thanks!"

"Secondly!" Michelle raised her voice, then dropped it. "Wanting sex, or not wanting it, is perfectly normal. I know this time has twisted and hypocritical attitudes towards women and sex, but you don't have to take those on board."

Gwyn stared at her, then threw up her hands. "This time? Even my time is messed up in its attitudes! Better, but still messed up. Ugh, why are we even talking about this? I get it, I can sleep with whoever I want, what happened with Cesare is not my fault, but we are still trying to fix history and… and…" She sighed helplessly. "I'm just so over it."

Michelle gave her own small sigh. "Me too. I've never been this long without support. We could both use a decent debrief and downtime. We'll get through the next few days then," she paused to think, "we'll give ourselves a holiday. We have time."

"A holiday?"

"Sure—we find somewhere nice, take a room and relax for a while. The Galician coastline is meant to be spectacular. Or there's Santiago de Compostela. People make the pilgrimage there even in your time, even if not for religious reasons. The architecture and scenery are meant to be amazing. No missions, no turning points, no agendas except relax and sightsee."

The prospect of a holiday cheered Gwyn up, and she let herself flirt with Matias in a very subtle way. Little touches of the hand when he brought her horse to her, small smiles. Her encouragement wrought results—on the first day's ride she found a posy of wildflowers tucked under the edge of her saddle blanket. The scent soothed Gwyn amidst Sofia and Marietta's apparent efforts to exclude her from all conversation. She ignored them and noticed Princess Juana did too. *Perhaps she's tired of their bitching.*

"You smile, Lady Gwynia," the princess appeared beside Gwyn and

Michelle as they prepared to ride after lunch on the second day. She had shed her minders, and was dressed once again for riding in a standard saddle, with breeches under her elegant skirts.

A great sense of calm washed over Gwyn. The next turning point was due to fall that afternoon—a lightning strike that would kill the princess outright if Gwyn didn't change it. She needed to be close to Juana, but her services as an interpreter hadn't been called upon, so her position had been further down the line thus far.

"It is a beautiful day, your highness." It was true—a stiff breeze had risen and cooled them as they wound through hills towards the coast. Gwyn knew it to be a harbinger of the storm to come.

Juana smiled knowingly. "I've heard whispers that you have an admirer, Lady Gwynia. It is true?"

Gwyn's blush must have given her away, because the princess laughed. "You'll have your own admirer soon enough, your highness," Gwyn said. "Your husband will adore you." *I hope.*

Juana's smile lessened and became formal. "I pray I shall be a dutiful wife to him."

Gwyn leant forward. "I think you will find him very loving, your highness. He is fortunate to marry such a brave and intelligent woman."

Juana looked astonished. "Do you not mean wealthy and beautiful?"

Gwyn felt Michelle tremble beside her and wondered if she, too, was suppressing a laugh. *You forgot 'modest', princess!* "That goes without saying, your highness, but you're more than that. I'm not saying it to flatter." She really wasn't, and the truth lent conviction to her voice. "You are brave, learning to ride without a side-saddle, and to question the priest. That takes courage."

Juana gave a small nod. "You shall ride next to me for the rest of today," she ordered.

Gwyn saw Sofia and Marietta circling behind the princess, scowling, and kept her face impassive as she curtsied. "An honour, your highness." She wished she could tell them that she had no desire to supplant them, that she would be gone soon enough. She supposed they saw her as a threat to the princess, not just to their positions of favourites.

Too bad. Just get on with the job, Gwyn.

Conversation with Juana proved awkward and difficult. Having made it this close, Gwyn didn't want to irritate the princess and be sent back down the line again. She saw Sofia and Marietta report back to Lady Valentina, who rode in one of the wagons with all the luggage, and—irritating though it was—decided she couldn't blame them for trying to protect Juana from an interloper.

"So your husband is handsome, I've heard?" she tried.

"I've seen a portrait of him. He is very handsome."

They fell silent again. *What can I say that won't piss her off? If I don't keep her engaged, she'll get bored and I won't be near when the storm comes.* The wind had picked up, whipping dust on the road in small flurries. Clouds on the horizon darkened and an earthy, electrical smell filled the air.

"Your highness, is there anything of concern that I might help with?" She was running out of ideas.

"Why should I be concerned, Lady Gwynia? We will reach shelter before the storm hits." Strands of her hair crept loose of the princess' hood, adding to her affronted expression.

Does she misunderstand me deliberately? "I mean, regarding your marriage. I'm being very presumptuous, I know, but if you wish to know anything, perhaps I can be of help." *There you go, will that hook you?*

"You *are* very presumptuous."

Gwyn chose silence over apology, bowing her head. *Take the bait, take the bait.*

"You speak… as if you have known a man, Lady Gwynia." Juana lowered her voice. Every fibre of Gwyn's being tuned to listen. She let her horse slow, knowing riders behind them would not dare pass the princess. Juana didn't seem to notice—she was eyeing Gwyn carefully.

Gwyn sighed and nodded. "I was not entirely truthful when I came to your court, your highness. The abbess at my convent wrote to my Aunt Maria and advised I was not suitable for the life of a nun. There was… an incident."

Juana was captivated, Gwyn could tell. The rumble of thunder that rippled across the sky didn't distract her for a moment. "A scandal?" She pressed her hand to her lips, shocked.

Gwyn nodded again.

"Your highness!" The captain of the guard rode up. "We need to seek shelter now. That storm is about to hit." They had slowed considerably thanks to Gwyn's dawdling; several of the party wore concerned expressions, glancing apprehensively at the sky.

Juana looked irritated at the interruption. "Can we not ride to the next village?"

"Perhaps we should take cover in those trees, your highness." Gwyn pointed and the captain nodded.

"Very well," Juana huffed. She turned her horse off the road just as a crack of lightning struck a lone tree farther up the hill from them. Ladies screamed and horses whinnied. Gwyn lunged for Juana's mount before it could bolt, hauling on the bridle and shushing to calm it, stroking her own mare's mane as she did so.

"Quickly, to the trees!" the captain ordered.

They huddled under a massive chestnut tree, its broad limbs wide enough to shelter the whole party. As the rain poured, Gwyn leant against the rough bark, glad the gathering darkness hid her dizzy relief.

"You okay?" Michelle sat quietly next to her.

"Yeah. Bloody pain having three turning points around the same person. If she didn't have another one I would have crash tackled her then nicked off." Her head thumped—she inhaled the cool smell of rain, yawning as she did so.

"True. You did well."

Gwyn scowled at Michelle. "You weren't much help. You could have screamed and caused a scene or something. That would have slowed everyone down."

"Or they would have ridden on without me—I'm just a servant, remember. As it was, I was flirting with the captain of the guards, distracting him from trying to hustle everyone onwards. Probably not the best impression—I think Valentina will tell you off for having an immodest servant."

Gwyn groaned. "She'll be telling me off for being immodest if she hears what I was saying. Let's just hope she leaves it till morning. I guess we're stuck here for the night."

It looked that way, but once the storm had passed men rode ahead and returned with torches to guide the nobles safely to the next village. Gwyn was relegated back down the line the following day and they reached the city of Bilbao in the evening. Gwyn admired the view of red-roofed houses clustered behind low walls between the river and the foothills. They ambled over the stone archways that spanned the silty waterway, the horses' clopping hooves a steady counterpoint to the splashing of oars below. Alongside the broad waterfront, a dozen half-galleys were moored at the utmost reach of the sea's tidal influence.

"Will you take one of those ships to France, my lady?" Matias appeared beside Gwyn, looking mournful. An attitude of calculated recklessness struck Gwyn. She resolved to make an opportunity to be alone with him, even if just to steal a few kisses before she and Michelle guided the timeline through the third turning point and vanished.

"I believe so." She glanced around quickly, making sure no one was listening. The rest of the nobles were ploughing through the peasants and townsfolk hastening across the bridge to enter the gates before sunset. Michelle rode in one of the luggage carts further back. Gwyn nudged her mare closer to Matias, foot brushing his as she did. "Perhaps you could find me later? I would like to say farewell properly." The blush wasn't faked. She wasn't used to propositioning people.

Matias looked astonished yet thrilled. He grinned but was saved from replying by a draught horse coming the other way, separating them. "Make way!" an irate farmer shouted in Basque from his wagon.

They were housed in a small palace quite a way back from the docks, whose rear gardens sat under the gaze of the steep hills, which were bathed in the light of the setting sun. Gwyn took the opportunity to scrub up before dinner, enjoying the smell of the sandalwood soap. Michelle had already bathed, and helped Gwyn plait her hair.

"Um, Michelle?" *Argh, how am I going to ask this?*

"Hmm?"

"Um, after dinner, I don't suppose you could stay out of our rooms for a bit?"

Michelle stopped plaiting and looked sideways at Gwyn. "Any particular reason?"

Gwyn reached back and took hold of her hair, finishing the plait herself as she mumbled, "Um, I maybe might have a visitor. Just for a bit. Um, if that's okay."

"Of course," Michelle responded, clearly fighting a smile. "It's not till tomorrow morning that we have to worry about Juana's food poisoning. I was going to check out the kitchens and see if anything looks particularly off. Might take me a while."

"Thanks. Um, appreciate it."

Michelle winked. "How about I tie a ribbon on the door so Matias knows where to knock? You can take it down when he's gone."

Gwyn coughed and concentrated on pinning her hair net into place. "Good idea."

Dinner passed in a blur, and fortunately, Princess Juana retired early. Gwyn slipped back to her room, seeing the blue ribbon around the carved handle and, gulping with nerves, wondered if she was doing the right thing.

A soft knock less than a minute later almost paralysed her. She took a deep breath, straightened her shoulders and opened the door.

Without a word, eyes shining, Matias entered. He too, had washed the road dust from his skin, combed his hair and short beard, and while the smell of horse was still about him, it was tempered by a citrusy aroma. From behind his back, he presented an orange. "For you, my lady," he said with a bow.

Gwyn lifted it to her nose and inhaled, loving the simplicity of the gift. "Thank you." She took his hand and led him into the bedchamber, seating herself on the bed and arranging her skirts while she considered her next move.

Matias took the orange back from her and produced a small knife. He sliced and peeled it carefully, catching the drops on a linen handkerchief, then fed Gwyn the orange one small piece at a time, gazing boldly at her face as he did. When the orange was finished, she took his hand and sucked the juice slowly from his fingers, feeling the heat crackle between them. Cradling her face in his hand, he leant in and kissed her deeply. Gwyn gave a small moan, which encouraged Matias. His hand slid down.

The door slammed open, and Lady Valentina strode in, followed by Princess Juana and her ladies.

Seven

1496 AD

Michelle knew something was wrong the moment she set foot in the kitchens. Servants stood gossiping—nothing unusual in that—but no work was being done, despite the haranguing from the irate cook.

"What's going on?" she asked idly. Immediately all attention was centred on her.

"Oh, you don't know?" one footman asked.

"Of course she doesn't know, you clod, she's the maid to the lady!" an older, female servant retorted, then returned to eyeing Michelle speculatively. "I'm not sure we want your type in here."

A male servant chimed in with a rude comment, and several servants laughed. Michelle pretended not to understand, turning instead and making straight for Gwyn's rooms. She cursed the distance between the kitchens, cursed the skirts that slowed her dash, and cursed Lady Valentina most of all when she saw that lady's tall figure leading the verbal attack on Gwyn.

"…disgusting, whorish ways into this royal household! Lady Maria has no niece from a convent in Italy, so whoever you are, you will be thrown into a dungeon and the Inquisition shall discover the truth. I have here a warrant from the Queen herself for your arrest—she is appalled and horrified that you would seek to corrupt her daughter and commit who knows what terrible crimes against her, and you shall be persecuted to the full extent of the law!"

Gwyn wore guilt all over her face, and given the circumstances in which she had been confronted (hair askew, Matias the groom standing terrified beside her) Michelle could forgive her for not bluffing it out.

What to do? They couldn't leave—the job wasn't done. This kind of notoriety was not the sort to be brushed off, however, not when their goal was to inconspicuously divert the princess from eating a dish of rancid seafood that would otherwise make her so ill she died.

A crowd was gathering at Michelle's back, jostling her forward. Gwyn caught sight of Michelle and they exchanged a wordless, desperate glance. Michelle racked her brains for a plan.

"I am a witch!" Gwyn yelled, silencing the room. Shock rippled through nobles and servants alike. Michelle cocked an eyebrow, unsure how she was meant to play this. "Yes, I am a witch, and I bewitched this man to seduce his innocent soul!" Gwyn carried on. "Even my servant I bewitched, but she broke the charm and ran away. *Michelle, get the hell out of here. I'll meet you one hour after midnight.*" That last was in Turkish, which, thanks to the chronokinetor, only Michelle understood. "You have discovered me, so I shall flee! *Michelle! Get lost!*"

She vanished in a cloud of blue smoke.

Sofia and Marietta screamed, Princess Juana paled but Lady Valentina was outraged. Michelle didn't wait to find out what would happen to poor Matias. She shoved through the crowd and bolted down the hallway, finding an alcove suitable for her purposes and flinging herself behind the heavy curtains, listening for the sound of pursuit. Exclamations and thudding feet decided her, so she performed her own vanishing trick and jumped ahead in time two hours.

I hope you know what you're doing, Gwyn. It was an odd feeling to know that while time passed for Michelle, Gwyn was circumventing these hours entirely, and when she reappeared it would only be an instant later for her.

If she reappeared.

* * *

The palace had gone to sleep. Michelle crept along the tapestried hallway using her wrist computer to light her way, and was relieved to discover that, while their bags had been torn apart and searched, the clothes remained—no doubt for a servant to dispose of in the morning, or perhaps for a priest to exorcise. Everything smelt of oranges, which was odd.

She tidied and packed, changing into men's clothes and stashing the rest into the less damaged saddlebag. The trunk of court dresses would have to stay, bar two she could carry. They could be useful, though from what she knew of the turning points after this one she and Gwyn would do better with both of them pretending to be servants. One would involve a deliberate poisoning.

She rested, shutting off her light and dozing on the bed until her body clock told her the hour after midnight approached. Michelle sat up, watching the space beside the bed intently.

She felt the rushing of time-travel before the blue haze even appeared. Like an oncoming wave it filled her senses and roared in her ears, momentarily overwhelming her. Gwyn appeared, facing the other way, and the cloud faded.

"Michelle?"

"Behind you." Michelle activated her light.

The girl spun so fast she overbalanced. Michelle grabbed her wrist. "It's okay, it's just me."

Gwyn heaved a sigh. "Oh, thank God. What happened to Matias? Did he get away?"

Michelle felt a pang of guilt. "Uh, I don't know. I had to jump away myself—more discreetly than you, obviously. I, uh, presume he sorted himself out."

Gwyn frowned. "I hope they don't do anything to him. I'll have to go by the stables and find out."

"Gwyn! I know I said to have an affair, but we still have to save Juana from food poisoning tomorrow." Michelle climbed off the bed. "Can you get your dress off, since Matias didn't manage it, and put on clothes for travelling? You'll need to go and let me handle the turning point."

Gwyn's glare intensified. "Why can't I dress as a man like you? And I'll thank you not to comment on what Matias did or didn't *manage* since you didn't *manage* to see if he's okay."

Michelle raised her palms placatingly. "Alright, alright. Look—you've done really well, but if all I do in the morning is to tip a dish of seafood on the floor, then I might need to clear off fast. You take the gear and hide out in the forest; I'll use my chronokinetor to find you. Then we'll have our little holiday. It'll be great."

Gwyn's face was inscrutable. She crossed her arms. "Fine. Am I stealing a horse? I'll need to go via the stables for that."

"Boat would probably be better. Take one upriver first thing. I promise I'll check on your lover before I go." Michelle offered a smile. Gwyn didn't return it. "I'm sorry it didn't work out, Gwyn."

Gwyn shrugged, eyes sliding sideways. "Whatever, it doesn't matter. I just feel bad for him. At least Juana will go on to have her happy marriage. That's the important thing."

Michelle felt like she was missing something. She decided to leave it for now. "Come on, let's get a few hours' sleep. I'll wake you before dawn, it'll be all officers on the bridge then."

Whether Gwyn slept, Michelle didn't know. The girl tossed and turned and rose bleary-eyed as the black night outside began to fade into grey. Dressed, they left the room and made a brief farewell.

"Head upstream. I'll come and find you," Michelle said.

"See you soon." Gwyn nodded and disappeared in the direction of the palace gate, dressed as a manservant and weighed down by their saddlebags. Michelle knew she could trust her to be inconspicuous and talk her way past the guards—the girl had a talent for blending in.

Alone, she made her way to the kitchens, shuffling past servants lighting candles and carrying supplies in from the pantries and cold rooms. Gwyn's vision had shown her Princess Juana eating a plate of fish, taking ill aboard the ship, and dying amidst horrible cramps and vomiting spells. *Not a nice way to go.* Problem was a city on a river close to the sea abounded with fish, shellfish and crustaceans. The smell permeated the kitchens and Michelle paused, wondering where to start. If she started tipping over dishes she would be in trouble pretty quickly and wouldn't be guaranteed to get the one headed for the princess.

"Can I help?" she asked in Basque to a maid muttering unhappily under her breath as she cracked open mussels and dropped them into a broth-filled pot.

"Who are you?" came the suspicious response. "Ain't see you here before."

Michelle smiled easily and passed her the next mussel from the string bag. "Brought in extra to help while the princess is here. Got told to make myself useful. Here, you whack them and I'll open."

The surly maid took the mussel. "Takes a knack to hit them without breaking the shell." She carried on, giving monotone answers while Michelle chattered inanely, assessing the rest of the kitchen's activities as she did.

"Take this up," the cook ordered of a large fish platter. Michelle abandoned her mussel-cracking and leapt to help. The maid's protests were drowned in the din of utensils clanging, and Michelle concentrated on negotiating the platter through the door with the servant on the other side of the dish.

"Heard there was a to-do yesterday," she exclaimed, acting the nosy newcomer. "It's all over town."

The other servant puffed as they manoeuvred the heavy dish up the stairs. "I'm… not surprised," he grunted. "Turns out one of the princess' ladies was a witch. She'd been seducing innocent men all over the place. She'd bewitch them and bed them then they'd crackle to dust, and every time they did she'd get younger."

Michelle marvelled at the way the story had grown overnight. *I'll have to tell Gwyn.* "Did the latest man survive? I heard a priest stormed into the room, chanting from the Scripture and banishing her with holy water just before she could steal the seed of her victim."

"Oh, he survived, but barely. Poor fellow was shriven and given fifty Our Father's to recite. They never caught the witch." He shuddered, making the platter wobble dangerously.

"Careful!" Michelle nodded to the carved double doors ahead. "Where's this one going down?"

"Sideboard. Servants in there will serve up to the lords and ladies."

Another problem awaited when they entered the dining chamber. None of the nobles were present, and half a dozen other dishes of seafood littered the sideboard, along with fruit, fresh bread and spiced rolls and pastries. *Dammit! I need an excuse to hang about to watch what Juana eats. Or do I just go crazy now and throw the lot on the floor?*

"Come on," the other servant encouraged. "They don't like kitchen staff to linger."

Michelle permitted him to lead the way back out then doubled over in a coughing fit. "Go on," she wheezed. "Just a bad chest. I'll be down shortly."

The manservant shrugged and carried on without her. The guards eyed her—one tapped her foot with the butt of his spear. "Go on, don't be keeling over here."

"Local trash," the other guard observed. They spoke Castilian Spanish, not the Basque Michelle had used with the other servant.

"Sorry," she coughed, leaning on the wall. "I'll be out of here before the nobles come."

"Clear off." The guard tapped her harder. Michelle nodded and stumbled to the side corridor which led to the kitchens. A maid passed, carrying a plate of strange long clams—the briny smell really did make Michelle cough. *Great that they're so resourceful but give me a plain insect-protein biscuit any day.*

The maid returned, empty-handed, giving Michelle a suspicious look. In the main corridor, a flurry of silk skirts signalled the arrival of Princess Juana and her ladies. Michelle watched them go past, listened to the clunk as the guards shut the doors. Michelle straightened. She used her hands to brush down her tunic, rearranged her cap, and considered which expression to use. *Urgent yet fearful. Let's do this.*

"Señors!" She burst out of the corridor and stopped short of the spears that clashed in front of her. "The cook sent me! The food is bad! Please, you must stop the princess from eating it!"

"What's this?" The guard who had told her to clear off earlier brought the point of the spear to Michelle's face. "What food is bad?"

"Please!" Michelle clutched her chest and did her best to look terrified. "The cook said the fish has gone bad—it will make the princess sick!"

"Come here!" The other guard grabbed Michelle by the collar. "Go inside and stop them from serving," he ordered his partner, who nodded and disappeared through the door. Michelle tried to ignore his garlic-breath as he snarled, "You swamp-trash can't even be trusted to serve proper food. I'll be glad when I'm back eating real meat, not bloody creatures that don't even have the decency to have the right number of legs."

The door opened again. Lady Valentina came out. "What is going on? The server says the food is bad? Which dish?"

"All of it! The fish, the cockles, the pulpo—only the bread is safe!" Michelle kept her gaze down, not wanting Valentina to recognise her, even dressed as a man. She pointed inside. "Please, my lady, don't let the princess eat it."

As if summoned, Juana appeared behind Valentina. "What in our dear Lord's name is going on? Why will no one let me eat?"

"I'm sorry, your highness, this servant says the food is bad. I am sceptical that an entire table of dishes has turned—it smells fine to me." Valentina pointed at Michelle. "Bring the cook up here."

"Forgive me, my lady. I will find the cook," said the guard who wasn't holding Michelle. She itched to break free. She didn't want the cook coming up here and ruining her story.

"The cook has fled with shame, your highness, my lady," she declared. "Please, I can show you which dishes are safe and which to send back."

"This is ridiculous!" Juana's expression was reminiscent of Gwyn—she wore a slightly deranged look brought on by hunger. Michelle would have thought someone used to fasting would cope better with a delayed breakfast, but perhaps mental preparation played a part.

"The bread is safe," Michelle urged.

"Show me!" Juana ordered. Michelle followed her inside under the gaze of the guards, the servants and the irritated nobles seated at the table. "Eat some!" the princess commanded when Michelle pointed to the round loaves. Michelle broke off a portion and munched slowly, enjoying the chewy crust. She sighed contentedly.

"The bread seems fine, your highness," Lady Sofia observed.

"And the fish?" Juana pointed to the large platter Michelle had helped carry up.

Michelle shook her head, looking at the ground. "All bad, plus the cockles and the pulpo. All of the seafood was cooked in a broth that has turned. One of the kitchen lads tasted some and it made him very sick, retching and emptying his bowels. It was a fright to see."

Lady Sofia made a noise of distaste, and Michelle felt confident that she was almost there. Even if the cook was found and challenged Michelle's story, enough doubt had been cast, and enough time would have been wasted. The nobles would be pressed to depart for their ship that would take the princess to France, and Michelle would slip away and rendezvous with Gwyn.

The princess' slender hand reached under Michelle's chin and tilted her face upwards. Juana's eyes widened. "You!"

Oh, damn. Convincing others she was insignificant and inconspicuous didn't bear up against intense scrutiny. Her cover was blown.

"It is the witch's servant!" Juana hollered, but Michelle was already moving. She dragged the large platter from the table and sent the much maligned fish to the floor, sauce and all. When the first guard came at her she was ready, using the platter as a shield against the sword swing that came overhead. The silver dented badly. Michelle kicked the guard in the kneecap, feeling a satisfying crunch as he screamed.

"Protect the princess!" she yelled, adding to the confusion as the second guard looked wildly about for Juana. Michelle used the time to duck under the sideboard table, brace herself and push upwards with all her strength, executing a massive table flip and sending plates and food crashing to the floor. With the table between her and the guards, one advancing, the other moaning and clutching his knee, Michelle hugged the dented silver platter to her chest and legged it for the door.

Bursting through, she ran at two more guards who raced towards the noise. Michelle didn't slow—instead she dropped into a perfect slide, glad she wore long boots and breeches against the hard stone. She held up the fish platter but the guards were too slow to strike. Flinging the platter behind her she kept her momentum and scrambled upright, sprinting down the hall.

Well, if that hasn't fixed that turning point, I don't know what will. Going to have to chance it. She'd become used to Gwyn confirming the turning point had passed—for now she would have to trust her own knowledge and instincts.

Eight

1496 AD

Gwyn stepped off the rowboat and passed a coin to the oarsman. He accepted it wordlessly and tucked it into his belt pouch, then gestured at the path that led from the weed-choked wooden landing.

"Thanks." Gwyn swung the saddlebags over her shoulder and strode up the path. Once out of sight of the river, she diverted into the trees and found a nice hollow at the base of an oak to lie down. Using one bag as a pillow, she closed her eyes and sighed.

A sharp pain woke her. "Ow!" Gwyn sat up and slapped her arm. A horsefly fell dead. She waved away another one buzzing about her head. "Jesus, that hurt!" She froze when she realised she had an audience.

A young woman sat on the bank, arms loosely clasping her knees as she watched with interest. Gwyn assessed her for a threat—no weapons, no visible companions—she seemed relaxed, curious even. "Why are you wearing men's clothes?" the woman asked in Basque. She tucked a strand of auburn hair back into her head cloth, quirking a fine eyebrow inquisitively.

"Um…" *I fooled the boatman and the men at the docks! How did this woman spot me so easily?* Gwyn could only suppose it was more obvious when she slept, without her conscious mind working to convince people otherwise.

"I thought you were a man, at first," the woman said, her warm voice melodious. She looked older than Gwyn, but younger than Michelle— Gwyn thought her extremely attractive and unconsciously brushed her tunic down. The woman went on, "I would have left if you were. Then I saw your hands. Too small for a man's, and too soft-looking for a commoner woman hereabouts. Who are you?"

"Um. Well." What story would work for this keen-eyed woman? "My name is Gwynia—I just travelled up from Bilbao. I'm waiting for a friend." There. The truth was simple and easy.

"You're waiting here?" Scepticism crossed the woman's face. "Bit of an odd place. And why are you dressed as a man?"

Hmph, persistent. It was time to take control of the conversation. "Safety," Gwyn replied brusquely. "I'm less likely to be harassed if people think I'm a man." Her assertive tone was undermined by her stomach rumbling. How long had she been asleep?

The red-haired woman laughed. "Are you hungry? I have blackberries." She lifted a small basket at her side. "I'm collecting herbs. You can help me if you haven't anything better to do while you wait for your friend."

Gwyn opened her mouth to say 'no' and heard herself say, "Sure, I guess I can." Perplexed, she straightened her own cap and fussed with the bags, tucking them under a huge crawling tree root. She turned back to find the young woman standing before her, offering a handful of juicy blackberries with a smile. "I'm Isabel," she said.

"Thanks." Gwyn accepted them and savoured the taste. She swallowed. "Like the queen," she added, for something to say.

A shadow crossed Isabel's face. "Yes, like the queen."

Gwyn followed her up the bank. They wandered slowly through the forest, Isabel pointing out various herbs growing in shady patches or on stream beds, getting Gwyn to hold the basket while she took a small knife and harvested what she needed. She found blueberries too, and large, flat mushrooms.

"Are they safe to eat?" Gwyn asked dubiously. She had never been game to try foraging for food.

"Of course!" Isabel laughed. It was a pleasant, kind laugh. "I'm not a witch to collect poisonous toadstools."

Gwyn thought she was too unguarded and carefree to be mistaken for a witch. Isabel's chatter was annoyingly charming; she described the uses for different plants and asked Gwyn when she expected her friend.

"I'm not sure," Gwyn told her. "Sometime today, hopefully." She glanced at the sky and was shocked to realise they had been walking for hours.

"I suppose you'll want to get back to your things, then." Isabel smiled. "Thank you for your help." She turned to go.

"Uh, wait!" Gwyn called. "Um, how do I get back there?"

Isabel raised her eyebrows. "Oh, I'm sorry—do you not know the way?"

Gwyn tried to keep her expression pleasant. *I wouldn't have bloody asked if I did.* "No. Can you point me in the direction of the river?" That should be enough to find the little landing stage and the path… she hoped.

"Does your friend know these woods well?"

"No." Gwyn was getting impatient. If she'd known Isabel was going to take her on a herb-collecting jaunt to abandon her in the woods she would have stayed put, blackberries or no.

"How will you two find each other, if neither of you have ever been here before?"

Gwyn cursed herself for being led into the verbal trap. Not that this woman posed much danger by herself, but who knew how long she might have to wait for Michelle. Isabel might tell other people from the village where she was. She didn't feel like fielding more questions. "A man in Bilbao described the path from the river to us. Michelle will find me there."

Isabel smiled conspiratorially. "Michel." She pronounced it the Spanish way, as a masculine name. "Is he your lover? Are you running away to be married? How exciting and dangerous."

Gwyn sighed, then decided that story worked. "You found me out. Our families won't let us be together but we intend to marry anyway. Now, can you please show me which way back?"

Isabel chuckled. "Of course. Here, carry the basket and I'll lead the way."

Gwyn pulled a face at Isabel's back—the basket was heavier now, full of berries, mushrooms and all manner of herbs. She was glad she didn't have long skirts to catch on bushes and tree roots, though her companion managed well enough now that her hands were free. They scrambled across gullies and along what were scarcely more than goat tracks. After an hour they emerged onto a wider path. "The river is that way." Isabel pointed. "Your hollow is beyond that chestnut and down the bank. I must go, now—it will be getting dark soon."

The late afternoon sun pierced the leaves above, but the shadows crept on. "Thank you," Gwyn said. She felt contrite now that this woman had gone out of her way to see her back safely. "I appreciate it." She passed over Isabel's basket.

Isabel smiled warmly and pulled several mushrooms from the basket. "Take these for your supper. Good luck meeting your lover, Gwynia, and may God bless you."

Gwyn felt bereft as she watched the other woman disappear back up the path. She made her way to the hollow and checked on the gear. It was still tucked under the tree root, untouched. Gwyn walked to the river and filled her drinking gourd, washing her face, hands and feet, then sat on the bank, watching mayflies dance above the water. She wished she knew how to fish. She wished Michelle would arrive. She wished Isabel hadn't left her alone.

* * *

She woke. The darkness was heavy and something rustled nearby. *It's just an animal. You've slept outside hundreds of times—calm down!* All the same, she hugged her cloak closer.

What would become of her once this was all over? Michelle focussed on their success or failure because the entire future of humanity and other species was at stake. Gwyn on the other hand… how would she ever fit in again? She was a year older than when she had first time-travelled—maybe two? She had lost track.

Michelle said they should have a holiday. Gwyn snorted. She and Michelle respected each other, but it was a working relationship. They would never be best friends.

Gwyn sighed. *She's the only one who understands any of this.* It wasn't enough, though. Michelle's time was too different. Gwyn's brother and sister believed her, but they would never understand what Gwyn had gone through.

She missed Gaius and Adi. She missed Meric. It would be nice to have someone travel with them, but while Gaius and Adi had survived and even seemed happy, it was Gwyn's fault Meric was dead. She couldn't ever risk that happening again.

She wished it could be different.

She must have dozed off because the birds were singing their morning chorus when she woke again. Gwyn shivered. Dew covered her cloak and the sun had not yet risen. She groaned and stood, then looked directly into eyes of a wolf standing at the top of the slope where Isabel had sat the day before. Gwyn barely breathed. The wolf sniffed the air, sneezed and vanished into the undergrowth.

Gwyn remained frozen until her heart stopped racing. Once she was calm she headed down to the river and stretched as she watched the sunrise peek through the valley cloud. She spent several hours foraging, careful not to stray too far and get lost, collecting berries and supplementing them with the last of the bread and sausage she had purchased before leaving Bilbao. Then she checked their gear, and tried to meditate as the day wore on. Yawns overtook her and she fell into a melancholy sleep.

When she opened her eyes, Michelle sat nearby and it was evening. Gwyn jumped up and gave the woman a hug. Michelle tensed, then patted Gwyn's back gently. "Did you miss me or something?" she gave a half laugh.

Gwyn shrugged and grinned. "No, I was enjoying the peace and quiet. I hope you brought food."

Michelle snorted. "Of course. And yes—*I'm* the chatty one. It's so noisy when I'm around."

They built a fire and cooked the fish and vegetables Michelle had brought with her. She filled Gwyn in on how she had handled the turning point—Gwyn laughed at the thought of Michelle table flipping and causing confusion.

"I thought you were the subtle one," she teased.

Michelle shook her head. She looked seriously at Gwyn. "It's definitely easier when we work together."

Gwyn blushed and looked down. "Thanks."

I guess a holiday with Michelle isn't such a bad thing. She's alright, really.

It was a nice feeling to go to sleep with that night, that their partnership had reached a comfortable balance. Gwyn felt less alone, and her haunting fears didn't bother her sleep that night. She slept well.

* * *

In the morning they packed up and followed the path deeper into the forest. Gwyn told Michelle about Isabel. "She said there are several hamlets and villages this way, as the river curves back around. People farm and fish and forage from the woods."

"I suspect we may have to hire a boat to take us back to Bilbao, or all the way to the coast, if that's the way we want to go. Isn't that what people in your time do? Have holidays by the seaside?"

Gwyn laughed. "Yeah, often. Or go camping. Or travelling. Really depends what you like. Some people want to relax, other people want to do activities, or visit museums."

"What sort of activities?"

Gwyn described water sports, snow sports, rock climbing and hiking. "Then there're people who want to do cooking classes, or visit wineries, or even go shopping."

"Snowboarding sounds fun. Cooking might be interesting—as unethical and un-environmentally friendly as it is eating animals, I do admire the variety of dishes and flavours people in these times manage to produce."

Gwyn frowned. "I remember you said people in your time mostly eat… insects?"

"Insect protein, and algae-derived products, as well as seaweed. Much healthier and much more sustainable."

Gwyn sniffed. "Someone's cooking something—smell that smoke!"

They continued on—the path widened and the trees thinned. They emerged from the woods and passed several cottages and empty fields. The river reappeared—curving around on their right and feeding irrigation ditches. Michelle halted and grabbed Gwyn's arm. "I thought you said this was a village? That's too big for chimney smoke." She stared at the billowing clouds rising up from further ahead, the source blocked from view by several houses.

Gwyn's stomach lurched. "It is a village, Isabel said. Is a house on fire?"

"No one's screaming." They listened. "It sounds like… cheering." Michelle frowned. "Gwyn, maybe we should go around."

Gwyn was already ahead, walking quickly towards the source of the smoke. She heard Michelle swear and chase after her, catching up as they entered the village square and witnessed dozens of people shouting and jeering. The foul smell hit them as the breeze shifted and Gwyn retched. Not just burning meat; the stink of charred hair and clothes clogged the air. Tied to a pyre was blackened corpse.

Gwyn lurched, dizzy—Michelle steadied her, white-faced. "Come on, we need to go."

"Bring out the other witch!" a woman in the crowd screeched, and her fellow villagers cheered. Two men dragged forward a struggling figure, a woman in a white shift. Someone lunged forward and ripped the cap from her head. Red hair spilled out. "Whore! Witch!" The crowd was an animal hungry for more blood.

"Ah, shit, come on, Gwyn!" Michelle urged. The men thrust the woman at the second, unburnt pyre and lashed her hands above her head. Tears streamed down the woman's face as she screamed for mercy.

Gwyn panicked. "It's Isabel!" She looked around wildly. "They're about to murder her!"

"And we'll be next if we get in the way! Let's go!" Michelle dragged at Gwyn's arm.

With an alacrity that astonished them both, Gwyn twisted free and swung her saddlebag at Michelle, hitting the other woman's midsection with an 'oof'.

"What in the stars are you doing?" Michelle gasped.

"Oh-one-thirty-six hours!" Gwyn yelled, and some of the villagers turned to stare.

"Gwyn!" Michelle bellowed, but Gwyn was away, shoving through the crowd. People cursed her, but most had no idea until she had pushed them aside, their focus on the macabre spectacle in front. Each short breath Gwyn took brought the tang of feral excitement, tinged with fear, from the shouting villagers.

She slid past a huge, sweaty man at the front and clambered up onto the wooden platform that supported Isabel's feet. The woman thrashed futilely against her bonds.

"Stay still!" Gwyn shouted. A hand yanked on her leg. She kicked free and threw her arms around Isabel, concentrating.

Blue haze rose. *Flick!*

The cloud faded. The pyre and platform were gone, but the timepiece stabilised Gwyn and Isabel on the ground. It was dark and the wind blew wildly. A rough hand hauled Gwyn away and she stumbled. "Of all the stupid stunts!" Michelle glared.

"What… what's happening? Am I dead?" Isabel's voice was a tremulous sob.

"No—we saved you." Gwyn tried to locate the woman in the darkness. "Michelle can you make some light?"

A blue glow emitted from Michelle's wrist computer. It cast eerie shadows up onto her face, making her look cold and grim. Not all of the grimness was due to the shadows, Gwyn realised, and hastened to placate her. "Look—they were about to murder her, and she knows about herbs and stuff. Maybe she could give us some advice for the next turning point." She turned back to Isabel. The woman had pressed ash-smeared hands to her face. "It's okay—I know this is really strange, but you're safe. We should probably leave though."

"You think?" Michelle hissed. "Come on, before we wake the village and they burn us all."

"Wait!" Isabel looked around. "We're in the village still? I need my medicines. Then I'll go wherever you want." She clasped her arms around herself and hastened towards the edge of the square, then stopped and looked back. Gwyn raised her eyebrows at Michelle, who huffed and swung a saddlebag at Gwyn.

Gwyn caught it and followed Michelle, who lit Isabel's way to a small cottage further back from the river. Isabel paused at the sight of the broken door hanging crookedly over the gaping darkness.

"What happened?" Gwyn whispered as they ventured in.

Isabel darted around the one room cottage, retrieving several miniscule clay jars from where they lay next to an upturned table. "An inquisitor came. Demanded to know why the priest tolerated witches and lapsed conversos." She shot a glance at Gwyn and Michelle. Despite the tear-tracks cutting through the grit on her cheeks, she looked defiant. "I never practised the Jewish rites—I simply kept my father's candles for Chanukah. They are an heirloom, nothing more!"

"I don't care who or what you worship, and neither does Gwyn," Michelle commented acerbically. "We need to leave."

Isabel threw a dress over her grubby shift and grabbed several more items, including a cloak, shoes and a box hidden in the chimney. She stuffed them into a pair of string bags and straightened. "Let us go."

Once Michelle deemed them far enough from the village they stopped by a burbling stream. Michelle increased illumination until they stood in a pool of light. "I'm not going to risk breaking an ankle in the dark, and besides, our body clocks think it's morning still. Isabel, get yourself cleaned up and respectable looking. Gwyn and I will stay dressed as men, but it will be better if you aren't all ash-smeared and unkempt."

Isabel peered at Michelle. "You… are a woman too?" She glanced at Gwyn, puzzled. "I thought you said you waited for a man named Michel?"

"Er." Gwyn sought for words.

"I'm Michelle," Michelle rubbed her forehead. "I'm as a man for disguise. Gwyn, what in all the stars did you tell this woman?"

"No, no," Isabel interrupted. "She was very discreet. I do understand even more now why you two chose to run away to be together."

Michelle was the picture of exasperation. Gwyn started to correct Isabel's assumption but Michelle butted in. "Just get changed. I need five minutes to clear my head. Gwyn, explain to her that she's about to see some real witchcraft, if that's what she wants to call it. I'm jumping us to the morning as soon as I get back.

She slipped her wrist computer off, hung it on twig and stormed into the darkness. Gwyn gestured helplessly. "She just needs to calm down. She won't go far. Er—do you want some privacy to get changed?"

Isabel gaped at her. "Did she say 'real witchcraft'?"

Nine

1496 AD

Michelle stopped within earshot and sat on a log. Once again, Gwyn had jeopardised everything by acting impulsively. Despite this, Michelle couldn't be bothered ruminating on the brief fury she'd felt. *I can't lose my temper over every stupid thing she does, or I'd be forever angry. Besides, she obviously doesn't learn. I'll just have to manage her as best as I can.*

A bubble of anxiety popped and relief seeped into her limbs. She could still smell the burnt flesh from the first execution. They had been too late for that victim, but Michelle found herself glad they had saved Isabel. Never mind it wasn't a turning point; in a small way, they had saved an innocent life. Michelle shook her head. Gwyn's influence must be rubbing off on her.

She found a spot to relieve herself, then returned to her log and sat, eavesdropping on the conversation between Gwyn and Isabel. Gwyn was giving a garbled explanation of how they had gone from daytime to the middle of the night in a flash. Isabel was taking it surprisingly well.

"You can travel through time." Her tone was flat. It was a statement.

"Um, that's pretty much it."

"Could you go back and warn me about what will happen?"

Michelle thought Isabel was surprisingly well-spoken for a villager. Perhaps her Jewish father had encouraged her education.

Gwyn was explaining they could not travel back in time, only forwards. "We used to be able to, but there's this thing called the Shift—it's a bit hard to explain. Basically we can only jump forwards."

Michelle listened to the pause. Then Isabel spoke again. "And what do you intend to do with me?"

"Um…"

Michelle pursed her lips. She stepped back into the circle of light. "I thought I said to get cleaned up," she said, her tone tired rather than harsh. "Gwyn and I will take you to Bilbao, if that suits? From there you can make arrangements for yourself. If you wish to skip the next year or two so that memory of you fades from this area, we can assist. A few years won't put you out of touch with social trends. Not that they will change much around here. The Inquisition will be in charge for a long time to come."

Isabel blanched, then hastily stripped off her dress and under-gown. Gwyn blushed and looked away. Michelle gave her a puzzled look. *Not like we haven't changed and bathed in front of each other lots in these past few months.*

"Please, would you pass me the gown from my bag?" Isabel asked as she stepped into the stream. Goosebumps raced to cover her skin as she hastily splashed water over herself, washing the worst of the soot away. As she stepped back up the bank Gwyn handed her the clean gown, looking away. Isabel dried herself using the old white shift, avoiding the worst of its tears and smudges, and dressed. "Let us go," she said, lacing her shoes. "I have no desire to be near this place any longer."

Flick!

* * *

"She didn't react too badly to the time-jumps." Michelle mused to Gwyn in twentieth-century English as they tramped along the muddy track. Isabel was well-educated and spoke Castilian Spanish, so Michelle spoke something Isabel would have no chance of understanding. "Barely looked nauseated, and she didn't freak out when we went from night to day. She must be one of those people with the genes to deal with temporal shifts."

"Yeah?" Gwyn skirted around a puddle, then squinted at the grey sky. It taunted them with the threat of rain. "Ugh, it's so muggy." She slapped a mosquito on her arm. Behind them, Isabel doggedly kept up, hampered by her skirts and waterlogged shoes.

"She needs a decent pair of boots," Michelle muttered.

"Maybe the cobbler was too busy trying to burn her alive than sell her boots—why do you care?" Gwyn snapped, slapping at more mosquitos.

Michelle chewed her lip. They would reach the next village soon—according to Isabel it was on the other side of the steep hill. From there they would hire a boat and make their way back to Bilbao, or even all the way to the coast.

"What if…" Michelle took a deep breath, more for pause than for oxygen. The walk was challenging but not strenuous.

"What if?" There was an edge to Gwyn's voice.

Michelle committed. "What if we ask her to come with us? You said she knows about herbs and medicines of the time—that could be handy." She used the expression hoping Gwyn would find it more accessible. "Plus a third set of eyes and ears is always useful. She seems mentally and emotionally stable, despite the fright of her near escape. She's a converso, and an outcast, and if she had any family she'd do them no favours by returning." Gwyn opened her mouth to interrupt but Michelle continued. "A third person would break up our dynamic—maybe stop us getting on each other's nerves so much."

Gwyn gaped. "Getting on… what the hell? I thought we were getting along fine! I was happy to see you when you rocked up yesterday."

Michelle attempted to soothe her. "We're still under a lot of pressure. It won't hurt to alleviate that somewhat."

Gwyn increased her pace and pulled away from an astonished Michelle. She caught up to Gwyn at the top of the rise and grabbed her arm, stopping her. "What is the matter? Did I say something to upset you?"

Gwyn's eyes grew wide. "Upset me? We have been working well together but it still isn't good enough for you. You tell *me* off for being impulsive, then you decide we need another person because obviously I'm too annoying for you to be around."

Michelle pinched her forehead and took a slow breath. She took a moment to reply, biting off the automatic retort "I'm sorry. I can see that I didn't think about how you might feel. I'm used to making all the decisions in the best interest of the mission, but the best interest is in us communicating effectively, and I didn't do that here."

Gwyn's mouth had dropped open during Michelle's apology, and she shuffled her feet. "Um, it's okay. I probably over-reacted going off at you like that."

"Hey—we're a good team, we just come at things from different angles." Michelle smiled and bowed, then remembered that people in Gwyn's time and culture tended not to do that. She stuck out her hand. Gwyn laughed and shook it. Isabel caught up to them.

"I fear I am the source of your disagreement," she said, looking from one to the other. "I am pleased you have resolved it. I do not wish to be the cause for dissent." Her cheeks were rosy, either from exercise or embarrassment.

Michelle looked at Gwyn, and gestured for her to speak.

Gwyn appeared to think a moment, then said, "Not really, no—Michelle suggested that you might travel with us, and I kinda took it personally, but that's to do with us, not you." She was emphatic, and Michelle sensed her leaning into the chronokinetor to convince the red-haired woman.

Isabel was taken aback. "You… want me to travel with you? I do appreciate how you came to my rescue but your magic frightens me." She edged away, and Michelle wondered if she and Gwyn seemed predatory.

"Look—no pressure," Gwyn said, "but if you have nowhere to go, please consider it. Otherwise we'll take you to Bilbao or anywhere along the river." She turned and started down the track, keeping to the side to avoid the muddy rivulet that flowed in the middle.

They reached the village, passing wooden huts on their way to the small jetty that marched a short distance into the river. A young man caulking a boat down on the mud frowned at them silently. A portly woman raised her eyebrows then carried on skinning and gutting fish on the worn planks, dropping scraps to the cat that crouched possessively beside her. A net-mender sat whistling, feeling his way along the twine as milky eyes stared into the distance.

"Hello, grandfather," Michelle addressed the net-mender. "We are pilgrims on our way to Santiago de Compostela. Would there be a boat we could hire to take us downriver?"

"Eh?" The old man squinted. "Pilgrims? How many of you be there?"

"Three. We are due to meet a larger party in Bilbao."

"Hmph. Mayhap Emmanuel can take thee, he travels to the city sometimes." He lifted his chin and yelled, "Emmanuel! Where are you, you useless good-for-nothing?"

The young man who had been working on his boat slouched over. "I'm here, Uncle."

"Don't sneak up on me! I tell you, young people these days," the old man grumbled. "These pilgrims want to travel to Bilbao. Is your boat sound or still full of holes?"

Emmanuel eyed Michelle and her companions. "They don't look like no pilgrims, Uncle. This 'un is dressed like a soldier, for all that he carries no weapons. The other is soft-looking, like a monk, but they have a woman, and I know her to be the healer from over the way. Didn't I hear there was going to be a burning yesterday, and she named a witch?"

Michelle kept her expression pleasant. "Does is matter what we look like if our coin is good?"

That perked the old man. "Hear that, you witless fool? Them's willing to pay, so you'll take them, pilgrim or no."

Emmanuel's grunt was identical to his uncle's earlier sound of derision. "How much?"

"I'll haggle over the price, you clod—you just see that your boat is river-worthy."

"Go with him, Gwyn," Michelle murmured. "Isabel, stay with me."

Gwyn followed Emmanuel off the dock to his wooden dinghy. She returned shortly after Michelle had agreed a price. "Looks okay, I guess. I don't know anything about boats really. You know I get seasick."

Michelle shook her head. "It's a calm river—you got up here alright, didn't you?"

"Does it matter than he's not finished caulking?" Isabel asked. Michelle and Gwyn looked at each other.

"Aye, it'll be fine," the old man said. "Soundest boat on the waterway. Have you down to the city faster than you can say a Hail Mary."

Michelle gave a small smile when Gwyn rolled her eyes. "Yes, he's got our money now," she whispered, "of course he doesn't want us to go back on the deal. Where'd the nephew go?"

Gwyn gestured back towards the village. "Went to fetch a few things. Said he'd be back shortly. Shall I see if we can buy some food for the trip?"

Isabel stayed with Michelle again while Gwyn followed directions from the old man to find the baker. The woman gutting fish had disappeared. Several other villagers strolled past the small jetty. Michelle waved away flies that buzzed over them, ignoring the old man who regaled them with tales of how Emmanuel was such a good boatman. Isabel made polite listening noises.

"If you want to stay, please do," Michelle said quietly to Isabel. "There is no pressure to come with us."

"No. It's too close. I don't like being here as it is." The woman hugged her shawl around her head, keeping her hair covered. "I'll be glad when we are gone."

"Michelle!" The yell came from the village. Michelle's head snapped around. "Michelle, we gotta go!" Gwyn appeared, running, a bundle clutched to her chest.

Michelle didn't wait for clarification. She grabbed the saddlebags and leapt off the jetty onto the muddy shore. "Come on, Isabel!" Flinging their packs into the boat, she shoved with all her strength.

Isabel appeared. "What's going on?" She, too, cast her possessions into the boat and pushed. The vessel groaned and slid along its rollers towards the water.

"It's a mob!" Gwyn gasped, joining them. The three women heaved and leapt into the boat as it splashed into the river, its momentum driving it forward. Michelle looked back at the bank.

It was indeed a mob—albeit a small one. A cluster of villagers surged onto the jetty, yelling insults and slavering for blood. Some brandished staffs, whilst others waved what must have been the closest implements to hand when someone had riled them up; a sickle, a rolling pin, a cleaver all made appearances, and Michelle didn't fancy trying to fight them all. "Where are the oars?" she hollered, clutching the side.

"Here!" Gwyn dragged one from beneath the sole bench seat and shoved it at Michelle. "Can you row?" She fished out a second oar, wobbling as she fought to keep her balance. The boat spun slowly in the current.

"No, can you?"

"No!"

Michelle stared at the oarlocks. "Just grab one and paddle!"

"Hurry!" Isabel urged. Michelle looked at the source of her concern. Several villagers had taken to their own boats. The rest had abandoned the jetty and kept pace with them along the river bank. Angry men and women scooped rocks from the ground and hurled them along with threats.

Michelle and Gwyn paddled. Neither woman was particularly practised but the urgency of the situation lent strength to their strokes. They steered away from the near bank, trying to avoid the missiles that rained down; some landing in the boat, others splashing around them.

"Don't take us too close to the other bank," Isabel warned. "We'll run aground in the shallows. We need to ride the current around the bend!"

Gwyn paused. Michelle cursed and paddled hard, bringing the prow around. They veered back towards the village side of the river and the mob cheered, sensing capture.

"Can't we jump the whole boat?" Gwyn shouted.

"It's a boat, not a bloody horse!"

"So?"

"A horse is a living animal, Gwyn! We'll land in the bloody water!"

"Will you two stop yelling and paddle!" Isabel yelled, getting their attention. "They're catching up!"

Michelle turned and swore. One rowboat was almost upon them, with a handful of exhilarated men. "Catch the witches! We've almost got them!"

"They stole my boat!" It was Emmanuel, looking furious.

"That bastard set the mob on us!" Gwyn turned back to paddle and copped a rock to the head. She crumpled, and would have fallen into the river had Isabel not lunged forward and grabbed her. Isabel lowered

Gwyn into the bow and took the oar, setting it into the oarlock.

"Give me the other," she ordered Michelle. "Can you not cast a spell against them?"

Michelle went to retort that she wasn't really a witch, then had an idea. She thrust the oar at Isabel, then took a wide stance in the stern and activated the light on her wrist computer, turning it to its brightest setting and covering it with her other hand. "Stay back or I shall curse thee!" she bellowed.

The men in the nearest boat barely hesitated. They were metres from Michelle, with two men readying themselves to leap. Michelle uncovered the light and directed it into their eyes. "Curse thee with blindness! Curse thee with pox!" she screeched in her best impression of a fairy-tale witch.

The first man yelled and threw his hands up. The second roared fury and reached for Michelle as their vessel scraped alongside. She grabbed his wrists and pulled him towards her just as she shoved his boat back with her foot. The second he was overbalanced she let go. *Splash!*

The second rowboat neared and Michelle shone the light at them. "Stay back or I shall curse thee too!" It was enough to give them pause and Michelle realised the distance between them was growing. She glanced around to see Isabel rowing hard, her face intent as she steered them back towards the centre of the river as the current straightened and tugged them downstream. The villagers on the shore cursed futilely and gave up the chase.

Michelle heaved a sigh of relief. "Gwyn, are you alive?"

No answer.

Isabel paused rowing in order for Michelle to clamber past her into the bow. "Gwyn?" The girl had a bloody gash on her forehead. Michelle checked her pulse and breathing. "She's just unconscious." Gwyn didn't seem to be injured anywhere else, but Michelle couldn't check her properly until they reached somewhere safe. "We'll have to put in somewhere downriver. I need to make sure she's alright, but we need to get further away first."

Isabel's back and shoulders strained as she rowed, facing upstream as trees obscured sight of the village. "There's a village further down that knows me as a healer. Hopefully they won't have heard of me being accused as a heretic. We can take her there."

Michelle was curious. "Do you travel up and down the river a lot?"

"I used to." Michelle couldn't see Isabel's face. The other woman sounded sad. "My father was a travelling healer. He used to take me with him when I was old enough to learn his craft."

Gently probing, Michelle asked, "What about your mother?"

This time the sadness was plain to hear. "She died when I was young. Women in the village cared for me and were kind but when my father died of the ague several years ago, people became… distant."

Having never known her parents, Michelle found it hard to relate. She did her best to soften her tone. "Do you have relatives anywhere that you wish to go to? We are happy for you to travel with us, but it'll be… strange."

Several ducks quacked noisily as they paddled furiously to avoid the oncoming boat. "Must I decide now?" Isabel asked at last.

Michelle raised her eyebrows. "No, of course not. I appreciate your help in the meantime. I can't afford to lose Gwyn." She frowned and looked back down at the girl, whose eyelids were fluttering. "I think she's coming around."

"Good," said Isabel tersely, increasing the pace of her strokes. "Because the boat is leaking."

Ten

1496 AD

Gwyn woke to a terrible headache and wet legs. "What the…?"

"You're alive? Good. Grab something and bail." Michelle scooped frantically using one of their wooden eating bowls. Water flew through the air and pattered onto the river, melding with the river in hundreds of circular ripples.

Gwyn sat up rapidly. "Are we sinking?" There were several inches of water in the boat; Isabel rowed with all her strength as they arrowed towards the bank.

"We will if you don't bloody help!"

Michelle hurled the second bowl at her. Gwyn fumbled, then scooped and flung water despite the dizziness that threatened to overwhelm her. Her shoulders sagged when she felt the boat crunch onto a pebbly shore, and together with Michelle and Isabel they grabbed their belongings and abandoned the doomed vessel.

The three women stood on the riverbank, panting. "That old bastard probably knew we were going to sink," Michelle spat. "Didn't stop him taking our money."

"Maybe I should have checked it better," Gwyn said. Her vision tunnelled and her legs collapsed from underneath her, sending her sprawling onto her butt.

"Mistress Gwyn!" Isabel dropped her sodden bag and grabbed Gwyn under the shoulders.

"I'm alright," Gwyn mumbled. "Just a bit… bit woozy." She heard the other two fussing and chattering but couldn't focus on what they actually said. She tried to help as they hauled her up the bank through some bushes to a patch of flat, dry ground. "Ow!" She rubbed her arm where a stick had scratched. Light and sound crept back to normal. "Ugh, I feel awful."

"Can you focus on me? Do you know your name?" Michelle's face hovered in front of her. Someone else—Isabel—bound her head wound with strips of cloth cut from the dryer regions of her skirt.

"Of course I know my name, it's Gwyn Turner." Gwyn tried to glare, but felt the effect was lacking as Michelle demanded varying other bits of information to establish her sanity, intelligence or memory—she wasn't sure which.

"She needs to rest," Isabel interrupted anxiously. "She'll catch a chill in these damp things. Have you blankets? We need to undress her."

Gwyn reluctantly agreed—her clothes clung to her uncomfortably, but she didn't fancy getting her kit off in front of a stranger.

"Everything is wet," Michelle pointed out. "How far is this village of yours? Or should I build a fire?"

Gwyn closed her eyes as Isabel replied, "It's close. Perhaps a mile. Can we carry her?"

Michelle must have noticed. "Gwyn! Don't go to sleep! You could have concussion!"

"I'm not asleep!" Gwyn replied crossly. "I'm just resting my eyes." She half sat up and put an arm out to stabilise herself. "I can probably walk, just… just give me a minute." Nausea rose and she swayed.

"I'll go for help," Isabel declared. "I'll be quickest on my own, without my things."

"What if they think you're a witch? They might attack you." Michelle sounded anxious, which surprised Gwyn. Was she so attached to this newcomer already? A spurt of jealously filled her stomach.

"I will be fine," Isabel said, "and I promise to return. I owe you both my life, twice over. I shall repay that debt."

Oh. Perhaps Michelle was just worried she'd run off on us. Idiot.

"I shall return soon."

Gwyn heard Isabel leave and felt Michelle settle in beside her. "Don't go to sleep, Gwyn, talk to me."

Gwyn sighed and cracked her eyelids. "I'm sorry. Got us into another mess. We'd be halfway to Bilbao by now if I hadn't jumped in to save Isabel."

"No, I'm glad you did. Burning is an awful way to die. She seems a good-enough person—I just hope she comes back."

Huh. "Could really use that holiday right about now."

Michelle chuckled. "River boat cruise?"

Gwyn snorted. "Pass. No boats. I'm happy to sit on the seaside but no bloody boats."

"We'll ride from now on, I promise."

Gwyn sighed again and fell silent, but made a point of keeping her eyes open, watching the sky through the trees. Grey clouds promised rain, and the smell of river weed and mud had her aching for a hot bath. A swallow landed on the branch above her and sang a warning, then fluttered onto their packs and pecked inquisitively. Gwyn let herself become mesmerised by the deep blue plumage and admired the dainty way the bird inspected each bag. "Laden swallow," she muttered to herself and giggled.

"What is it? Are you alright?" Michelle felt Gwyn's forehead and took her pulse.

"I'm fine." She chuckled again. "Guess we're not witches, or we'd be lighter than ducks!" She giggled at Michelle's apprehensive face, then forced herself under control, feeling a smile twitch the corners of her mouth. "I'm fine, really, just a joke from my time."

Michelle didn't believe her, Gwyn could tell. The other woman stood and paced the small clearing. "I hope she comes back."

Gwyn agreed, however a more insistent urge was clamouring for her attention. "Michelle, I really need to use the privy. Can you make sure I don't fall over? I think I'm fine to get up."

She was. Michelle helped her sit and stand and balance against the trunk of the tree. She was back sitting by their packs when a shout from the river gained both their attentions.

"Michel! Mistress Gwyn!"

Michelle plunged through the bushes and returned mere moments later. "She brought help." Gwyn smirked at the note of surprise in Michelle's voice. *Too cynical, Michelle.*

"Wait, didn't she walk in that direction for the village?" Gwyn jabbed a thumb behind them.

Michelle smirked right back at Gwyn. "Yep. I hope you'll make an exception to your 'no river cruise' decision, because she brought a boat."

* * *

While the village of Lemoa hadn't heard of her accusation and attempted burning, Isabel was glad to leave it behind. It wouldn't be long before news travelled downriver. She had kept up the pretence that Michelle was a man, and spun a story of Gwyn as the injured wife, promising money to the fisherman who rowed upstream to rescue them. Michelle hadn't quibbled at the reward, and paid the fisherman twice as much the next day to convey them all downstream to more civilised reaches of the river.

They took rooms in a house more expansive and luxurious than any Isabel had ever seen. It had a high wall with a quiet courtyard garden, where shrubs of pink and white camellia sat in corner pots, infusing the air with their scent. Upstairs, soft woollen blankets and feathered pillows adorned the beds in each of the three bedrooms, and a cook and a maid came for a few hours each afternoon to prepare meals and clean.

"Normally we stay at inns," Michelle explained, "but I want some peace and privacy while we have a break from work."

What their work was, Isabel couldn't say. The first morning they emptied saddlebags and packs and spread the contents across the courtyard paving stones. Some items of clothing were still damp; all needed cleaning or mending. Isabel was astonished to see Gwyn pull out a beautiful gown worthy of a noblewoman. *Courtesans,* she thought, but what courtesan carried weapons? Michelle set about cleaning and checking all sorts of knives, a short sword, and a wire that looked like a cheese cutter but felt sinister considering the company it kept.

Given the male disguise, Isabel suspected Michelle was Gwyn's protector. They were not lovers as she first assumed. The idea had shocked her, but a secret part of her mind found it fascinating. Sisters? Perhaps. They shared some features—dark brown hair, a certain set of the jaw—but some of the things they said made it seem as though they hadn't known each other for very long.

She knew Michelle watched that she didn't touch their things, or gossip with the cook or the maid. Isabel was friendly with both servants but suspected it was easier for them to avoid eye contact and conversation. They were being paid for discretion. If anyone asked, they could say they had seen nothing, heard nothing.

Gwyn appeared to find this hard too. "I'm not used to people doing things for me," she confided, mending her skirt whilst they sat in the courtyard on the second day.

This made Isabel feel kindly towards her. When a light shower drifted in, they retreated to the covered walkway, and Isabel disappeared into the kitchen briefly to put together a small tray of food for them to share. "When you visit people as a healer you tend to wait on them," she said. "I've become good at finding things in other people's kitchens."

Gwyn frowned. "We don't expect you to wait on us. We didn't bring you along to be a servant."

Isabel smiled. "You can clean up then."

With that, Gwyn happily shared the lunch and took the dishes and tray back to the kitchen, returning when everything was clean and away. They continued with their personal chores into the early afternoon. Isabel sorted her medicine box, noting which herbs and powders she was low on, and which she might sell for coin. She couldn't rely on the generosity of these women—it might disappear as quickly as it came— and if she were to earn her keep she would need to establish herself as a healer again.

"You say you are not used to servants, yet you appear comfortable with money." As soon as the words were out Isabel cursed herself. Worrying about funding made her consider sinister reasons Gwyn and Michelle could have for wanting her around. She hated secrecy—let them declare themselves!

Gwyn's tone was unbothered, however, as she replied. "Michelle's seen to it that we're okay for cash. I've usually had to pretend to be a servant when I've travelled on my own." She put down her needle and smiled. "It's a long story, as they say. I noticed you haven't asked us too much. Don't you want to know? Or are you afraid of what we might say. It's not really magic that we do."

Isabel chewed her lip. "I like stories." *I do want to know, but…* She had no desire to end up on the stake again mixing with real witches. Her conscience was clear in that regard—perhaps she wasn't as pious as she ought to be, but she was no heretic. Coming close to being killed and having to flee quelled her natural curiosity, yet it crept to the fore, overcoming the urge for caution. The puzzle of Gwyn and Michelle niggled at her. Even the gash on Gwyn's forehead was healing well, despite Michelle forbidding Isabel from putting a poultice on it.

"I have antibiotics," the strange woman had said, cracking open a tiny stone and jabbing Gwyn with the sharp needle inside. "I know you're a healer, but we do things differently where I come from, and where Gwyn comes from too."

Where do you come from?

The rain stopped, leaving the smell of wet earth and leaves. Michelle came out of the house and began a series of fighting exercises in the courtyard. "Gwyn, you should practise these too, when you're up to it," Michelle called, grunting as she skidded on the wet stone.

"I will!" Gwyn replied, then turned back to Isabel. Without the rain, the coolness vanished and mosquitos whined in the humidity. "Some of what we say might be hard to believe. If you want to know, we'll tell you. We'll probably stay here a week, then we'll be moving. We think we might ride to Santiago de Compostela."

"Oh," said Isabel. *I've always dreamt of going there.*

"We can leave you here with some money, enough to get set up, like Michelle said, or you can come with us. I was annoyed at first when she suggested it, 'cause I thought she was sick of me, but maybe we are better with a third person." She half-shrugged, smiling. "But you'll need to know what you're in for." She rose. "Maybe after dinner tonight."

The ease of getting what she wanted made Isabel nervous. *Surely if they were trying to trick me they would not be so open? Are they dangerous or not?* Michelle and Gwyn *had* risked their lives, and while she had repaid them with rescue from the river, the debt was still well and truly weighted on her side of the scales.

She would hear them out.

* * *

That night, Isabel felt as if she had fallen into a dream world. Talk of travelling through time, of tricking kings and queens and popes, left her boggled. Surely it could not be true? Nothing else she could think of made sense, however. And the things they spoke of made her hungry to learn more.

"You mean women are respected healers in your time?" The idea of learning from great physicians, being able to read ancient texts, was thrilling. If it was a wonderful fantasy.

"We come from two very different times," Michelle corrected. Gwyn rolled her eyes. "Gwyn's time is much more advanced than now. My culture is even more tolerant and sophisticated."

Gwyn poked her tongue out at Michelle but her tone was mild as she said, "Yes, yes, and that's the future we're trying to save. Make the world a better place, and all."

Isabel's mind raced. "And you say it's not magic. But the curse you did on the boat…?"

Gwyn looked at Michelle, confused. Michelle shook her head. "This device," she lifted her right wrist, which held a metal and crystal bracelet topped by a metal disc, "is a light, amongst other things." She tapped it. A faint white glow emitted from the disc. Isabel gasped. "I can make it brighter." The glow increased until it was an eye-smarting brightness. Michelle tapped it off.

"How did you use that to curse people?" Gwyn asked sceptically.

"You were unconscious." Michelle's smile hinted at smugness. "Isabel gave me the idea—I screeched witchy words at the guys trying to board us and shone this on its brightest setting right in their faces. They'll be lucky not to have permanent retinal damage."

"What does that mean? Is it like the pox?" Isabel was determined not to be left behind in the conversation. Her head whirled as every question she asked was answered, even if the answers triggered more questions.

As Michelle described the anatomy of the human eye, Gwyn yawned and excused herself. "Plenty of time to tell you whatever you want to know, particularly if you decide to come with us. I want to start planning our ride to Santiago de Compostela—I'll be asking around stables tomorrow to look at horses to buy."

Trepidation crept across Isabel's heart. Should she go with them? She wanted to trust them—being open and truthful came naturally to her. She knew not all people were the same—how quickly the people of her village had turned from friends to aloof neighbours when she had become fatherless and without prospects. *They stopped greeting me with smiles, and they warned their sons not to court me.* Remembering the rejection stung her heart anew.

And again, how quickly they had stirred to hatred when the Inquisition came preaching fear. They had burnt old Juan for complaining the Church should not take its tithe when his crops had failed. They would have burnt her as a witch just because she liked to wander the forest looking for herbs, because her father was a converso, because someone's baby had died and they needed someone to blame. She shivered.

No—as much as she liked them, she could not trust Gwyn and Michelle just yet.

Eleven

1496 AD

"That nag won't do—look how hard his mouth is, poor thing!" Gwyn rejected the gelding and moved on to the next stall. This horse chewed hay and looked at them mournfully. Gwyn sighed. "Feed this one up a bit and maybe I'll consider her. Come on, Isabel, let's try somewhere else."

The smell of hay, manure and horse clung to her as they left the stables but Gwyn didn't mind. The prospect of riding again—not subject to the whims of a river or sea—made her happy.

"I don't actually know a heap about horses," she confessed to Isabel as they made their way back to the market street. "But you have to pretend that you do, or they'll rip you off."

"And the amulet you wear helps trick people into thinking you do?"

Gwyn nodded. "Some people aren't as susceptible to it. You don't seem to be. But you have to be confident to pull it off. It's like when I want to go unnoticed, I dress inconspicuously. I also *think* I'm inconspicuous, and I kind of drift on past people."

"Yet you say it's not…" Isabel lowered her voice and waited until a carter wheeled his barrow of nightsoil past, crinkling her nose at the whiff. "You say it's not magic."

"Not the way I understand it—there are rules and physics that don't make sense to me, but I know someone has thought out very carefully the technology behind it, just like…" Gwyn searched for an example. The road reached the top of a hill and through the gaps between houses

Gwyn could see the river. "See the bridge there." She pointed.

Isabel looked. The peaked bridge over the River Nervión was made up of three stone arches—a large centre arch, and two smaller ones on either side. It was high enough for the smaller sailing ships to pass under, though the larger ones tended to be seafaring and clustered by the dockside, ready for the run back to the coast.

"You don't know what size arches a bridge can have, exactly, before it collapses under its own height and weight," Gwyn said. "But you know there are people who do know. Masons and bridge builders—in my time we call them engineers—who have learnt the facts of weight distribution across different spans, and what shapes hold strength better than others. Cathedrals are another excellent example—any large building made of heavy material, you have to build it in such a way that it will support itself."

"That is so," Isabel replied ponderously. "So you are saying that you don't know exactly how your amulet works, but the men who built it do, and you trust their knowledge."

"Exactly!" Gwyn almost jumped with excitement at Isabel's quick grasp. "Except not just men. Women and… other people too." She wondered how to describe aliens to Isabel, and decided that was probably best handled with the help of Michelle. They hadn't touched on it in the explanation of how they were trying to fix the timelines. "So it's not magic—it's science!"

"And they keep this knowledge locked away, these men… and women?" They continued down the street. "My father's people prize knowledge, but it is mostly the men who are educated. Michelle said that people in her time are warring over the right to that knowledge."

Gwyn bit her lip. "It's a tough one. I think each side thinks only they know how to use that knowledge responsibly, so they are fighting to keep the technology from each other. But I've been to that time, and I know that Michelle's side want to keep things fairer and more tolerant of all peoples, whereas the other side—they hate anything that's different. They'd see the whole world burn rather than see everyone live together in harmony. I know that's pretty simplistic, and Michelle could probably explain it all a lot better, but that's the gist of it. And besides, if I don't help fix these timelines now, I'll never get back to my own time."

Sadness clouded her heart. "I'll never see my family again."

Isabel stopped and put a hand on Gwyn's shoulder, who looked at her, startled. "That sounds like a world I would like to help build. I want to go with you and Michelle."

* * *

"I like her, she's smart." Gwyn mused to Michelle. *She's beautiful too.* Gwyn felt oddly guilty and disrespectful, so pushed the thought aside and tried to remain professional. "But… do you really think we should take her with us? She says she wants to come." They were doing exercises in the large downstairs room, having pushed the wooden chairs back against the wall and laid a rug on the brown tiles. Isabel had gone to buy cloth from the market, saying she needed a dress for travelling.

Michelle finished her push ups and stretched her shoulders. "Are you concerned you'll feel responsible if she gets hurt or killed?"

Gwyn's eyes opened wide. "Wow, go straight for the heart. Of course, I don't want a repeat of Meric." She bit her lip, fighting the sudden tears. Blinking hard, she said, "I'm just surprised that you suggested she join us without even knowing her. You said yourself you don't make friends easily. So why the snap judgement on her?"

Michelle knelt and folded her hands, considering. "I don't quite know. It was an instinctive decision, one I'm waiting to be confirmed by evidence, though thus far she seems compatible with us. She was brave on the boat, capable, thinks on her feet, loyal enough to return with help, or at least intelligent enough to recognise that we were a good ticket out of there."

Gwyn felt her frustration grow. "That was all *after* you asked her to come with us!"

Michelle nodded. "I don't know yet, Gwyn—but my instincts are good. I daresay my subconscious mind noticed things about her, and my decision will be confirmed over time."

Michelle's confidence irritated Gwyn. She quashed it, hiding her face as she leant forward and stretched her legs. *You were never that confident about me.*

"So you think you've found some decent horses for us?" Michelle asked.

Gwyn grunted. "Yeah, and a pack mule. We have a few choices for which road to travel. We can follow the coastline, but it's not as popular these days apparently, and quite hilly. If we cut inland to Brugos we can pick up the French Way and follow the pilgrimage route all the way to Santiago de Compostela. Supplies should be easy enough to buy along the way—there are hostels and villages that cater to pilgrims, we just need to get ourselves some scallop shells to wear."

"Scallop shells?"

"It's a Saint James thing—shows you're a pilgrim. We'd better dress simply and hide our fancy clothes."

"Hm, fair enough."

Gwyn hesitated. "There's one other thing."

"Yes?" Michelle raised her brows expectantly

"Well, some of the traders I spoke to said we should hire a guard if we aren't travelling in a larger group. A lot of people get robbed. Easy targets, I guess."

The suggestion hung in the air between them, along with the implication that Michelle wasn't enough to protect them if they ran into trouble. Gwyn shuffled awkwardly.

Michelle rubbed her forehead. "I suppose that's fair. It was different when we were just two and could jump away from trouble. And the mountains of Galicia are wilder than the roads of Castile."

So now you're happy to take on yet another person? "Look, maybe this is all too hard," Gwyn said. "We've had a nice week of rest, maybe we should just get organised for the next mission and jump to then. It's Juana again, except she'll be queen, right?"

Michelle shook her head. "Santiago de Compostela is scarcely out of our way from A Coruña, which is where we must find Juana in 1506. Yes, it would be quicker to take a ship from Bilbao to A Coruña, but you said no more boats. And this next turning point is not going to be pleasant. We have to shift the balance of power to Juana and Philip. When Philip dies her father Ferdinand will do his best to discredit her as queen and take power himself."

Gwyn slumped. "I know. Juana the Mad and all that. I didn't really like her but she doesn't deserve that."

Michelle nodded. "Deserved or not, we have to make sure she lives even as Philip dies. The rest is out of our hands."

Neither of them said anything as they finished their stretches. "So we might as well take a break from it all," Michelle suggested. "We'll follow the pilgrimage trail. I'll sort out weaponry tomorrow—I want crossbows for us both—and I'll ask around for a soldier or guard who'd like to earn some easy money babysitting some pilgrims. Do you want to ride as a man or a woman?"

Gwyn thought. "Woman. I don't think Isabel is up to maintaining a disguise and it would look indecent if she was a woman travelling alone with two men. I don't think we'd all pass for siblings—you and I can, everyone says we look enough alike."

"Fine. I'm your brother, she's our cousin; I'll say I want another man to protect my womenfolk—they'll believe that easily enough."

Gwyn chewed her lip. "Assuming, of course, Isabel definitely wants to come."

"Wants to come where?" Isabel stood in the doorway, a bolt of cloth under one arm.

Gwyn looked at Michelle, who seemed unbothered at the interruption. She moved furniture back into place while Michelle outlined the plan to Isabel. Was she waiting to hear the redhead declare that she wished to stay here, amongst people she understood in a time she was familiar with? Gwyn thought about it. She liked Isabel, plus someone to share the load of cooking, foraging and all the other work that went with being on the road would be useful. But why was Michelle so in favour of her, based on instinct?

Another tendril of jealously curled through Gwyn's stomach. She had worked so hard to be accepted by Michelle; it had only happened when she could 'see' the timelines, could 'feel' the turning points, in a way Michelle could not. But they still weren't friends, not like she and Meric had been friends.

This is stupid—none of this even matters. When you're back home you can make real friends.

Twelve

1496 AD

Mountains gave way to high green hills as the road climbed away from the coast and met with the famed pilgrimage route of the French Way. From the Pyrenees to the Atlantic, fervent Catholics walked for weeks, if not months, to reach the great cathedral and supposed final resting place of the bones of Saint James to earn indulgences for their sins.

Some pilgrims had come from farther afield, travelling across parts of Europe in dedication of their goals. Most walked. Others rode like Gwyn and her party, crossing the rich green meadows and golden farmlands as peasants sought to bring in the late-summer harvest. Cattle grazed, impervious to the showers of rain which drifted over them occasionally. Gwyn was grateful they weren't stuck down in the mud like many of their sackcloth wearing, staff-bearing contemporaries. Not all pilgrims were dressed as paupers, but many were thin from illness and lack of food. Gwyn wondered how all of them would make it to their destination, let alone back home, and realised uncomfortably that many would not.

Stone fords and bridges took them across burbling crystal streams and wide rivers. When they stopped to buy food, villagers were reserved but kind, respecting the scallop shell and not overcharging them. Gwyn and Michelle decided they would camp most of the time, weather permitting, instead of staying in the spartan hostels run by local monasteries.

As they left the farmlands behind, the grassy hills and wooded valleys were laced with game trails traversed by wolves, deer, and smaller animals.

Gwyn paused at the top of one hill to breathe the fresh air and take in the view. It held a hint of chill and the faintest breath of wood smoke, as well as lavender from the bushes that adorned the side of the path, interspersed by small yellow flowers. She smiled. They had been on the road a week and she loved it. The weather was fine and the sense of freedom invigorating. *Michelle was right—this was a good idea.*

"Daydreaming?" Michelle ambled past on her bay mare, the pack mule trailing from a rope looped onto her saddle.

"It's so beautiful. People will hike this road for centuries just for the sake of it, not even for religious reasons."

"Perhaps that is for the best." Isabel rode behind the mule and caught Gwyn's statement. "Faith is tearing the harmony of this land apart. Our queen fought a war to drive out the Moors so that Christians could have peace, but there is no peace for those left behind, no matter what God they believe in."

One of the extra members of their group, sitting on a gelding just ahead of Gwyn, grunted in disapproval. "Best not say that where the Inquisition could hear," he said. "They'll have you burnt as a heretic." The three women exchanged glances and nudged their mounts on wordlessly. Diego was one of the soldiers they had hired as a guard for the trip. Both were tall and muscular, but Diego was the darker of the two, and wore his curly hair cropped short. His handsome face was marred less by various small scars than by the constant pout he wore, looking unimpressed with his employers, the job, and the world at large. Rafael, fair with long hair tied back in a queue, smiled and joked, chatting with Michelle and flirting with Isabel and Gwyn.

Both men could fight—Michelle had tested them, posing as a well-off merchant's son taking his sister and cousin on pilgrimage. Gwyn hadn't seen the brief bout—Michelle had scoured various taverns alone in search of men—so had to be satisfied with Michelle's account that both men sparred well and could shoot straight with a crossbow. They were Castilian-born After the fall of Granada four years prior, they had found soldiering to be in less demand. They had made their way north, ending up in the Basque countries.

The road took them down into one of the heavily wooded valleys, autumn leaves carpeting the trail in red and gold. "Let's find someplace to camp in the next few hours," Michelle called out to the group. "There's no need to press on in a hurry, we've plenty of food."

Diego looked sour. Gwyn muttered to Isabel, "Don't know what he's unhappy about—he's getting paid by the day, so what's it to him if we take a few extra days?"

Rafael heard her. "Ah, nothing makes old Diego happy." He drew up next to Gwyn and winked. "Me, on the other hand, I have the sky above and the company of beautiful ladies—I couldn't ask God for anything more!"

Gwyn rolled her eyes. Rafael continued to banter as they rode through the valley, making Isabel giggle and Gwyn smile tolerantly. As usual, he was quick to offer help to dismount when they stopped to camp, bowing chivalrously and keeping one eye on Michelle.

Gwyn made sure she swung off her horse before he could assist. He had started out circumspectly enough, but over the days had become too handsy for her liking. "I'm fine." She untied her saddlebags herself, not missing the bemused look on his face before he turned to the other 'lady' of the group.

"Just let me or Michelle know if he's bothering you," she muttered to Isabel as they unloaded their things. "But if you don't mind him, we won't get in your way." In another time she would have subtly enquired as to whether Isabel liked women. She knew better than to do so in this century, no matter how beautiful she thought Isabel was. She felt proud of herself for taking on Michelle's approach to other people's liaisons, and felt she was setting the tone nicely for the three of them getting along well. They were all adults, after all.

Isabel looked appalled, then glanced over a where Rafael stood teasing a grumpy Diego. "I don't know what you think I am, but I am not a whore!" she hissed.

Gwyn blinked. "No! I didn't think you were. Ah, dammit—look, it's none of my business, I was just trying to—"

"To imply that I was loose and without morals!" Isabel flushed red and stamped away.

Michelle sidled up to Gwyn. "What did you say to upset her?" she asked quietly.

Gwyn frowned and threw up her hands. "I was trying to do what you did for me—let her know that she doesn't have to answer to us, but if she wants Rafael to back off to let us know."

Michelle nodded sympathetically and put an arm around Gwyn's shoulder. "Drastically different morals of the time, remember."

"Yeah," Gwyn mumbled, cross at herself. "I guess because we were getting along so well I forgot. I'd better go apologise."

Michelle squeezed Gwyn's shoulders. "Let me know if… no, you can handle it."

Gwyn sighed. "Let's set up camp first."

* * *

Isabel could tell Gwyn was going out of her way to apologise—Gwyn laid out bedrolls and cooked stew for everyone's dinner, serving Isabel first. Nothing was said—perhaps she didn't want the soldiers to hear—but Gwyn's actions showed she was sorry.

Seeing the girl's anxious face, Isabel couldn't find it in herself to stay angry. She smiled and gathered the wooden bowls to take to the nearby stream to clean.

"Let me carry those for you." Rafael leapt up to help. His winks and little smiles told Isabel that if she was so inclined, like Gwyn had implied, she could show favour to the flirtatious soldier and he would no doubt have her on her back in the woods before they had finished washing the dishes.

It wouldn't be the first time—boys in the village had stolen kisses, several even courted her before she became a penniless orphan with no dowry and no prospects. That didn't stop married men from smiling at her when their wives weren't looking. One even told her she should be grateful someone was looking out for her.

If the Inquisition hadn't come looking for heretics, maybe I would have ended up as the blacksmith's mistress and shunned even more. Anger rose in her and she scrubbed furiously at the cooking pot.

"Steady there," Rafael put a large hand on hers. "You'll wear a hole through the bottom and next time you cook all the stew will fall out!" He grinned.

Isabel gave a polite smile. "Could you perhaps go and ask Gwyn to come and help me?" He had carried the dishes down to the stream for her, but sat idle while she cleaned.

"Oh, you don't need her surely." He looked intently into her eyes.

"I'll help." Diego's gruff voice came from the trees behind them. Rafael looked up and frowned as Diego came down the bank. "Michel wants you to scout."

"Why can't you?" Rafael asked rudely.

Diego shrugged. "Michel is paying us—I don't ask questions." He squatted down next to Isabel and grabbed the next bowl to clean.

Rafael made a *hrmph* noise and stalked away. Isabel noticed Diego's shoulders stayed tense even after they finished scrubbing in silence and carried everything back to camp. Gwyn glanced up from where she was checking the tack. She joined Isabel as she packed the cooking things away. "You okay?" she asked.

She is kind. Strange, but not false like the people in my village, people who I thought cared for me. Isabel smiled. "I am fine, thank you."

Gwyn bit her lip. "Look, about what I said before—I really didn't mean to insult you. Things are different where I come from, and again in Michelle's time."

Isabel held up a hand to silence her. "I understand. I didn't realise how different in… personal matters… your time must be. You meant no ill-intent."

Gwyn's relief was tangible. "It must be confusing for you. Michelle and I get our wires crossed all the time because of different expectations, but we're getting better at talking it through."

"Wires… crossed?"

Gwyn grinned. "We mean different things to what the other person thinks. Probably that's why she wanted you to travel with us—when we talk to you it highlights our different thinking, so we explain ourselves more carefully." Her grin faded. "We had a friend with us in Italy—he was from this time. He balanced us out."

Isabel saw the sadness wash over Gwyn despite the fading light. Stars crept into the evening sky and a cool breeze had arisen. "What happened to him?" she asked tentatively.

Gwyn looked away. "He was murdered," she whispered. She sniffed and straightened abruptly, walking over to where they had hobbled the horses, checking the knots.

Isabel wanted to comfort her, but did not know if she would be intruding. Perhaps that custom was also very different in Gwyn's time?

There was so much to learn. Despite the great uncertainty that travelling with Gwyn and Michelle held, Isabel found herself wanting to know more. Her old life was behind her. It had been burnt away even before the pyre had been lit. She shivered. She would have to make a new life, for good or ill.

It was only then she noticed Diego watching from the shadows, and shivered again. The soldiers might be there for their protection, but she wondered if they were better off alone.

Thirteen

1496 AD

Michelle frowned at the stew as she gave it a stir. "Gwyn, did you use all the salted beef we bought? There is a lot more meat in here than I'd rationed for." They were still over a week away from their goal, and Michelle had hoped their most recently purchased provisions would last until that time.

Gwyn glanced up from the horse blanket where she was laying out bowls and spoons. "No, Diego shot a rabbit. Fancies himself a hunter, it seems."

Michelle lifted a spoonful from the bubbling pot and blew on it. "Mmm," she said appreciatively. "Got that gamier taste—I quite like it. Did you bury the entrails?"

Gwyn hacked the loaf of bread apart with her knife and set a piece in each bowl. "Diego took care of the yuk bits. All I had to do was chop it up and chuck it in." She gave a little laugh and shook her head. "Such a grumpy bastard. Stomped up with the rabbit, sat there without a word and skinned and gutted it," she indicated a nearby log. "Then said, 'this be for the stew' and walked off before I could say thanks."

Michelle shrugged and smiled. "Can't complain, I suppose. I'll go and thank him. I want to see if they've sorted out watches for tonight. Rafael gave me some bullshit story about scouting the perimeter when I caught him sneaking around our things the other night."

She left Gwyn and wandered into the surrounding woods, nodding to Isabel who carried a pan of water from the stream for Gwyn. Where was Diego? Hiring guards would be useless if they weren't around to guard.

Rafael's voice sounded up ahead, a wheedling note to it. Diego's gruff response was deeper and Michelle couldn't make out the words. Instinct told her she had stumbled upon a disagreement. She slowed, stepping on clear ground where she could, avoiding the crunch of leaves.

"I'm telling you, that Michel has a lot more gold than he's letting on! He barely haggled over our fee. Most pilgrims don't have two reales to rub together." Rafael sounded excited. Michelle crept closer, stopping behind a stand of thick bushes.

"They ain't real pilgrims," Diego said flatly. "Something's off about them. They hardly pray, and he ain't built like a fighter, but he moves like one."

"So he's a noble in disguise. That'd explain the money!"

"Why the hell would a noble dress as a commoner? He'd have his own guards. Makes no sense!" Diego sounded more irritated than usual. "Better to bloody well leave it alone. Nobles be trouble."

Rafael chuckled, and Michelle could practically hear him shaking his head. "Oh, Diego. Ever the pessimist. I'm telling you, we clean out this Michel and we'll have enough to pay back the captain and get back into his good graces. I'll have a bit of fun with the redhead—you can have the brown-haired wench."

Michelle let out her breath slowly. This was turning ugly.

"I don't like it," Diego was saying. "We'll take our fee as agreed. You can ask for a bonus, but leave the women alone."

"You're just jealous! Fine, you have the redhead—I've seen the way you look at her. Maybe if you smiled a bit more she wouldn't think you such a mopey bastard!" Rafael raised his voice and Michelle realised Diego was coming towards her. She moved away as swiftly and silently as she could, then turned around and whistled tunelessly. Diego came into view and eyed her suspiciously.

"There you are!" Michelle exclaimed. "Gwyn told me you'd added rabbit to the pot—I was coming to thank you. I think it's almost ready. Do you know where Rafael is?"

Diego grunted and jerked his thumb back the way he had come.

Michelle thanked him and pretended to look for Rafael, mulling over the need to warn her companions.

She found the opportunity the next day. They stopped off the side of the track where a cairn marked a smaller path. Other pilgrims on the trail had told them of a holy spring nearby and, keeping the pray comment in mind, Michelle advised they would all stop for an extended lunch so they could give thanks to the saint of the spring.

"Would you stay with the horses while my sister and cousin and I spend some time in prayer?"

Rafael smiled smugly at Diego. "Of course, Señor Michel."

Diego scowled. "Only need one to guard horses. I'll bag another rabbit for the pot." He lifted a crossbow from his saddle and swung a small pack on his back, disappearing into the trees.

"I'll take good care of your things." Rafael assured, patting the nearest horse. Its ears went back and the horse's head swung around to bite Rafael. He removed his hand hurriedly.

"You know he's going to go through our stuff," Gwyn murmured to Michelle as they follow the path.

"I know. I'm counting on it keeping him busy while we talk."

"What's wrong?" Isabel struggled to walk as quickly as the others, her legs not used to horse-riding. Gwyn waited and guided her over several tree roots.

"I remember when I was like that," the girl smiled sympathetically. "Your body gets used to it."

"Come sit here." Michelle decided they had gone far enough. The spring burbled nearby.

"Can I get a drink first?" Gwyn shook her empty water skin.

"Hurry up, this is important." Michelle stood, arms crossed, trying to quell her agitation. There were no other pilgrims here, but that could change if the group they had passed earlier caught up. It was quiet, with only the rustling of leaves above and the chirping of the occasional bird to add to the ambience of the trickling stream. Soft-topped clouds marched across the infinite blue of the sky, their flat grey bellies casting shadows across the hilly landscape below.

"Right, what's up?" Gwyn returned and sat with her back against a tree, offering the skin to Isabel, who took it gratefully.

"I overhead a conversation between Diego and Rafael last night. They were discussing robbing us and raping you two," Michelle said matter-of-factly, using Basque so Isabel could follow without effort. "Rafael was advocating, Diego didn't sound too enthused but I don't know what his motivations are. It seems they owe money, and suspect I have a lot more than I'm letting on."

Gwyn's eyes were wide with alarm. "I never should have suggested we hire guards!"

Michelle held up a hand. "I went along with it, remember. And they were a deterrent yesterday."

"True." Gwyn frowned, distressed. Michelle suspected she would blame herself regardless, much as she had with Cesare Borgia. The soldiers had come in useful. The day before they had crossed a bridge where a band of dirty peasants clustered. The peasants stared sullenly rather than demanding payment as they might have done to other, less guarded travellers. Michelle also hoped that as they neared Santiago de Compostela, hawkers and petty thieves would give them a wide berth, choosing instead to harass pilgrims who were distracted and excited about almost reaching their goal. Which made deciding what to do unclear.

"How dare they!" Isabel looked angry. "You hired them in good faith, and they want to turn on you. They will burn in hell!"

Michelle nodded. "If there is a hell. I'm more concerned with the now. We have three options: jump forward in time to get away from them, carry on as planned and hope Diego isn't tempted to go along with Rafael's plan, or I could… put them out of action, as it were."

"What do you mean?" Isabel was puzzled.

"She means kills them," Gwyn replied, looking sick.

Isabel looked awed. "She can do that?"

Gwyn nodded. Michelle continued. "The problem with options one and three is we'd be left without a guard and vulnerable to any other robbers who might look for small parties of pilgrims to prey on. Option two—Rafael might convince Diego to turn on us at any time. Gwyn and I can escape, but you, Isabel, will be left behind unless you are in contact with one of us. We might lose our horses and gear too, though I can probably fight my way to one of them. Not ideal, though."

Isabel pondered. "You mean, go forward in time like you did with me before? You said it was not possible to go back anymore."

Michelle grimaced. "Correct. We used to be able to, but even then you can't be too close to yourself or you get very ill. We call it proximity sickness. It's not an issue now, though—we can only jump ahead."

"Just before dawn," Gwyn interrupted. "If we have to jump separately, let's go to just before the next dawn. Otherwise we'll be stumbling around in the dark again."

Michelle nodded. "Agreed. So are you advocating for option two? Isabel, what do you think?"

Isabel looked alarmed at being consulted. "You are asking me to decide if these men should live or die?"

"Perhaps just Rafael? He seems to be the instigator. You should also consider what happens when we reach Santiago de Compostela. We intend to jump ahead eight years and begin our next mission. If you decide you want to stay in this time, we can help you get set up somewhere. I know things are hard if you don't have family. Once we are on our mission, however, you will have to stay with us if you want our protection."

Isabel looked overwhelmed. Gwyn noticed and patted Isabel's hand. "We'll stay the course for now. You stick close to Michelle or me, and we'll get you out of trouble if need be. We'll have to sleep in shifts." Her shoulders slumped. "Well, the holiday was nice while it lasted. Back to people trying to murder and rape us, what's new?"

Michelle wondered if she should take matters into her own hands and arrange an 'accident' for Rafael, then sighed. "At least we know to keep a close eye on them now."

The quietest snap of a twig behind her had her whirl, hand on the long knife she wore at her waist.

"What is it?" Gwyn rose in alarm.

Michelle gestured for silence, staring into the trees. Nobody drew breath for several moments. "Nothing," Michelle said unconvincingly. She glanced at the other two. "Just keep close over the next few days."

* * *

Five more days riding brought them close to Santiago de Compostela, where Isabel would have to decide whether she would join Gwyn and Michelle in the future. They made it clear to her that the next eight years would pass in the blink of an eye, that there was no going back.

"Princess Juana's older brother and sister will have died by 1500 and upon the death of her mother in 1504, she will become queen. Her husband Philip will become king of Castile but her father Ferdinand won't want to give up power in Castile. He obstructs them wherever possible."

Isabel listened to Michelle's account carefully. Despite what she had experienced, doubt lingered in her mind. They called it science and technology, said people understood it, how masons understood how to build bridges and cathedrals, but… eight years? *Surely the world will not be so different?*

She mulled on this as they made themselves comfortable in a barn generously offered by a farmer to them and another group of pilgrims. The village of Sarria was used to providing hospitality to those on the road to the great cathedral of Saint James—any cost to the villagers was made up by sales of holy relics; such as saints' toenail clippings. Chatter and brief arguments punctuated the late afternoon until Isabel was swamped with noise, despite the presence of the soldiers discouraging the hawkers. Since Diego and Rafael had given no sign of turning on their employers, Isabel left the barn and climbed the small hill nearby. Ivy carpeted the lower trees. As she neared the grassy summit the cool breeze picked up, whispering of rain later that evening. The wind brought a sense of trepidation that she had never experienced in her river valley home. A gust might pick her up and deposit her who-knew-where, just as Gwyn had picked her up from that burning pyre, and could drop her at any moment.

As if summoned, Gwyn emerged from the tree line and made her way to Isabel's side. "Rafael is looking for you," she puffed. "Thought I'd better warn you."

Isabel frowned. Rafael's flirting had become more insistent whenever Michelle wasn't looking. Isabel tried not to encourage it but didn't know how to tell him to stop in a way that wouldn't make him angry. She had asked Michelle to pretend to be the stern cousin protecting his womenfolk, but Rafael had merely smirked and assured Michelle he was here to protect their party, then carried on whenever Michelle wasn't around. Diego's face grew thunderous when it happened, but did nothing to stop Rafael.

If Isabel left this time with Michelle and Gwyn, it was only eight years. She would still recognise the towns, even the people. She could settle somewhere, be a healer, make a life.

Then what?

"Isabel?" Gwyn looked at her enquiringly. "Are you coming?"

Time to confess. "I am afraid, Gwyn." Isabel stared out at the campfires that winked into existence on the slopes below.

Gwyn put an arm around Isabel's shoulders. "I don't blame you. Michelle and I will do our best to look after you. She's pretty bloody good at what she does."

Warmth kindled in Isabel's belly at Gwyn's protective words and nurturing touch. "She thinks highly of you too," Isabel said, feeling impervious to the cold evening air.

Gwyn's bemusement was clear. The light of the setting sun outlined her angular face and lent golden highlights to her plain brown hair. A single lifted eyebrow gave tell to her thoughts.

"She does!" Isabel insisted. "When you were struck down in the boat, she said she couldn't afford to lose you."

"Hmph, I suppose. She's not very good at showing it sometimes." Gwyn smiled and Isabel's heart skipped. What was happening to her? Despite learning that Michelle and Gwyn were friends only, the possibility of two women loving each other had lingered sinfully in the back of her mind. Isabel shivered, trying to shake the embarrassing thought away.

"You're getting cold. Come on, let's get back to the fire." Gwyn hugged Isabel closer for a moment then let go, leading the way back down the hillside.

It was then Isabel knew that, despite the sin, she wanted to follow Gwyn, no matter where it might take her.

Fourteen

1496 AD

Michelle reined in her mare and addressed Diego and Rafael. "Thank you for your service." It was mid-morning and while the walls of Santiago de Compostela were not yet in sight they expected to reach their destination by lunchtime. "Here's the rest of the amount we agreed on, I wish you well in all your endeavours." She tossed two purses at the men.

Diego grunted in surprise, catching his purse with a clink. Rafael looked sly. "Best we escort you all the way into the city. Plenty more pickpockets will be itching to get at your gold, not to mention such pretty ladies will attract the attention of more than thieves."

No doubt you'd like some more of that gold yourself. Michelle hid her thought with a bland face. "Thank you, but no. My sister and cousin and I will do just as well as a smaller party in the city." *Let them think it's because I'm tight with my money and don't want to pay for their lodging too.* She clicked her tongue to the horse and made to ride on.

She heard Rafael sigh. The scrape of metal didn't surprise her—she whirled her horse. Rafael already had his sword at Gwyn's neck. The girl froze. Michelle met her eyes calmly. "At least we're on the horses."

Gwyn gave the tiniest nod, wary of the blade across her throat. "Isabel, get to Michelle."

"Shut up!" Rafael barked.

"Raff, what the hell are you doing?" Diego demanded. "We talked about this."

"I talked! You mewled excuses. This is easy money, Diego! We need it."

"We'll find another way!"

"Isabel, come here," Michelle ordered quietly.

"No one move or I cut the wench!"

Isabel stopped trying to nudge her mare over. She stared at Gwyn, eyes wide, mouth quivering.

"Isabel, it's fine, get to Michelle!" Gwyn froze when Rafael pressed his sword against her skin. Michelle could see her trying to calm her breathing, and hoped the girl wouldn't have trouble finding the mental calm one needed to connect with the timepiece. She was so much more experienced—surely she wouldn't fail now?

"Here's what's going to happen," Rafael said, addressing Michelle. "You, señor, are going to get off your horse and hand over all the gold and any other valuables you might have to Diego. Your womenfolk are going to spend a little bit of time with us in the bushes, but I won't make you watch." He smiled toothily. "I'm not a complete monster."

"No, you're a fool," Diego growled. His hand inched towards his sword. "Something ain't right about them—we should take our pay and go. And leave the women be."

"Don't hold with a bit of fun? Don't be such a softcock." Rafael laughed.

Michelle sighed. "Gwyn, just go. I'll take Isabel. Time we agreed?"

Gwyn closed her eyes briefly, then looked at Isabel. "I'll see you soon, Isabel. Just get to Michelle."

The familiar blue haze rose up around her and Rafael shouted in confusion. Michelle kicked her horse and grabbed Isabel's arm, making her own connection and jumping them both out of there.

Flick!

* * *

Gwyn blinked as the haze faded and she patted her startled horse. "Ssh, easy there." Her mount whinnied and shifted.

"Gwyn? Is that you?"

Gwyn dismounted and led her horse to the sound of Michelle's voice. Isabel rushed out of the bushes and caught Gwyn in a hug. "Thank the Lord you are alright, Gwyn! We were so worried when you didn't appear!"

Gwyn patted the anxious redhead on the back, comforted by the embrace. "What do you mean? It's only been a few moments."

"It's almost sunrise, Gwyn." Michelle sounded relieved. "You said just before dawn!"

Gwyn looked up at the swiftly lightening sky. "Oh. I must have mistimed it. I was a bit distracted—sword at my throat and all that." She smiled shakily.

Michelle put a hand on Gwyn's shoulder. "You did well."

Isabel had let go of Gwyn but still stood close. "We have a problem," she whispered.

Gwyn looked at her, then Michelle. "What problem?"

A man cleared his throat as he stepped out from the shadows. Gwyn tensed and grabbed Isabel's arm. "What's he doing here? Where's Rafael?"

Diego ran fingers through his short curly hair. "He rode on. He was terrified—wanted to find a priest to bless him, get the taint of witchcraft off the gold he was paid."

Gwyn cocked eyebrow, disbelieving. "And you happened to hang around? Aren't you frightened? You should be. You don't know what we're capable of." She spoke in Basque, knowing he would understand well enough. Her tone and body language said the rest.

Diego drew his sword and laid it at his feet. "I ain't a threat to you. Also—I want to come with you."

"What?" Gwyn turned to Michelle, baffled. "Did he tell you this?"

"Turns out he's been eavesdropping on us a fair bit—must be one of those suspicious minds that isn't affected by the chronokinetor. Isabel's the same."

"What do you mean, I'm the same?" Isabel queried. Her eyes flicked apprehensively from one face to another.

"I'll explain later." Gwyn touched her arm reassuringly. "What is this bullshit, Michelle? He's been listening in so he thinks he knows what we're about and wants to come with us? Tell him to get lost! He would have let Rafael rob and *rape* us."

"I would've stopped him!" Diego protested, angry.

"You did nothing!"

"Gwyn, calm down," Michelle ordered. "He did try to dissuade Rafael, back when I overheard them arguing in the woods. He says they didn't speak of it again and Rafael simply acted when I tried to pay them off."

"And you believe him?"

"I'm no liar!" Diego's face flushed dark—Gwyn realised she could see clearly. The sun had risen, though it would be some time before its light pierced the trees to where they stood. A light breeze rustled the dry leaves—several detached themselves from bony branches and drifted to join the autumnal carpet below. Gwyn glared at Diego. His presence was a sour note in the serenity of their surroundings.

"It does tally with his behaviour when Rafael attacked. Anyway, let's sit down and talk about this. You're probably hungry, Gwyn, let's have something to eat and work out what we're going to do." Michelle took Gwyn's horses reins and led the mare back through the bushes. Diego stormed after her, retrieving his sword as he went.

Isabel anxiously looked at Gwyn, who said "Don't worry, I'm not ticked off at you. Just Michelle making decisions for me again. Now she gets to decide when I eat!" Gwyn was loathe to admit that she struggled to concentrate when she was hungry, so she simply pressed a hand to Isabel's back to guide her to the others.

Bread, cheese and sips of wine didn't restore her temper completely. She glared at Diego as he sat across from her. "Our body clocks are going to be out if we don't correct soon, it was late afternoon before. Let's just leave this joker behind a year so he doesn't pull the same stunt and hang around."

Michelle sat against a large rock, her legs stretched out in front of her. They had picketed the horses, still saddled, where they could forage on bushes and low leafy branches. Diego didn't ask for any food, nor was he offered any by Michelle, which mollified Gwyn somewhat.

"Alright, Diego," Michelle addressed the tall soldier. "State your case. You suspected we weren't pilgrims, so you spied on us to confirm your suspicions. You heard about the time-travel. Rather than call us out as witches you decided you'd like to hitch a ride. Why? And why should we take you with us?"

Diego's thick eyebrows drew together. "Me and Raff owe money. We ain't friends, but we fought together. He wanted men for this scheme of his. I trusted him, put my coin in, all my savings. I wasn't the only one— he got the captain to invest. Trouble was, job went bad, our share was worth nothing."

"So you lost your money. How is that our problem?" Gwyn said rudely.

Diego glared but continued. "The captain was right furious. Would've let the boys string him up, but… I spoke out. Said he'd never see his money if Raff got no chance to pay him back. He'd lost money too. He deserved a second chance." He frowned more heavily. "At least, that's what I thought. Now I knows he's a low-life who'd rob pilgrims and rape women. I don't hold with that."

Gwyn raised an eyebrow sceptically. Michelle said, "You're a soldier. Surely you've seen that sort of thing."

Diego looked down. "It happens. But we're Christians. Our King and Queen would be shamed—soldiers treating countrymen so. Battlefield pickings is different to robbing pilgrims."

"Back to the money. How did it become your debt? You'd lost your savings too."

Diego slumped. "Nay. The captain said if I cared about Raff's neck so much I could put mine on the line too. Said we had until winter to pay him back or he'd let the boys cut both of us up. They was baying for blood. But I can't, even if a dozen more jobs like yours come up." He straightened and looked Michelle in the eye, then Gwyn, then Isabel. "But you could use a guard—a real one, not a crook like Raff. You're a fighter," he pointed at Michelle, "but you're a woman too, for all that you fool most as a man. I didn't say nothing to Raff, not when he started talking about rape an' all, that woulda pushed him to it sooner. But you could use a real man; I hunt and I know these lands well enough to serve you."

Gwyn and the other two women were silent at this speech. It was the most Diego had spoken in the several weeks they had known him, and despite her irritation with the 'real man' comment, Gwyn could see the effort it took him to put his plea together. He was sweating despite the morning chill, and despite his claim to believe they wouldn't harm him, she guessed that he wasn't entirely sure.

Isabel broke the silence. "He has acted in good faith, Gwyn, Michelle. Why would you save me yet leave him?"

Gwyn argued, "You were about to be murdered. He's just in debt."

"His comrades will kill him all the same. Just as the people in my village turned on me."

Diego looked at Isabel gratefully. Gwyn narrowed her eyes, then looked at Michelle, who tapped her finger against her lips, saying nothing. Gwyn tried to guess what Michelle was thinking. Michelle the logical one, the ruthless one. If Michelle saw value in letting this soldier tag along, perhaps there was some angle Gwyn hadn't considered. Maybe she should let logic guide her, not her initial emotional response.

Michelle quirked a smile at Gwyn and lifted an enquiring eyebrow.

"Oh, what's one more?" Gwyn burst out, speaking Turkish so only Michelle understood her.

Michelle laughed. "I thought you liked rescuing people, Gwyn. Isn't it your thing?"

Gwyn glared, and started to respond, then realised that Michelle was trying to think like her, and went quiet. Sadness washed over her as she looked at the handsome but dour Diego, so different to the grizzled but cheerful Meric.

Isabel demanded to know what they had said. "He can come," Gwyn said softly. She gave Diego a hard look. "Let's hope you're as honourable as you say you are."

He nodded stiffly.

"Some ground rules, however," Gwyn carried on. Michelle raised an eyebrow, gesturing for her to continue. "One: Michelle and I have a mission—you are not to get in the way of that. We have to fix history and save the future." It sounded ridiculously grandiose when she said it out loud but how else could she explain it? "Two: you might not hold with rape and robbery, but I bet you aren't used to letting women tell you what to do. If you want to tag along, Michelle gives the orders. You'll also listen to Isabel and me."

It was fortunate Diego was not the sort to smile. He merely studied the three women before him for a good minute before giving another, cursory nod. "It will be so."

"Three." Gwyn relaxed somewhat. "We value your input. If you have knowledge, experience or questions—please share them with us. We'll do our best to listen, and to answer."

An inscrutable look passed over Diego's face. Did he think her weak for not being more authoritative? Too bad—he'd learn to fit in, or he could walk. Just because he seemed honourable didn't mean she would trust him, and she knew Michelle well enough to be confident the woman would remain on guard.

"Ain't you wanting me to swear an oath to obey?" Diego sounded puzzled.

"Uh… if it makes you feel better?" Gwyn caught Michelle's tiny expression of exasperation and wished she had said something else.

"Yes, you shall," Isabel interjected, smiling encouragingly at Gwyn. "Swear on the blood of our Lord Jesus that you shall obey and respect our wishes."

Diego looked more comfortable with this arrangement. He drew his sword and rested its tip on the ground as he knelt. "I swear by the blood of our Lord Jesus that I'll be obeying Michelle as my captain, and I'll be respecting the words and wishes of Gwyn and Isabel as I would my fellow soldiers."

There was a pause as he waited, and Gwyn realised he required a response. "We accept your oath," she said. "And in return you may travel with us into the future. If you wish to leave us at any point, just tell us and we can part ways on good terms."

Isabel nodded and Gwyn turned and smiled at her. "Same goes for you, but you know that already. Once we're finished in Spain we'll be jumping much further ahead. We'll try to find you both somewhere safe before then."

A moment of silence fell upon them, broken only by the dawn chorus of nearby birds. "Well, if that's all settled, I don't want to stay awake until nightfall." Michelle rested her palms upon her knees and stood. "Gwyn, can you handle jumping with Isabel and your horse? I'll take Diego and the other horses—Rafael stole the pack mule, apparently."

Gwyn hid her annoyance that Michelle didn't think her capable of taking the extra horse. The other woman had let her take the lead in the impromptu council about Diego, after all—that counted for something. *Still doesn't think I'm as good as her.* At least she was splitting the load.

"So… you'll be casting us into the future?" The only sign of Diego's unease was the tenseness with which he grasped the hilt of his sword, now sheathed.

"It's not magic," Isabel said breezily. "It's technology." It was difficult to tell that she had only encountered this concept recently herself. "Others have knowledge that make it possible to skip hours or years in the blink of an eye."

Gwyn hid her smile and went to her horse, hauling herself into the saddle. "Come on, then." She held out her hand for Isabel, pulling the redhead up behind her.

"One year and say, nine hours? That should bring us to mid-afternoon." Michelle mounted her own horse and pulled Isabel's close, laying her hand on its withers. "Diego, I'll need to touch your horse, too. Put your hand on my shoulder."

The soldier hesitated for one moment, then complied. "Will I… fall asleep or anything?"

"Nope," said Gwyn cheerfully. "But you might feel a little sick. Some people don't cope well with time-travel. Shall we?" Isabel's arms tightened around her waist. Gwyn smiled.

"See you in a moment." Michelle nodded, then the blue haze rose.

Flick!

Fifteen

1497 AD

"I see it!" The excited voice of a woman cut through the babble of the dozens of pilgrims that crowded the road. Gwyn, Michelle, Isabel and Diego were forced to slow their horses as they climbed Monte de Gozo. They reached the top of the hill and saw the cause of the excitement. The three spires of the cathedral peaked against the clear blue skyline, and many people fell to their knees to give thanks that the end of their journey was in sight. The road ran down the hill and curved to enter the city walls via the northern gate. The hills opposite gleamed a rich green in the patches of sunlight that pushed through a pale grey blanket of clouds. Gwyn could smell wood smoke from kitchen fires.

"Only a few miles to go," Michelle said. "We'll be there by midday."

Diego and Isabel crossed themselves. Even Gwyn and Michelle shared a sigh of relief. "Hot baths tonight!" Gwyn declared, and found herself on the receiving end of many—literally—dirty looks from the more devout. She widened her eyes at Isabel, who giggled. Diego frowned, but that was nothing new.

Baths were indeed had, and hot meals, and even Diego couldn't complain that Michelle's coin bought them more comfortable rooms in an inn rather than the bare boards of a pilgrim's hostel. "You're a soldier, not a pilgrim," Gwyn chided him.

He shrugged and tucked into his oyster stew. They all ate as much as they wanted and slept well that night.

The next day they attended Mass in the cathedral, marvelling at the

Romanesque architecture. Isabel whispered to Gwyn, "I never knew a building could be so tall. How does it not collapse under its own weight?"

"Remember the bridges? Builders learn what angles are strongest, and what materials can hold the weight," Gwyn whispered back. She noticed Diego listening. Michelle had her eyes closed. "In the last few hundred years they have been relearning knowledge from ancient civilisations. The Moors were responsible for bringing a lot of it back to Spain."

"Ssh!" The man in front of them glared. Gwyn bumped Isabel with her elbow. They shared a smile and bowed their heads.

After Mass they filed out past a cluster of pilgrims reverently laying their hands on the pillar just inside the doorway of the cathedral. The pillar was shiny in that spot. Gwyn wondered how many hands it took to wear a mark into the stone.

"Listen up," Michelle got their attention, scowling at the salespeople who clutched scallop shell badges or Virgin Mary statuettes. One hawker persisted until she snarled, "Go away!"

He shrugged, shells on necklaces clinking as he looked for his next target. Michelle turned back to their group. "Right, listen up. Next couple of days you can rest, sightsee, mend or replace any gear. See me if you need money—meals will go on our tab at the inn." She gave Diego a hard look. "No gambling, no fighting, or getting drunk. You bring trouble to our group, you're on your own."

He stiffened. "I ain't that sort of man."

Michelle stared him down. "Then it won't be a problem."

Diego grunted. "And then?"

Michelle exchanged a glance with Gwyn. "Start planning… tomorrow afternoon? Somewhere private—find a garden or something, I don't fancy people overhearing us at the inn and misconstruing what we intend."

"I'll have a look about today," Gwyn said.

"Do you want us there?" Isabel asked tentatively.

Michelle gave her a brief smile. "Sure. It might get confusing, but if you mean to stick with us then you'd best know what you're in for."

"I'll be there," Diego declared.

"Good," said Michelle. "But for now, enjoy your day."

Isabel elected to go with Gwyn, much to Gwyn's pleasure. The pair of them chatted as they moved through the streets. In a market they bought bread, olives and cheese for lunch and climbed a hill to where a convent overlooked the city. They found a field for their picnic and spread their cloaks on the grass. As they ate, Isabel peppered Gwyn with questions. They had been circumspect in their conversation during the trip from Bilbao, not wishing to alarm or confuse the soldiers. Now Isabel's curiosity poured forth.

"Tell me of the places you have been," Isabel asked eagerly.

Gwyn smiled. "In what time? Let's see…" The story of how she had travelled back in time to Masada turned into a long and convoluted tale, with many stops for explanations. Gwyn arranged leaves and twigs as substitute maps. "So, if this pebble is Bilbao, and this is Santiago—imagine the distance between to represent what we rode over the last few weeks."

"But… that means the Holy Land is… years travel from here!"

"On foot, or even horse, yes, but you can sail there much faster. And Europe itself is only a small landmass in the world."

"Incredible," Isabel breathed.

Gwyn's enthusiasm for travel sparked—it had lain dormant for so long. It was more than the desire to impress Isabel, though the redhead was plainly enthralled at the thought of the big wide world. Gwyn could have recounted the horrible tales; the deaths, the wars, the loss, but she didn't want to ruin it for Isabel. Something must have shown in her expression, because she blinked and realised Isabel was saying her name.

"Gwyn? Are you… unwell?" Isabel touched Gwyn's hand, then felt her forehead.

Gwyn shook her head and smiled reassuringly, ignoring the tingles from Isabel's touch. "I'm fine—just remembering some of the not nice things."

Her friend looked concerned. "I'm sorry—here I am making you speak of such things when you have bad memories. Are they what give you the dreams?"

Gwyn stiffened. She thought her nightmares had gone unnoticed. "Yeah," she muttered. "It's okay—I should probably talk about it. In my time we have people you can talk to for counselling; to help you feel better and deal with negative thoughts."

"Like confession?"

Gwyn laughed. "Maybe—except they don't force you to say Hail Mary's or Our Father's."

"What do they do then?"

Gwyn rubbed her forehead, trying to think of the best way to explain psychologists. "They… get you to talk about how you feel and why you might be feeling it. They usually let you know that it's normal to feel that way, whether it's sad, angry, anxious, and try to teach you strategies to deal with those feelings so they don't get out of control. Better than pretending you don't feel it then having it burst out at a bad moment." *Which is what I've been doing.* She faced the guilty thought, squirming.

To her surprise, Isabel was nodding. "My father used to say there was much what ails the body, and even more what ails the mind. But most folk preferred a brew with harmless herbs if they thought it would help them sleep. Some things were never talked about." She hesitated, then reached over and squeezed Gwyn's hand. "If you need an ear, please feel you can talk to me."

Warmth bloomed in Gwyn's belly, and she squeezed back. "Thanks, I might just do that sometime." Isabel was very easy to be around. "We should head back soon, before it gets dark."

"Oh! I forgot." Isabel rummaged in her skirt pockets. "I got these when you were buying the bread." She produced a paper twist of sugared almonds. "For dessert."

Gwyn's delight knew no bounds as they consumed the dainty treat, licking their fingers for every last scrap of sweetness. "Amazing." She sighed.

Isabel laughed. "You're the picture of contentedness. Like a cat with cream."

"Mmm. I don't think they've invented it yet, but in my time we have a dessert called ice cream. It's whipped frozen cream and sugar and often other flavours like fruit. It's amazing."

"I wish I could try it," Isabel said wistfully, and Gwyn felt bad for describing something her friend could never have. Isabel caught her expression and shrugged with a half-smile.

What is she going to do when it comes time for Michelle and I to leave? Am I supposed to just leave another friend behind?

* * *

"Right, what's the plan?" Gwyn sat cross-legged on the ground, yawning. Michelle shot her a level look and Gwyn straightened. She and Isabel had spent the morning exploring the city and after a substantial lunch, Gwyn felt a nap was in order. They sat in the deserted courtyard of a quiet tavern—the owner had closed the doors and gone for a siesta. Michelle had tipped generously and he had left them with carafes of wine and water rather than kicking them out.

Michelle cleared her throat. "We need to alert Juana and Philip to Ferdinand's machinations. He'll play the fatherly role around her, telling her it's in her best interests and he just wants to use his experience to guide her. There are nobles in the Castilian Cortes that don't want Ferdinand to gain more power—if we can encourage them to support Juana and Philip that'll undermine Ferdinand. And if we can obtain correspondence between him and the Cortes of Castile that demonstrates he tried to grab power, that'll put her on her guard."

"What father wants to disinherit his child?" Isabel asked, frowning. "My father taught me all he could and hoped I would take up his mantle of healer when he was gone. I did my best…"

"You were his only child," Michelle pointed out. "And no threat to his own status as healer."

"Ferdinand gets what he wants," Diego rumbled. The others looked at him, surprised. It was rare he contributed something without being asked first. He shrugged. "I've soldiered in this land awhile—you gets to learning which way the wind blows. He was equal to Queen Isabella in Castile… but only as far as she let him be. He ain't going to play second fiddle to his daughter, much less his foreign son-in-law."

"I wonder how he would have handled it if his son survived," Gwyn mused.

Diego shrugged again. "Son was his own blood. Man has his pride."

"Be as that may," Michelle carried on, "we need to make Juana see it's greed driving this, not pride and *not* fatherly affection."

"Then let's get in Philip's ear," Gwyn suggested. "If she's so in love with him as history says, surely she'll value his opinion."

"You said she was opinionated." Isabel fidgeted with her plait. "Do you think she'll have changed?"

"Opinionated sounds like a bad thing," Gwyn countered. "She was headstrong, but she had to be or her mother would have squashed her spirit. She'll need those qualities if she isn't to be ridden over by her father. She's supposed to rule a country, after all."

Michelle tapped her fingers. "We'll need to observe her and Philip together to ascertain their dynamic." The others gave her blank looks. "See what their relationship is like."

"What about King Ferdinand?" Isabel asked.

Michelle nodded. "We want him to overstep in his grab for power. He needs to be desperate enough to make an attempt on Philip's life."

"What?" Isabel gasped.

Diego shifted uneasily. "You be calling the king a murderer. That's treason."

"I'm not his subject," Michelle shot back. "It's just slander if it's unfounded, but in this instance we're going to make sure it happens."

"It's convoluted," Gwyn explained. "But Philip dying leads to his son Charles inheriting. He's only six when he becomes king of Castile but when Ferdinand dies Charles inherits Aragon too—as well as all his Austrian and Burgundian territories through the Habsburg side. It becomes one of the largest empires of the time; almost half of Europe plus all its overseas colonies that it pillages for gold and slaves." She and Michelle had spent enough time discussing the timeline to be well-versed in the general history of the period.

"So, this is what you are working towards?" Isabel asked slowly. "An empire?"

Michelle sighed. "Sort of. Charles is a powerful ruler, and the nephew of the Queen of England—Juana's sister. When the King tries to divorce Katherine of Aragon, Charles has enough power to make the Pope refuse to grant an annulment. This leads to England breaking away from the Roman Catholic Church."

Isabel nodded, obviously trying to keep up. "And you want this schism?"

"This schism leads—in a very bloody and roundabout way—to a Protestant England, which seeds the kernel of another Empire—this time an overseas one. It eventually collapses too." Michelle held up her hand in a 'stop' motion. "Before you ask, no, this is not what we are working towards. It's simply another part of human history, one that eventually leads through some even more horrific times to something better. It's all many hundreds of years from now."

They were all silent. "It's still all bloody depressing," Gwyn muttered. She met Michelle's eyes and nodded sadly. "But it has to be done."

Diego looked overwhelmed, but Isabel was frowning. "How will you make his majesty kill Philip?" she asked.

"What do you mean?" Gwyn cocked her head. "Michelle said, we make sure Juana and Philip don't let Ferdinand walk all over them."

"Yes, but to kill his son-in-law… He is the most Catholic King, his faith would never allow it. Jealousy and greed are one thing… this would condemn his soul to hell…" She pointed at Diego. "Even men who kill for duty have honour."

Diego gave her a little bow. "Thank you, señorita."

Michelle and Gwyn exchanged uneasy glances. They had discussed this turning point only lightly, focusing on the prior ones. "Have we missed something?" Gwyn ventured.

Michelle drummed her fingers on the table. "I need to consult the history texts I have. Let's leave it there for now." She looked about the shady courtyard. "How about we have a rest? We'll think how best to convince Castilian nobles to support Juana and Philip, and make Ferdinand paranoid that he's going to lose power in Castile."

Their rooms back at the inn were sweltering so they elected to remain in the courtyard where it was cooler. With rolled up cloaks for pillows, the four of them arranged themselves in shady corners and dozed. The smell of camellias and humming of bees soothed Gwyn to sleep until she woke with a start. Michelle and Isabel were gone. Diego leant on a wall, sitting with his legs stretched out in front of him, ankles crossed. He noticed her wake and stopped whittling.

"They went to find a tailor," he rumbled. "Something 'bout another set of breeches." He shook his head.

"Oh." Gwyn dragged herself up and rubbed sleep from her eyes.

Isabel had borrowed a pair of Michelle's breeches when they'd left Bilbao, but the seat was close to wearing through.

"No one came in the courtyard while you slept," he reported.

"Ah, thank you."

Diego nodded, stood, cracked his neck and put his knife away. "I mean to see a smith to sharpen my blades. Shall I be escorting you anywhere?"

Gwyn wondered if he thought she needed escorting. He appeared to have decided to guard her while she slept, or perhaps Michelle had asked him to. Either way, she smiled and shook her head. "I'll go check on the horses where we stabled them. Thank you, though."

He gave a brief bow, then paused, an air of hesitation about him.

"Forget something?" she prompted when he didn't seem inclined to speak.

His brows drew together. He faced her. "Where you come from, things be different, I know. You and Michelle are worldly, but speak to me as an equal. Also Isabel, for all that she be a village healer and the daughter of a converso."

Gwyn wasn't sure how to respond to this statement. "Well, yes. It's how you treat people. Doesn't matter where you've been or who your parents are. That's why we took you along—you weren't a complete arsehole like Rafael. You tried to do the right thing."

He looked affronted at her choice of language, then shook his head. Stepping towards her, he bowed deeply. "You be truly good and noble, Gwyn. I am your servant in all ways."

"Thanks," she muttered. He rose and walked away, and she tried to unpack what she felt. Diego was handsome, but there was no frisson between them. It made her nervous that he paid attention, innocent though it seemed. She could misread his intentions and end up embarrassing them both, or worse. She shivered then scolded herself. Diego was *not* Cesare. *Not every man wants to get into your pants, Gwyn. Get over yourself!* But he wasn't Meric either, who had been like a brother or even father to her.

She missed Meric.

Sixteen

1497 AD

"I've been thinking about it, Gwyn, what if we split up?"

Gwyn looked at Michelle, startled. "Are you kidding?"

They walked the streets near the cathedral while Isabel and Diego attended Mass. A misty rain had started, not hard enough to make them seek shelter, but the cool air prompted them to keep moving to stay warm.

Michelle made a placating gesture as they strolled past a baker. She smiled as she saw Gwyn inhale the warm aroma of fresh bread. Perhaps they would walk back this way and buy some. "It'll be like when we worked both sides of the negotiations in Segovia."

"That was different—we were in the same city. What are you thinking of?"

"I'm worried we focussed too much on Juana and Philip. When it was just the two of us it made sense—we couldn't afford to separate—but with two extra people…"

"Hang on, we don't know when Diego plans to leave us, and same with Isabel. We could be back to two tomorrow!" Gwyn wiped her face clear of the moisture beading, flicking her fingers.

"They seem inclined to stay. I spoke to Isabel yesterday at the tailors—she was resolute." Michelle wondered if Gwyn had noticed the way the redhead looked at her. She guessed not.

"What about Diego? We're a year ahead—what if he decides he's left his debtors behind and wants to go back to soldiering."

Michelle shook her head. "Spoke to him too, while you were asleep. A year isn't enough in these times. A man might be gone a year and come back to the same problems. He said he has a duty to ensure the future of Castile, and not see it consumed by the greed of Aragon."

Gwyn sniffed. "He sure takes his honour seriously. I suppose that's a good thing."

"It's an excellent thing, Gwyn—if he supports us he's a valuable resource. I feel comfortable sending him with you to A Coruña to meet Juana and Philip while Isabel and I go to Segovia and work on Ferdinand."

"Send me… what?" Gwyn halted, flushed. "Michelle, this is crazy. We can't just go splitting up like this. We'll be hundreds of miles apart! We'll have no way of communicating and you know the geo-locating trick only works when we're in the same time! Juana and Philip aren't due to arrive in Spain until 1506. Ferdinand starts trying to take over as soon as Isabella dies at the end of 1504!"

"I know." Michelle was glad the drizzle had stopped. She would rather keep this conversation out in the half-empty street than huddle under a shelter with other city-goers. "But convincing a man to assassinate his son-in-law is going to need some work. I'll need to build his fear up over time."

"Maybe it'll happen anyway! It's Juana and Philip we need to work on—making sure they put on a show of force that'll make Ferdinand back down. Then we can work on Ferdinand plotting murder."

"But they won't have the confidence to do that if the nobles of Castile don't support them, and that won't happen if Ferdinand doesn't get them really offside by seeking a marriage alliance with France. We've been thinking about this all wrong. We need to do the ground work before they arrive; put the fear of Philip calling on French support into Ferdinand in order to provoke him. I've been reading up on it—this is much more complicated than we realised. Juana's turning points were simple compared to this—we just had to keep her alive. We need to set the board before Philip is dead."

Gwyn blew air out through her cheeks. "So we can't just top him ourselves?"

Michelle raised an eyebrow. She jogged Gwyn's elbow and they started walking again. Gwyn had said 'we'—did that mean the girl was prepared to make the hard decisions? "Correct. If we assassinate Philip, and all the other pieces—the French alliance, the Castilian court—aren't set correctly, I worry that we'll send the timeline in the wrong direction."

Gwyn chewed her lip. "And we can't afford to leave it to chance. But why send Diego with me? Surely you and he get along better—being fighters and all?"

"That's exactly why he should go with you. I want someone protecting you—he's perfect for the job." She didn't mention that if Isabel made her feelings known, Gwyn might get distracted by an affair. And if Diego was infatuated with Isabel, as Michelle suspected he might be, the last thing she needed was a love triangle. That could change, but for now there was no such thing as being too cautious.

They entered the great plaza in front of the cathedral. The sun peeked out briefly then hid behind grey clouds, doing nothing to alleviate the chill which settled on the vast area of stonework.

"Do you feel uncomfortable at the thought of travelling with Diego?" Michelle asked carefully.

Gwyn looked at her sharply. "No. Well, yes, a bit—but not because I think he's a bad man. He seems the opposite. But…" They stopped and gazed up at the two square towers either side of the ornate middle belfry, all three topped by spires bearing the Christian cross. "I just feel nervous, being away from you."

Michelle's heart panged at how she had failed this young woman, used her and led her to being hurt. To still have Gwyn's trust—well, she didn't deserve it. "You'll be safer with Diego," she said gruffly. "Like you said, he's an honourable man. We lucked out with him." She felt guilty for entrusting Gwyn's care to someone else, for using her still—as a resource that needed to be put to best use. Gwyn's innate ability to use the timepiece didn't make her less susceptible to Michelle influencing her, and Michelle was leaning heavily on that now, as she had leant heavily on Diego the day before.

The guilt multiplied when Gwyn hugged Michelle. "I'll miss you. I know you think I'm annoying and immature—I really am sometimes, but I've gotten used to travelling with you."

She is one of those people who needs stability, needs a home. The irony that she, Michelle—the transient, the Agent who never stayed in one time or place long—was providing Gwyn a sense of security, was one of the biggest jokes in this whole venture.

* * *

They had assembled for the evening meal, sharing fish, scallops and seasoned vegetables, accompanied by a carafe of dry red wine. As a guitarist strummed quietly in the corner, Michelle outlined her thoughts regarding splitting up.

Isabel heard the new plan with trepidation. Diego took it in his stride. "My loyalty be to Castile and the queen," he said. "I will not see the Crown of Aragon consume it." He slumped.

"Before I came here," Gwyn said to Isabel, "I didn't realise the people of Spain were so very different. I feel quite stupid, assuming otherwise."

Isabel barely heard her. "Michelle, why do you wish me to travel with you, and not with Gwyn?" She couldn't interpret the speculative look Michelle gave her, but felt uncomfortable all the same.

"Gwyn asked me the same thing," Michelle responded. "I can protect you in a fight, she can't. She can defend herself well enough, but I'd rather Diego was there to protect her."

Diego straightened his shoulders. "I be honoured you place Gwyn's safety in my hands."

Isabel gave Michelle a sidelong look. "We haven't seen you fight. You can pass for a man well enough, but how do I know that I wouldn't be just as safe with Gwyn to spirit me away from danger, as she did back in my village?"

Michelle grinned darkly. "You want to see me fight? Diego, would you oblige me tomorrow morning? I could use a sparring session."

Diego looked as if he had swallowed a fish bone. "You be a woman, I cannot fight you," he muttered.

"See!" Isabel declared triumphantly. The strumming of the guitarist grew louder, building tension with deep staccato notes.

Michelle put her hands flat on the table. "You vowed to follow my orders. We are not fighting, we are sparring. I refuse to insult your manhood and will settle instead for seeing you in the courtyard before breakfast." She stood, looming for a moment. Isabel shrank, regretting causing this situation. If Michelle got hurt she would be angry at Isabel for questioning her word. The music of the guitar built to a crescendo then stopped abruptly as the player finished the song.

"See you in the morning." Michelle smiled at Isabel before she left for their rooms.

Gwyn patted Isabel's hand. "She's not angry, don't worry. You've given her an excuse to show off. I'm curious to see how Diego here fares against her." She half-smiled. "I'm not entirely happy about it either, but if everything goes to plan we'll be back together in a few weeks. Just ten years from now."

* * *

Diego watched apprehensively as Michelle bounced on the balls of her feet, and wondered, despite his outward calm, what he had gotten himself into. Desperation had given him the initiative to go with these strange women a year into the future. Plus there was Isabel. While he had never chased after a lady before, providence meant he had escaped debt and death in the company of the kindest, most beautiful woman he had ever met.

Now was not the time to be distracted by the thought of Isabel, however. Diego stepped carefully as Michelle circled him, feeling the packed dirt of the courtyard under his boots. They were weaponless, as he had insisted, but as a seasoned campaigner he could tell his instincts had been right—Michelle moved like a fighter. Beyond that she was unpredictable.

She moved in a blur, lashing out with fists and feet. Diego blocked, took several blows on his torso and stumbled when she connected with his knee.

She skipped back when he swung, all desire to not hit a woman overridden by the instinct to fight back. He snarled at her grin, feeling the rage that overtook him in a fight rise up despite his effort to maintain control.

He attacked. Michelle blocked and dodged, moving too fast for

Diego to land anything solid. His vision narrowed to her whirling form. He wasn't losing this sparring match, but he wasn't winning either.

Michelle stepped too close, teasing him with an opening. He chopped down on her arms and kicked hard. As his boot connected with her midsection, she let out an *oof* and flew backwards, rolling as she landed and springing to her feet, albeit with less bounce than she had initially started.

"Good shot," she croaked, still grinning. He charged. She ducked and hit his knees with a curious lifting sensation that reminded him of the time he had been thrown from a horse as a child. Then he was flat on his back, all the wind knocked out of him as he stared at the blue sky, struggling to breathe.

Michelle appeared in his vision, eyebrow raised sceptically. "That was good, you made me work." She held out a hand. Humiliation pressed down like a weight on his chest, but he squared his shoulders and accepted her assistance.

"I've… never seen… anyone fight like that before," he wheezed, clasping her hand and hauling himself upright. "Are you that good… with a blade?"

Gwyn and Isabel hovered behind Michelle. Isabel was pale, Gwyn merely looked concerned. "She doesn't usually muck around that long with a blade," Gwyn said. "If she wants someone dead, they're dead."

"Shush, Gwyn." Michelle rubbed her stomach and looked rueful. "You've got one hell of a kick. Feels like a mule got me. Plus I'll have bruises on my arms for days." She looked around at Isabel. "Satisfied?"

Isabel nodded frantically. "I am sorry for questioning you, please forgive me."

Michelle waved her down. "It's okay—we told you to ask questions. Better now than when things get really hot because I won't have time to prove myself then." She shrugged and looked at Gwyn. "I'm still getting used to having to explain myself, but I've found it makes for better teamwork."

She reminded Diego of one of the better captains he'd had. That man had taken the time to explain his tactics to soldiers before the fight, but punished any man who disobeyed or questioned him during a battle. It had been so unusual, so different to every other sergeant, captain or lord he had ever met, he had been devastated when the man caught an arrow to the neck. That had led to his current captain taking over the squad, and the whole mess with the money and Rafael.

"I thank you." He bowed formally to Michelle, then shook his head. "If we be short for coin we could travel the towns and take wagers. No one would think a skinny woman could put a man like me on my arse, even if you be dressed as a man."

She returned the bow. "Won't be necessary. I'll allocate funds for you and Gwyn." She hesitated, then smiled, and leant close so Isabel and Gwyn couldn't hear. "I'm glad you take your honour seriously because if you break your oath and betray us in any way, I will hunt you down and kill you."

If he had thought Michelle convincing before, he was utterly persuaded now. She was not a woman to cross.

Seventeen

2623 AD

"What have you done?" Jaysen Fitz stormed into Owen's lab, his mood the opposite of when he had visited last time.

Owen stepped behind a table, trying to hide the fact that he was shaking. "I-I haven't done anything!"

Fitz narrowed his eyes. "*Why*, then, is the timeline repairing itself? My scientists tell me that turning points in the fifteenth century are resolving themselves. They say it's inexplicable. I say, explain!" His breath was in Owen's face, and the space-born technician recoiled at the waft of sour air. Was that alcohol he could smell? He had never drunk it, knowing it fuddled wits and killed precious brain cells.

"They are resolving themselves." Owen gestured at his digital display of the timeline with its bright stars of turning points. There were fewer than when Fitz had come to see him previously.

"I don't believe you."

Owen tried to outstare Fitz, but didn't have the nerve. The kidnapping, the trips through time to study the time-space energy waves that had engulfed Earth during the nineteenth and twentieth centuries, Michelle's aborted rescue attempt... It had all shaken him so badly he just wanted to curl into a sleep pod and wait until the whole horrible drama had finished and he could be left alone again to study and tinker and conduct quiet research with the Shanista scientists who had pioneered the Time-Space Agency.

Where were the Shanista in all this anyway? They were meant to be the leaders of the Allied Planets. Why hadn't they stepped into this debacle on Earth and neutralised the Earth First party and their maniacal ideas of placing humans above all other species? Was sending Michelle back into the eighteenth century to rescue Owen when he had been held prisoner there the best they could do? He wasn't in the past now—why couldn't they send in a brigade of Mayash troops and extricate him from this mess? Then he wouldn't be quivering and shaking and trying not to whimper under the aggressive glare of Jaysen Bloody Fitz, the epitome of all things xenophobic, violent and arrogant.

"Someone is fixing them!" Owen burst out, unable to keep quiet any longer. "I don't know who, or how, but someone is back in time fixing the turning points, preventing the timeline from going awry!"

The fury of Fitz's face doubled. His skin flushed and his lip curled. "*Who?*"

"I don't kn-know!" Owen squeaked.

"Tell me!"

"It's Michelle, it must be!" Owen babbled. "She's the only Agent unaccounted for, she must have gone rogue. She's the best—she must be back there fixing things!"

Fitz blinked slowly. When he reopened his eyes the fury was still there, simmering close to the surface. "I want to send someone back to kill her. Build me a chronokinetor."

Owen stared at him. "The Shift is here. There is no going back—only forward."

"You're the best—build it!"

"I can't!"

The terror in Owen's voice must have convinced Fitz, though by all appearances he didn't like it. "If we can't go back, then neither can she. If she misses one turning point…"

Owen's knuckles were white from gripping the stool. "She can't go back and fix it."

Fitz smiled, showing all his teeth. "Then we just have to wait until she fails. She can't possibly do them all by herself. I know your Agents were only supposed to do one at a time. They were supposed to have support and down-time and alternate on missions. She's all alone, under pressure, and if she misses one turning point she cannot to go back and repair her error. She will fail."

Owen sank onto the floor after Fitz left, clutching the legs of the stool. "She will fail," he whispered, feeling sick.

When he finally brought himself to rise, he glanced at the display of the timeline on his computer.

Another light winked out.

Eighteen

1505 AD

Ferdinand II, King of Aragon and—up until a few months ago—King of Castile, was worried, though he took care not to show it in his handsomely bearded face. He re-read the report from his useful young spy, Michel, and pondered his next move.

Curse those infernal Castilians. Half a lifetime of ruling over them—albeit with the blessing of his beloved late wife—and they still saw him as a foreigner, an outsider, one to be treated with suspicion and mistrust.

Isabella's death had not come unexpectedly, and Ferdinand thought himself prepared. He mourned the loss of his partner, that remarkable, extraordinary, at times infuriating, woman—a queen unlike any other—untiring, pious, practical yet ever dutiful to her subjects and her realm.

He missed her. She had never been afraid to point out his faults, irritating though it had been. She had given her life for Castile and Spain, and now he was left to carry on the work alone.

Why was the Cortes of Castile subverting him? Couldn't they see that he was the future? He had manoeuvred carefully, discussed the matter at great length with his wife as she organised her funeral and the disposition of her estate, and they had decided it was best to put a codicil in her last Will and Testament that Ferdinand would act as Regent should Juana be absent, unwilling or unable to govern. *How much more absent can one get? She lives in bloody Flanders with that Habsburg pretty-boy of hers.* If only his troublesome daughter hadn't become heir. If only Isabella had lived longer. If only the bloody Castilians weren't so arrogant, thinking they were superior to every other kingdom of Spain.

"Majesty?"

Ferdinand started. He had forgotten the spy, Michel, stood there still, silently waiting for further instruction. Ferdinand sucked his teeth—a habit his wife had always hated, but she wasn't around anymore, was she? "That little Flemish upstart is a thorn in my side, Michel. Arrogant pup tells me to quit the regency and go back to Aragon." He waved the scroll at the slim young man, whose impassive face was framed by dark hair topped by a soft black hat in the latest fashion.

"It is expected that he will use his connections with France, your majesty, to try to intimidate you into relinquishing your rightful rule over Castile."

Ferdinand nodded. "You said as much in your report. I tried to tell the Cortes he was an inexperienced and incompetent foreigner, yet they would take someone who sides with France over me!"

"Perhaps you could prevent him from gaining French support, your majesty?"

Ferdinand looked sharply at his spy. He didn't quite know why he spoke so freely to this young man. He hadn't known Michel that long, but he had come highly recommended from one of Ferdinand's ministers. Perhaps it was because he was convinced of Michel's loyalty. He wasn't currying favour or promoting his own agenda like so many of his advisors or nobles from his respective kingdoms of Aragon, Catalonia and Valencia. Wearing the Crown of Aragon was hard work, and no one seemed to appreciate the constant demands on his energies. Isabella had understood, ruling over Asturias, Galicia and the Basque countries in addition to Castile, but at least her nobles weren't as damnably independent as his were. Until now. *Damn them inviting Philip and Juana to come and rule. The insult to me!* "What are you thinking, Michel?"

Michel bowed respectfully before he spoke. "If the Cortes of Castile aren't put off by a French alliance, perhaps you should seek one first. It might solve the issue of Naples at the same time…"

A man less controlled than Ferdinand would have let his jaw drop. *That. Is. Brilliant!* He stabbed a finger in the air. "You are saying, by negotiating with France, I could drive a wedge between Philip and King

Louis…" He frowned. "But Naples?" The French claim to Naples had been a sticking point for him for the last decade, with two invasions of Italy to claim that territory—trying to steal it from the Crown of Aragon, its rightful overlord.

Michel shrugged. "What is the best way to secure a treaty, your majesty? You are a widower now."

The pieces fell into place. Ferdinand permitted himself a wolfish smile. "Any princess of France could bring Naples as part of her dowry. Our son would inherit and his claim would be secure."

"You have a truly discerning mind, your majesty." Michel bowed again. "The nobles of Castile are foolish to ignore the greatness you will bring to their country and to Spain. Ignore their petty complaints. Concentrate on weakening Philip. Without him they have no reason to resist your rightful governorship."

Ferdinand laughed and clapped Michel on the back. "I shall discuss this with my advisors at once, and draw up a list of suitable candidates for a French bride. I wish you to write letters—find out for me from Paris who might be best to approach with this wonderful proposal, and who might convey our cause to the ear of the French king."

He dismissed Michel and, still chuckling, rang a bell for a servant to bring wine. He would visit his mistress tonight—out of respect for his wife's passing he had refrained for several months. Now it was time to celebrate.

* * *

Isabel dismissed her last customer with a nod of thanks and sent them on their way with a sachet of willow bark to brew into a tea. There was nothing she could do for the woman's failing eyesight, only recommend she didn't sew by candlelight and leave the finer stitching to her daughter. Willow bark would help with the headaches. Isabel's heart ached at the disappointment in the woman's voice—as a seamstress, she needed her eyes for her profession.

When the little shop bell rang, Isabel glanced up and sighed in relief. Michelle slunk in, barring the door behind her. It was scarcely more than a front room with a counter, a curtain that could be drawn across one end to give privacy to a small table and two stools, and a backroom with pallets for sleeping. Michelle had bought it outright for the time they were in Segovia, giving Isabel somewhere secure to practise her herbal medicine and Michelle peace of mind that she wasn't leaving her companion alone in an inn while she masqueraded as a spy.

"Good day?" Isabel asked, as Michelle doffed her cap and hung up her gloves and cloak. February in Castile was cold but not freezing, and usually sunny, which Isabel found pleasant after the rainy winters of her home.

"*Extremely* productive." Michelle's grin was catlike in its satisfaction. "Got him thinking of a French alliance, and dismissing the fact that it will irritate the Castilian nobles even more. Naples was a nice drawcard, though I'm concerned about Navarre. There's an issue there I have to resolve once we're done with this turning point."

"What issue?" Isabel crouched and poked the small fire and hung the kettle over it. Michelle and Gwyn had introduced the concept of boiling water before drinking it. She needed to draw water from the nearby well before nightfall, but there was enough for now.

When Michelle didn't answer, she turned to see the other woman tapping her fingers on the counter, an expression of reluctance on her face.

"What is it?" Isabel asked, puzzled. *Why bring something up if you don't want to talk about it?*

Michelle cricked her neck and gave Isabel a direct look. "I don't know if Gwyn mentioned that while we were in Italy, she was... attacked by a man called Cesare Borgia."

"The old Pope's son!"

"That's the one. I don't say this to break confidence—I honestly don't know how best to support her in this because in my time it's unheard of. I believe in her time there is still a great deal of stigma around it, though far less than now."

"Stigma..." Isabel's mind worked quickly. "He raped her, didn't he?" A layer of sadness settled on Isabel's heart—she knew these things happened. In her village any incidences were either hushed up for fear of shame, or dealt with swiftly by arranged marriages to preserve family honour. "This is why she has the nightmares?"

Michelle nodded, eyes downcast. "Amongst other things."

"But what does this have to do with the Kingdom of Navarre?"

"Ferdinand covets Navarre as well as Castile, so King John of Navarre has been forced to negotiate treaties with him. He occasionally fights battles, as well, but lacks a strong military commander. When Cesare Borgia escapes Spanish captivity–"

"Why is he being held captive?"

"Long story. After his father the pope died, he didn't have enough support to maintain a grip on the territory he conquered in Italy. The new Pope hated him and betrayed him to the Spanish, who have held him prisoner since. He will escape, however, and his wife's brother is King John of Navarre."

"So of course he will flee there." Isabel used a potholder to remove the kettle from the fire, pouring steaming water into clay mugs. She added chicken bones and herbs to the remaining liquid and rested it near the fire to simmer into soup stock.

Michelle retrieved the wooden bucket from behind the counter. "I'll go and get water in a minute."

"You haven't said what the problem is," Isabel reminded her.

Michelle grimaced. "After we deal with this turning point, where Philip of Flanders dies, we must go to Navarre and make sure Cesare Borgia is killed in battle."

Isabel pondered this. "You are afraid this will upset Gwyn? Perhaps she will be glad to know the man who hurt her is dead."

"Probably, though I don't presume to know how she might feel. I would rather keep her right away from Cesare, rather than relive the trauma. I wondered if you and she might wait somewhere, and let Diego and I handle that one, assuming Diego still wants to work with us."

The idea of being left alone with Gwyn sent confusing thrills up Isabel's spine. Sinful thoughts kept creeping into her mind when she thought of Gwyn, imaging her soft brown hair unbound and her eyes, so expressive and kind, intent on Isabel.

She shook herself, then blushed. "Cold in here, isn't it?" She added wood to the fire. "Perhaps we should discuss it later. I need to make this soup." She busied herself retrieving vegetables from the basket under the bench, peeling and chopping.

She heard the door open and close. Michelle had gone to fetch water. Isabel sighed. Should she go to a priest and confess? If only she had one of Gwyn's counsellors to talk to. Michelle was friendly enough, but hardly warm and understanding. Travelling together without the others had been solemn—Gwyn was quicker to joke, laugh or even just chat. Isabel wondered how she was getting on with the taciturn Diego.

Nineteen

1506 AD

Once more, Gwyn found herself missing Meric. Diego was quiet, serious and formal to a point where Gwyn wanted to throw something at him just to get a reaction. She didn't, though, and she berated herself for being dissatisfied with her travelling companion. He took her safety seriously, scouting the woods around any campsite they made, checking the entrances and exits of any inn they stayed at and sleeping across her doorway with a knife to hand. When she had told him to sleep inside the room at least, he looked shocked and shook his head abruptly, muttering that he would not compromise her honour.

Gwyn sighed as she thanked him. It made for lonely travelling as they rode from Santiago de Compostela to A Coruña, skipping ahead in time to the year when Juana and Philip would arrive in Spain. Diego vomited profusely when they had completed the jump.

"I wasn't that sick… last time." He sipped water from his leather bottle, swirled it in his mouth and spat. "Why?" His sickly pallor contrasted with his usual olive hue. Gwyn felt sorry for him.

"Bigger jump?" she offered. "We only skipped a year before. This was eight. Some people just handle it differently." She glanced down and patted her mare's neck. "Doesn't seem to bother animals, though I've only ever jumped with horses."

Diego grunted. "Let's make camp."

He left Gwyn with a loaded crossbow and disappeared into the woods to hunt, returning after a couple of hours with a brace of pigeons. By that time Gwyn had readied the fire for cooking, laid out bedrolls and brushed down both horses and the mule, which, contrary to everything she had heard about the nature of mules, was accommodating and affectionate. It nuzzled her, searching her pockets for carrots or apples while she scratched behind its ears.

"It's like an oversized dog," she declared. "I'm glad Rafael stole the other one—I hope it bit him." She spoke with no heat in her voice.

Diego gave her a puzzled look, then shook his head. "You don't sound as if you mean it"

Gwyn raised an eyebrow. "Oh I'm annoyed, for sure, but I can't get hung up on it. Gotta concentrate on the mission, as Michelle would say. Guess she's rubbed off on me a bit."

"You two have not… worked together long?" It was the first time Diego had shown any real curiosity about his employers themselves, not just their intentions. Gwyn had thought it strange, then realised that questions would hardly be encouraged if he served a lord or captain.

She filled him in on the basics; her time in Masada, serving Vlad the Impaler. He advised Gwyn all of Europe knew Vlad to be a vile and dishonourable prince, despite fighting the Moslems of the Ottoman Empire. She spent more time talking about Domitian's assassination, but glossed over her efforts to install the Borgia Pope and start the Italian Wars—he had heard of those. The name Borgia was infamous. Diego glowered most disapprovingly at the mention of how that corrupt family had shamed their Spanish homeland.

"Hmph, what would you expect, they are Valencian," he declared, showing his Castilian prejudice against all kingdoms under the Crown of Aragon.

Gwyn shrugged and agreed.

"Where did you learn Castilian?" Diego wanted to know.

As they ate, she explained that the time-travel device (or magic amulet, as it was easier to say) gave her the ability to speak the language of those around her. "I would have a lot of trouble fitting in if I spoke a different tongue! I'll have to decide what to speak to Philip of Flanders when I present myself to him."

"You won't approach La Infanta… Queen Juana?"

"I haven't decided." Gwyn chewed thoughtfully on a roasted pigeon wing. "I'm scared she'll throw me out. A Coruña might be a remote town, but there will still be men and women seeking favour from their new queen."

"Men will seek favour from King Philip," Diego pointed out.

"Men, yes. I'm hoping as a woman I can approach him and stand out. If he's curious enough to grant me an audience, I'll ask him to invite Queen Juana to see me too."

Several days later, she was ready to put that theory to the test.

"Lady Gwynia of…" the herald paused over the unfamiliar word, "Australia." His back was as rigid as the rod he used to tap on the wooden floor. He banged the rod again now, and silence fell as curious glances turned Gwyn's way.

She advanced slowly, careful of the elegant skirts that covered her practical boots. She sensed Diego stop just inside the door, and imagined him standing at attention, taking in the view of the long audience room just as she was now. The early spring sunshine cast fleeting rays through the windows to her right, shutters open to take in the fresh air. Dust motes swirled out of her way as she approached the dais where a pale, clean-shaven man with shoulder-length brown hair sat on a backless wooden chair, surrounded by several gentlemen dressed similarly in voluminous surcoats over exquisite linen shirts. One grey-haired gentleman nudged another, quizzical, whereupon his companion shrugged. Both looked Gwyn up and down, at a loss to why she was there.

Philip of Flanders was not as tactless as his companions. He offered a gracious smile that couldn't erase the concerned agitation written in frown lines at the corners of his blue-grey eyes. "Mademoiselle." He gestured she rise from her clumsy curtsey. "Does she speak French, Pieter?" he asked a rotund gentleman with salt-and-pepper hair. It was he who Gwyn had approach with an elegantly written note it be presented to King Philip. Pieter bowed, but Gwyn answered.

"Oui, Majesty." She smiled, hoping she looked interesting. *Why on earth is he called Philip the Handsome? He's pasty and has no chin.* His eyes were his best feature—with them he peered down his long nose at Gwyn and raised his brows expectantly.

"What can I do for you, Mademoiselle? You wish to petition me?"

Gwyn took a deep breath. "I came to warn you, Majesty, that your father-in-law does not mean to give up Castile without a fight. This may not surprise you, but I do not wish you to be taken in by false promises of conciliation. You must beware."

Silence greeted this astonishing statement.

"And who are you to speak of Ferdinand of Aragon so?" Philip demanded. Gwyn wasn't surprised. Royalty tended to get tetchy and close ranks, despite their personal and political differences.

Gwyn curtsied reassuringly. "I was briefly a lady-in-waiting to Her Majesty, Queen Juana, before she left Spain to marry your excellent self, but we did not depart on the best of terms because she thought me a spy for her mother. I have remained loyal all this time, and I will do my utmost to see her take her rightful place on her throne."

Philip looked uncertainly at his entourage. Whether advisors or sycophants, Gwyn didn't know or care, but she knew in that moment Ferdinand would eat this man alive. She remembered a story where a young scientist and an old scientist both claimed sole credit for a brilliant idea. The detective solving the case purported that the old scientist had more motive to lie, being at the end of their career and with an illustrious reputation to lose. The story it reminded her of how the potential to lose all that one had grown accustomed to, made people desperate and dangerous.

"Your Majesty," she spoke emphatically. "I ask only for the chance to serve my queen. I beg that you ask her to receive me."

This seemed to give Philip direction. "Return tomorrow at the same hour," he instructed. "The queen and I will receive you then."

* * *

"You think this'll work?" Diego trudged behind Gwyn. Nothing she said persuaded him to simply walk beside her—she hated talking over her shoulder. "No guard walks equal to his lady," he declared. Gwyn knew he was right.

"I've done this sort of thing a few times before," she replied, pulling her cloak more tightly around her shoulders. The brief sunshine had retreated behind banks of endless grey clouds, rolling in off the ocean to dowse the town with yet another shower.

"What then?" Diego wanted to know.

"First, I make sure Juana isn't inclined to trust her father. If she is, out of daughterly duty or love, I'll have to persuade her otherwise." Gwyn picked up her pace as they neared the street of the inn where they were staying. She could see a squall blowing in from the sea—dark sheets of rain advancing with surprising speed across the water. Shutters slammed shut above them as residents prepared for the inclement weather. They ran the last dozen yards, hurtling through the inn door as the rain blasted in behind them. "Whew!" Gwyn wiped her face. "Sure rains a lot here. I see now why this place was cheaper than inns on the port-side of town, even though it's nicer."

The innkeeper cackled and emerged from behind the bar to lay two pokers in the fire. "Spot of mulled wine to warm you up?"

Gwyn thanked him and sat with Diego at a corner table. There were no other customers at this hour. Once the innkeeper had served them and disappeared into the kitchen, Gwyn spoke openly to Diego. "Michelle gave me several names to recommend to Philip and Juana to approach for support, so that they can establish a political base before confronting Ferdinand. I understand they've brought some German mercenaries, but Philip needs Castilian nobles to back him, otherwise he's just another foreign king who married a Castilian queen."

Diego nodded as he sipped slowly. The wind howled outside, whistling through the cracks in the taproom door.

"If I can set them on that path, and if Michelle manages to get Ferdinand to snub the Cortes of Castile by marrying a French princess, then our work will be mostly done. Ferdinand will get desperate and murder Philip."

"And after that?"

Gwyn hesitated. "Michelle was a little unclear on the next one. Something about Navarre—some military leader there needs to die." She grimaced. "There were so many turning points, we only focused on the first few. We figured we had plenty of time to sit and study the texts once we'd ensured history was on the right track." She yawned, the mulled wine seeping relaxation into her bones. Rain battered against the shutters. "Won't be going out anywhere again today—I might go have a nap."

Diego nodded and remained by the fire, drawing his dagger and a piece of driftwood from his pocket and whittling.

* * *

The rain hadn't cleared by the time they presented themselves at Philip and Juana's temporary court the next morning. Gwyn fussed for some time in the antechamber trying to make herself look presentable. Diego was no help—he had sheltered her as best he could with his cloak as they hastened along the rainy streets, but refused to assist in tidying her hair or sponging mud off her skirts.

"It is not seemly," he rumbled. "You should have a maid." Gwyn rolled her eyes and did as best she could, finger-combing bedraggled strands of hair and pinning them under her hood, shaking out her skirts in an attempt to dry them.

"I don't want to be at a disadvantage," she muttered to him under the steely eye of the herald who had announced them the day before. "You know how appearances matter to royalty."

The herald beckoned for her to come into the hall. "You will wait until I announce you," he instructed, as if she hadn't been through the drill the day before. Gwyn nodded and used the time to examine the scene before her. Yesterday, there had been only gentlemen in attendance on their king; today, ladies in elegant gowns swirled around their queen too. Juana sat next to Philip on the dais, listening with pinched lips as her husband nodded gravely to the beseechments of a townsman.

Almost ten years older than when Gwyn had seen her last, Juana had grown into her striking looks. Youthful uncertainty had given way to poise and beauty, though Gwyn couldn't help but cynically consider that, being royalty, Juana would always be dressed in the most flattering colours, fed the most nourishing food, and have wet-nurses and nannies to fulfil the exhausting duty of caring for his children. Gwyn then felt guilty—royalty or not, the future that awaited Juana was horrible.

Eyes turned her way. Gwyn realised she had missed the herald announcing her. She stumbled, then recovered herself as she advanced, ignoring the titters at her clumsy, unkempt state. Philip looked dismayed as Juana turned a disbelieving pout his way.

"Majesties." Gwyn managed a respectable curtsey. "I apologise most sincerely for my bedraggled appearance. Storm or blizzard would not stop me, much less a little rain." She gestured to the windows—closed today against the weather. My loyalty is such that I would face far worse to bring my warnings and advice to you."

One of the gentlemen applauded quietly, offering Gwyn a half bow. It was Pieter. He stood back from the monarchs' field of vision. Gwyn took heart from his encouragement.

Philip gave a half-smile and placed a quietening hand over his wife's beringed fingers. "You approached yesterday, Lady Gwynia, with dire warnings about my dear and cherished father-in-law. You also said you were a lady-in-waiting to my noble wife. She does not recall you."

"I do not," Juana declared. "And the punishment for slandering my father the king will make you wish you had never presented your miserable self here."

Gwyn smiled as though her heart wasn't thumping. "Do you still ride side-saddle, your majesty," she asked conversationally in Castilian Spanish. "Or do you ride as I taught you? And does Lady Valentina still serve you? She hated me, I know. She didn't understand I was there to help you."

Juana paled so quickly Gwyn imagined she could hear the blood rush from the queen's face.

"My love," Philip asked, concerned.

"Everybody out," she whispered. She looked at her husband, wild-eyed. "Out!" she screamed. Gentlemen and ladies rushed to obey. "Not you." Juana pointed at Gwyn with a finger wearing a ruby as red as her sudden flush. "You stay."

Gwyn felt Diego at her side. "It's alright," she murmured. "Wait outside and don't talk to anyone." He joined the throng leaving the room.

The doors swung shut and only Gwyn, Juana, Philip and Pieter were left in the hall. Gwyn and Pieter stood in silence; Philip stared at his wife, bewildered but seemingly resigned to her extreme behaviour.

"Are… are you a witch?" Juana stammered. "Why are you here?"

Gwyn pitied her. "I am here for the same reason I was there ten years ago. To help you, your majesty. Your life was in danger back then, and it is in danger again now. I was sent to protect you."

"Are you seriously saying my wife's father seeks to murder her? This is outrageous!" Philip declared, standing.

"Stay, husband." Juana put out a hand, halting Philip. "It is true, I remember her now. There were… strange occurrences the month before I left Spain to marry you."

"I am not a witch," Gwyn said earnestly. "I was an agent of your mother's, sent to watch over you. I was not noble, so a story was concocted because it was felt that only as one of your ladies could I be close enough to you to protect you."

"Why did my mother say nothing of this?"

Gwyn sighed and painted the most heartfelt expression of pained reluctance on her face. She pressed a hand to her heart. "Your dear departed mother, rest her blessed soul, did not… trust that you would listen to her."

Juana's nostrils flared ever so slightly. She drew herself up. "It is true that my royal mother, the queen, and I did not always… agree."

"Then you do understand the unfortunate need for deception," Gwyn jumped in, pressing the point and distracting her listeners from her sketchy half-truths. "But that is all in the past. It is the present that concerns us." She leant forward. They mirrored her, captivated. "The Cortes of Castile needs its queen. I have the names of those who will support you, but you must show that you can stand up to your father. It is a terrible thing that he would try to unseat his own daughter, but… he already told your nobles that you were incapable of ruling."

Juana's eyes flashed. She simmered visibly but made no outburst. Philip's advisor, Pieter, whispered in Philip's ear. Philip flicked his eyes at Juana and nodded slightly. "Perhaps we should discuss this elsewhere, my dear," he said in Dutch. "Pieter will take you to a more private room, mademoiselle," he continued in the same language, "so we can speak away from prying ears."

Gwyn pretended not to notice the way Pieter scrutinised her, and smiled in polite confusion. "Forgive me, majesty, I do not understand."

Pieter's tiny quirk of the lips confirmed her guess, although Philip's poor acting was a fair indication. "Oh! Forgive me, mademoiselle!" he reverted to French. "We speak Dutch in private." He waved a hand and repeated his direction in their supposedly common language. Gwyn followed Pieter through a door at the back of the hall after curtseying to the falsely smiling Philip and tight-lipped Juana.

"My guard will be concerned for me," Gwyn told Pieter.

"I shall send for him." Pieter bowed her into a spacious sitting room. "You shall wait here until their majesties are ready to speak to you again."

He bowed as he drew the doors shut behind him. Gwyn heaved a great sigh and selected a large, straight-backed chair with armrests and overstuffed cushions to lower herself into. *They don't trust me, and they think they are being clever speaking Dutch. Good. If they think they are smarter than me I can play them. Philip is easy—he's unsure and easily influenced. Juana is… Juana is unpredictable. I wish I knew what she thought.*

The next few days would be critical.

Twenty

1505 AD

Ferdinand brandished the scroll triumphantly. "I hold here, Michel, a letter from the French king, stating how delighted he would be to welcome me into his family by marrying his sister, Germaine de Foix."

"Congratulations, majesty!" Michelle bowed deeply and offered a sincere smile. "A most noble marriage for a most noble king."

"She was the foremost of your candidates for a French bride. She has family claims to Navarre, and Louis will bestow Naples on her as part of her dowry." Ferdinand poured himself wine into a silver goblet and took a long draft. "He wants money for the war he waged in Italy, but we can pay in instalments. Plenty of time for that."

"You have been most successful, majesty. The nobles of Castile would be foolish indeed to turn to Philip now, when an experienced king with a strong French alliance is at hand." Michelle sighed in quiet satisfaction. The letters and the secret meetings had paid off, and despite being followed by court spies several times, her cover appeared intact.

Rather than wait out the months until Ferdinand was due to confront his daughter and son in law, she and Isabel had skipped ahead several times, pretending to depart on journeys to France. Michelle had paid couriers to run her French letters and checked in with them upon their return.

"I have indeed." Ferdinand sounded smug. "They won't dare stir from those sodden fields they call Flanders now."

Oh. That's not good. "That is true, majesty." Michelle nodded pensively.

"I only hope their absence doesn't foster discontent and rebellion against you."

Ferdinand opened his mouth to rebut, then closed it. "That is a remote possibility."

Michelle shrugged. "Very remote, majesty. I'm sure the nobles who invited him to reign as king will abandon their plans to foment rebellion against you."

Ferdinand pursed his lips. He tapped a finger against his goblet. "Indeed."

"Castile cannot afford another civil war like the one a generation ago. They will desist." Michelle nodded as if assuring herself of her own words.

The king stroked his beard. "Perhaps I should take measures to be certain."

Michelle shrugged again. "If Philip and Juana were to present themselves to the Cortes of Castile, they could declare in front of all the nobles that you are regent, and they will not interfere with your rule. None could act in their name then."

A smile grew on the king's face. "That would certainly stymie any plots."

"Would they come, though? Surely Philip is too afraid of you to leave his homeland." Michelle made herself sound puzzled. She had avoided any flattery when she had first inveigled herself as a spy with Ferdinand, to have him believe her sincerity now.

"Hmph. A sweetener, perhaps. Half the revenue of Castile? I'll call it Juana's inheritance—that should be enough for him." Ferdinand smiled as he planned. "He's just a boy—he'll be tempted."

Michelle was unsurprised Ferdinand disregarded the potential that his daughter might have something to say on the matter and hoped Gwyn would put that element to good use. Michelle certainly wasn't going to put into Ferdinand's head that Juana could be a threat.

"When would you have them come, majesty?" Michelle asked, as if it were a sure thing now, this idea of Ferdinand's.

Ferdinand poured more wine. "Not before I've ratified this treaty with France. I've plenty of time to solidify my claim and hopefully get a son on Germaine before they even arrive. I'll instruct my daughter and her husband to present themselves early next year, so we can resolve this issue once and for all. That will suppress any murmurings that call for a different king."

Michelle felt her heart rate slow again. She bowed as Ferdinand dismissed her. It was strange to think that Gwyn had yet to meet Philip and Juana, and that all this groundwork was being laid so that in just under a year, they would arrive in Spain and push Ferdinand back into Aragon.

After that, Michelle had to make sure that Ferdinand was desperate enough to murder his own son-in-law.

* * *

1506 AD

"Juana, surely you cannot believe this wench?" Philip whispered in Dutch to his wife. His uncertainty showed through his courtly smile as his eyes flicked sideways at the strange young woman who had reappeared in Juana's life so precipitously.

How Juana hated this tentative, unsure version of her husband. Away from his beloved Flanders, catapulted into Spanish intrigue, he was polite instead of charming, cautious rather than canny. Only in bed did her true Philip return—the passionate man who stoked her fires and made her feel like the only woman in the world.

Which she was not. Juana pursed her lips sourly at the reminder, eyeing Gwynia, who stood by the fire, stifling a yawn. Juana snorted imperceptibly. As if her husband would sniff the skirts of someone so plain. But he had strayed before, and Juana worried that the mystery of their visitor would intrigue Philip. She turned a comforting smile on him. "I doubt my life is in danger, my love, but it is true that my father is used to being in charge. Only my mother could overrule him. With her gone..." Did her father truly intend to unseat her? Would he plunder her inheritance? It was true she had never expected to rule Castile—being Duchess of Burgundy these past ten years had been immensely satisfying, despite her husband's indiscretions. He always returned to her; placated her temper and pledged words of love and passion. She could not be replaced.

But her father had replaced her mother, with a French princess, of all things! And so soon! She was under no illusions that her father was a saintly man—he was much like Philip in that way—but the insult to Castile was tremendous. And as much as Juana had been loathe to return to the land of her unhappy childhood, she would not be put aside! She was the daughter of a great queen; her sisters were queens. It was her time.

She straightened. "We must consider, husband, that this woman speaks the truth. The names of those in the Cortes of Castile who would support us concur with the letters we have received from those nobles. We must gather our strength, so my father sees you are not a man to be trifled with, and I would look him in the eye and seek to know whether he truly means me ill." As ludicrous as it sounded, she knew her father for a ruthless man. He had already issued coins in his name while Juana and Philip had travelled to Spain—the months they spent waylaid in England due to storms had cost them dearly. They needed to gather support before Ferdinand entrenched himself further.

"Gwynia." Juana switched from Dutch to Castilian Spanish. Gwynia's head snapped up.

"Majesty." She gave an atrocious curtsey.

Juana raked her gaze over the girl—how had she aged so well? Juana felt as though there was something she was forgetting, but all she could think of now was how different and exciting Gwynia had been. No wonder Valentina had taken against her, accusing her of all manner of terrible things. Valentina had travelled with Juana to Flanders, then bemoaned the rain, the society, and the questioning attitudes of Dutch scholars so much Juana had sent her home, tired of the fustiness and nagging.

"You say you act out of loyalty to my mother and Castile," Juana said. "Yet surely you wish for some reward? Who pays you?" She felt Philip shift in surprise as her directness. She smiled. She had learnt a thing or two from his German relations.

Gwynia did not appear fazed. "Don Juan Manuel, who first wrote to you and King Philip begging you to take up the crown of Castile, pays my master," she said matter-of-factly. "I am merely an agent. To deliver my warning to you is sufficient—whether you would have me stay and serve, or send me back, is entirely up to you."

"Of course it is," snapped Juana.

"My love," Philip interrupted in Dutch. "Perhaps we should keep the wench close. That was if she is lying we can mete out justice."

Juana hesitated. It was a sensible suggestion, but how close did he mean?

Philip seemed to sense what she was thinking. He placed a hand over hers and smiled. "You are my jewel, my queen—nothing shall shift my gaze from you."

His words, as always, undid her. "I have a jealous heart, my love," she whispered. "You know this to be true."

"Your passion is what draws me to you," he murmured in return.

Juana caught the nauseated expression on Gwynia's face and glared, then remembered the girl couldn't understand Dutch. "You will stay with us, as a companion for me," she ordered stiffly. "We will ride to meet my father and resolve this matter once and for all."

Twenty-One

1506 AD

"So Ferdinand's new bride isn't pregnant yet?" Isabel asked as they rode north from Segovia in a long train of horses, carts and mules. The summer heat flooded her nostrils along with the dust, the smell of sweat and manure pungent on the air.

"Doesn't appear so," Michelle murmured. She swished the end of her reins to keep flies away from her face. The road dipped and curved to meet the edge of a light forest where intermittent shade was not enough to cool the travellers. It only emphasised the scorching sun.

"Will we see Gwyn and Diego?"

"Possibly." Michelle shrugged, pursing her lips. "I advised Ferdinand there is a spy in Philip's party so I want to sneak across to their camp. I doubt I'll be able to take you with me."

Isabel hid her disappointment.

"Cheer up, we'll see them soon enough." Michelle wore an amused look. Isabel wondered why. "You like her, don't you?"

"Do you mean Gwyn? Of course—she is kind and generous." Her mouth felt dry and she had trouble swallowing.

"I mean, in a romantic sense. We haven't seen Gwyn in weeks but you light up every time she is mentioned. Even before that, your eyes always followed her. I thought it was hero worship, because she rescued you from the stake. But it's more than that, isn't it?"

Isabel must have tightened her hands on the reins, because her horse stopped. Michelle stopped too. Other riders cursed as they veered around them until the last wagon passed them. Once the dust settled, the only sound was the sough of wind through the trees.

"Are you alright?" Michelle asked. "Did I offend you? I think you know me well enough now to know I don't intend to upset people unless it serves a purpose. I have no reason to upset you."

Isabel found it hard to swallow. "You… you don't think it is a sin?" she whispered.

Michelle sighed. "Definitely not. I know that goes against everything you've been taught, but in my time, and even in Gwyn's time, most people are more open-minded about romantic relationships. I don't know exactly how she feels about you but I believe she might be interested."

This information left Isabel floored. *How does she know that? Has Gwyn told her?* She remembered girls in her village would giggle and gossip over the miller's son. Gwyn and Michelle didn't seem to share such private information with each other, unless Isabel had misunderstood their partnership?

"Your mouth is open." Michelle wore a half-smile on her face. "And before you ask, no, I'm generally not attracted to women." She looked ahead. "Come on, we'd better catch up or we'll get left behind. All I'm saying is, you might not get to see her this time, when Philip and Juana meet with Ferdinand, but next time you do see her, you might want to say something. You never know your luck."

With that, Michelle kicked her horse into a trot. Isabel scrambled to follow. The conversation replayed over and over in her head as they rode on for the rest of the day and the next, until they reached the plain where they were to camp. It was here Ferdinand would treat with his rivals, and attempt to settle the question of who was to rule Castile.

* * *

"Psst, Gwyn!" Michelle crouched outside a tent, hoping the object of her search was awake. She listened hard. A shadow moved around the side of the canvas, sword out. "Diego, it's me, Michelle!" she hissed.

The sword lowered a fraction. "Show yourself," Diego rumbled.

Michelle illuminated her wrist computer enough to light her face.

"Where's Gwyn?"

"Asleep." Diego put a finger to his lips.

"No I'm not, I'm awake," Gwyn grumbled from inside the tent. "Wondered when you'd show up. Don't know why it had to be the middle of the bloody night."

"Just let me in," Michelle ordered. "Diego, can you stand guard?"

"I will return to my post."

Gwyn pushed out the tent flap enough for Michelle to crawl in. "He sleeps across the front of the tent," she whispered to Michelle. "Got really strict ideas about my honour. Kinda annoying sometimes."

Michelle shook her head. "If he's protecting your honour, he's protecting you. I ordered him to keep you safe."

"Yeah, yeah, I know, I do appreciate it. He's just like a Dobermann—growls if any dude even looks at me."

"A what? Never mind. How are things with Juana and Philip?"

"Yeah, fine." It was too dark to see Gwyn's expression, but Michelle thought her voice sounded rueful. "Juana's pissed her dad is undermining her husband—those coins you sent with Ferdinand's head on them really helped. Philip sent for a bunch of German mercenaries— he wants to give an impression of power, that he's not to be messed with."

"So what's the problem?"

"Who said there's a problem?" Gwyn sounded defensive.

"Keep your voice down. If everything is going to plan, why do you sound as if a xanbar sat in your finbar?"

A heavy sigh. "They're just so hopeful and determined, and it's all going to be cut short—wait, a what?"

"Alien species from my time. Rather icky. Never mind, it's just an expression."

"Uh huh. Well, it's hard knowing he's going to–"

"Try to think about what it will achieve. We're that much closer to you going home."

A brief silence from Gwyn. Michelle wondered if she had overstepped.

"Isabel misses you," she told her. "Shall I take a message to her?"

This time Gwyn's silence was puzzled. "Uh, sure. Tell her I miss her too. It'll be nice to hang out when this turning point is over. Hey, you haven't told me much about what's next."

"Don't worry about it now," Michelle ordered. "Just focus on this turning point—you're doing a good job. I'll keep working on Ferdinand and we'll come to find you soon. After this meeting, do you think you can jump ahead to the week before Philip's death?"

Gwyn grunted. "She keeps an eye on me—she and Philip don't trust me entirely. If I disappear and reappear I'll need a good reason."

"Hmm, let me work on it. Alright, I'd better go."

"Wait, how're things with Ferdinand? You didn't say."

The breeze shifted, bringing the smell of smouldering campfires. A horse whinnied and stamped. Michelle suppressed a sigh. "He's realised the French alliance was a mistake in that it got more Castilian nobles offside. He's doubling down, though, trying to get his wife pregnant so that he appears a more secure prospect for succession. The court doesn't see her much—she's young and pretty and he gives her no opportunity to be anything more than a broodmare. Who knows if she has any talent for politics?"

"Hmph, typical."

"Yes, definitely not the partnership he shared with Queen Isabel. We'll see how he is after the negotiations tomorrow." She paused. A dog barked in the distance; there was a rustle outside as Diego shifted position. "I'll be in a precarious position because I've been feeding him false reports, telling him Philip has been too afraid to meet him, that's why he's been avoiding this meeting."

Gwyn murmured agreement. "Philip by himself probably would be, but Juana has steeled him. They've been meeting in secret with lots of nobles, gaining support. Ferdinand will likely be in for a big shock tomorrow."

"Let us hope so. Now I really must go. I'll find you again."

Michelle crept out and made her way through the darkness to the edge of the camp. She slipped past sentries without incident, crawling into the tent she shared with Isabel. The other woman didn't stir, for which Michelle was grateful. She didn't want to answer questions at that moment—she would need all the sleep she could get to deal with tomorrow's fallout.

Twenty-Two

1506 AD

The field was set. Bright morning sunlight shone on the armour of several thousand sweating German mercenaries, lending a military air to the proceedings. Juana watched carefully as her father's horse picked its way towards them; a handful of guardsmen and finely dressed gentlemen accompanied him. Ferdinand's distinctive red and yellow striped banner snapped in the wind, the standard-bearer resting the base of the pole in his stirrup. Juana was pleased to see he hadn't used the joint coat of arms he had shared with her mother. He was too savvy for that.

Juana and Philip's own standards decorated the open-sided tent. The stripes of Aragon were quartered with the lion and castle of Castile-Leon and pierced at the bottom by the pomegranate of Granada. These arms were quartered again with the Habsburg arms representing all their different lands, making the flags far more complicated and, in Juana's mind, more impressive than her father's simple banner. The weight of Austria and Burgundy stood behind her, never mind her father's alliance with France.

Thinking of France, and Ferdinand's new French bride, incensed Juana so much for a moment she had to grip the carved armrests of the backless wooden chair upon which she sat. Her chair was identical to her husband's, resting on the wooden boards that had been hastily nailed together to make a smooth platform for the meeting royals. The boards were angled, so that Juana and Philip's seats were a fraction higher than the ones set opposite for her father and his advisors. Juana took a deep breath to calm herself. The air brought the aroma of rich red wine and fresh fruit from the table set between the places of the opposing parties. If she closed her eyes she could almost forget her fury, but instead she banked its fire and chose to smoulder instead at her father dismounting and walking towards her, arms outstretched.

How could he? As a girl Juana had always loved her father more than her mother. Ferdinand was jovial while Isabella was sombre. He encouraged while her mother sought to crush Juana's spirit. She had chosen to believe that her mother's coldness had driven him into other women's beds, and had vowed that would never happen to her. She loved Philip with a passion, yet he still strayed. Reluctant as she was to admit it, doubt had crept into Juana's mind like a cold draft through a broken shutter, and she had begun to wonder if perhaps her husband's, and therefore her father's, unfaithfulness had less to do with their wives and more to do with their own weakness of character. On the voyage from Flanders, a storm had washed them ashore in England, and she had reunited with her younger sister Catherine for the first time in many years. Catherine had recounted the affection and devotion of her poor dead husband, Arthur Tudor, and Juana had been envious. *Which does not make sense,* she had thought. *My husband is alive, after all.*

"My new betrothed, Henry, is much more like your Philip, my dear sister," Catherine had said. "Passionate, full of life—but Arthur, bless his dear soul, was special. Still, I was destined to be queen of England, and I will do great things here."

The reminder that her sisters, alive and dead, were queens or would become queens, reinforced Juana's resolve as she rose to meet her father. To avoid trembling hands, she brushed down her Spanish style dress—much lighter than the heavy wools to which she had become accustomed in Flanders. A confusing rush of old affection combined with anger that he would supplant her mother so easily led to a stiff embrace, outmatched in awkwardness by the formal greeting given to Ferdinand by Philip. Juana's husband ignored Ferdinand's outstretched arms and gave a short bow instead. Juana silently cursed him for showing submission to her father instead of greeting him like an equal.

"My children!" Ferdinand spoke comfortably, apparently unswayed by the show of force and formality. He looked genuinely relaxed and pleased to see them. "I thank God for your safe arrival into Spain. I was expecting you months ago!"

"We were waylaid by a dreadful storm," Philip replied, a little too enthusiastically in Juana's opinion. They weren't here to talk about the weather, after all. "We spent some time in England as guests of King Henry."

"And how is that tight-fisted old usurper?" Ferdinand laughed. "Though I shouldn't call him that, seeing as I legitimised his reign by marrying Catherine to his son, Arthur. Won't repay her dowry but won't marry her to his other son! A canny player, if ever there was one."

Juana found herself smiling at her father's description of the grim English king, then stopped. *Canny player indeed! Don't think to distract us from why we are here!* "My husband and I are here to assume our duties as monarchs of Castile. We thank you for ensuring a smooth transition while Philip and I made our way from Flanders, father. We would not see you torn away from your own duties to the Crown of Aragon any longer."

Ferdinand's head swivelled slowly as he turned from Philip and fixed on her, his effortless smile tinged with puzzlement. He blinked several times. "My duty is to your mother, my beloved queen. She stipulated carefully in her last testament that I act as regent should you be… incapable or absent."

Juana bared her teeth, feeling much like the lion that graced her banner. "I am present now, father, as is my husband, and we are very capable of ruling."

"Oh, I've no doubt!" Ferdinand jumped in. "In Flanders, I'm sure, he has much experience ruling, but as I mentioned in my letters," he spread his hands wide, "ruling Castile is a very different matter. They don't like foreigners."

"Fortunately, he has me to guide him," Juana replied swiftly, "and I am Castilian to the core." She sensed Philip beside her watching the battle of wills. *Don't let him ride all over you!* She wished her husband would say something.

Her father seemed to wish that too, as he faced Philip again. "My lord, let us attempt to resolve this matter. There seems to be some confusion over what is best for Castile."

Philip frowned. "No confusion, my lord. Juana and I are here to take our rightful places on the throne. I understand you wish to continue receipt of some income from Castile—perhaps that can be agreed upon as thanks for your service to the realm and in memory of Queen Isabel, God rest her soul. Though no doubt the dowry brought to you by your new bride is a comfort to you in these times."

Ferdinand's smile faded as he looked from one stony face to another. His eyes drifted behind Juana and she knew he was considering the soldiers arrayed at her back. His own gentlemen, elegantly dressed but few, were a paltry statement in comparison. Ferdinand's eyes also scanned the nobles standing behind and to the side of the negotiating tent, and Juana decided to play her winning card. "I have a letter here, father, signed not just by those nobles who stand with me here today, but by many other lords of Castile and Leon, citing their confidence and support for my husband and me." She raised her arm and flicked her fingers forward without turning her head. A secretary stepped forward, bowed, and presented the scrolls to Ferdinand. One of his gentlemen accepted it, unrolled it and passed it to his king.

Ferdinand's eyes scanned the document. He smiled again, but it was tight. "There are… a considerable number of names in this letter. How wonderful you should have such support."

"So you see," Philip picked up where Juana had left off, "you may return to Aragon without fear you are neglecting your obligation to Castile. Of course, your obligation now is to support your daughter's reign. She shall be Queen like her mother before her, with a husband as equal partner such as you were. God be praised!"

Several of Juana and Philip's supporters echoed the sentiment and Ferdinand's smile grew tighter. "God be praised, indeed." He rose. "It would seem there is no more that needs to be discussed here. I shall return to Aragon. How wonderful to see you again, daughter. You are truly your mother born again."

Triumph bloomed in Juana's heart as she formally embraced her father farewell, then watched him ride away, but it soured when she thought of the comparison to her mother. *Will I never escape her? Why cannot I just be myself, without her shadow looming over me?*

"That went rather well, I thought," Philip murmured in Dutch.

"He did not expect to lose," she replied, staring at the retreating riders.

Philip put a hand over hers and squeezed tight. "I am proud of you for standing up to him. You are so strong, my love—a true queen indeed."

She smiled at him. "You always know what to say to me, my dear heart." She had a husband who loved her, a father who respected her. She was a great queen.

So why did she feel so hollow?

* * *

Ferdinand threw the wine glass across the room, watching it smash with a sickening splash of red on the stone wall. He sent the wine jug after it, then a silver plate of sweetmeats. His knife and his fork—a wedding gift from Germaine de Foix, forks being the latest fashion in France— followed. The metal clanged to the floor, and Ferdinand gripped the table, tempted to overturn it to vent his rage.

"Dammit!" he screamed, thumping his fists on the wood instead. "Damn them all to hell! Curse that pasty Flemish weasel and curse that presumptuous daughter of mine! And curse every Castilian noble who went behind my back to kiss their usurping arses!"

His closest advisors hovered in the room. He looked at their unsure faces. Their normally calm and suave king was losing his temper, and they didn't know how to react. He hated them.

"Get me, Michel, my spy," he commanded. "And bring me more wine!"

He paced as he waited, wondering how his intelligencer could have got things so terribly wrong. He would have to upbraid the minister who had recommended him… if only he could remember who it had been. There had been letters, and Michel had seemed highly competent and full of information, Ferdinand hadn't questioned his credentials. There was something so unassuming about the spy. He could well imagine Michel as a field agent, quietly listening and gathering news for his king.

The object of his thoughts was shown in. Ferdinand glared at Michel, who bowed but didn't grovel. Could it be the spy was a fool and didn't realise how badly he had failed? That didn't match what he knew of the young man, and it jarred him briefly from his anger.

"You told me Philip was weak. You told me to concentrate on a French alliance and ignore the nobles of Castile. Now I have alienated them, and they went scurrying off to that Flemish boy!"

Michel waited until Ferdinand had finished his tirade, then spoke. "Philip *is* weak, majesty. Without Queen Juana to encourage him, he never would have dared make such demands. My agents failed to identify that she would have such resolve and likely did not intercept letters sent from her to the wives of many of those nobles. Their plans slipped under our noses."

Several advisors shifted uncomfortably at the talk of intercepting letters. *Pah! Everyone does it, whether they like to admit it or not! It's why we all use cyphers and codes.* He refocused on Michel, who frowned as if presented with an intriguing puzzle. Calmness stole over Ferdinand despite the situation—he found himself less irritated with his spy than the quaking nobles around him.

"Do you have a plan?" He asked hopefully. He would never usually ask for help so blatantly, but Michel had such a confidence about him, and he had been vital in bringing about the French alliance. Ferdinand did enjoy his new bride's bed, even if she wasn't in foal yet.

Michel nodded slowly, tapping his beardless chin thoughtfully. "We have vastly underestimated your daughter, majesty."

Ferdinand grunted. "Never would have thought she'd turn on me like that. She was not interested in politics when she was younger."

"She was a rather… passionate young woman, your majesty?"

Ferdinand glanced sideways at his advisors. "Get out," he ordered shortly. "Come up with a plan for Naples. I can't concentrate on Castile when Naples is falling apart at my back! I'll send for you all when I need you." The nobles bowed and shuffled hastily from the room, leaving Ferdinand facing Michel.

"Juana was always passionate—like her mother but without Isabella's control."

Michel nodded. "The reports I have conclude she still is. She is devoted to her husband—wildly jealous of anything that takes him from her. Without him, her resolve to rule Castile will fall apart. They are only strong with the other—separate them and your regency will be unimpeded."

Ferdinand frowned. "How do you suggest I do that? I can't very well send him back to Flanders and keep her here, or vice versa."

Michel spoke carefully. "I would never suggest you raise your hand against your own blood, but Philip is a foreigner, and unused to the climate of Spain."

A chill went down Ferdinand's spine. The notion that had been presented was… evil.

Michel gazed at the wine stain on the wall, still speaking slowly and deliberately. "Just because it is not on the battlefield does not mean it isn't a war."

The chill turned to boiling hot anger. "Get out," hissed Ferdinand. "How dare you suggest such a thing? Begone from my sight!"

Michel bowed deeply and said, "Forgive any misunderstanding, your majesty," then departed. Ferdinand sat heavily in a high-backed chair and gazed at the wine stain. He poured himself a fresh glass from the tray a fearful servant had replaced earlier. Sipping, he tried to banish from his mind the evil suggestion his spy had made.

But the thought lingered.

Twenty-Three

1506 AD

Michelle entered the little shop and barred the door behind her. She took deep breaths, closing her eyes, and tried to calm her racing heart.

"Are you alright?" Isabel emerged from behind the curtained section of the shop. She peered at Michelle with concern.

"I'm fine," Michelle managed.

"You're all flushed—have you got a fever?" Isabel rested a palm on Michelle's forehead. "You're not burning up. What happened? How did the meeting with the king go?"

Michelle let out a deep breath and sagged. "I may have pushed him too far. I thought I had gauged him correctly—he overlooked the fact that I gave him bad advice, took out his anger on his ministers. There's a lot that the chronokinetor can do in the hands of someone who is naturally adept at influencing people. But he reacted quite strongly when I alluded to… murdering Philip."

"Come and sit down." Isabel led Michelle to a stool. "You have been confident up until this point. The way you worked your way into Ferdinand's court, tricking ministers and the king into thinking that the other had appointed you as a spy. Why, the way you fooled him into underestimating Queen Juana was incredible! Why lose faith in yourself now?"

Michelle nodded. "There's just so much riding on this. We can't simply take care of Philip ourselves—it has to discredit Ferdinand so he won't be named regent again. I was sorry he sent his advisors from the room—the more people who know, the more chance it gets leaked that Ferdinand had a hand in his son-in-law's death. Whether that'll even happen now…" She rubbed her face in her hand. "I used to live for these moments. Plant an idea in someone's head, watch it grow, watch them think they came up with it themselves. The thrill of manipulating a turning point just so in order to fix the timeline."

Isabel listened, a slight frown of worry etched on her face.

"But there were always safeguards, back up plans. There were other Agents we could call upon if things went awry. I messed up a turning point once—it was awful, but the Agency had resources to fix it. Here, I have nothing. The entire future of my world rides on me not stuffing this up!" She tried to shove aside the self-pity—she had never been one to indulge in it before—but the overwhelming wave of hopelessness made her feel as if she was drowning, choking, and suddenly she couldn't breathe. Her vision tunnelled into pinpricks of light, and Isabel's voice sounded echoey and far away. Beads of sweat broke out on her neck but she was so cold and couldn't move.

Her vision slowly returned. She was kneeling on the floor—how had she got there? She focussed on her hands resting in front of her face—if she just looked at them everything would be alright, surely? Everything else would go away. Worn hands; little nicks and scratches and scars. Ink stains—might as well be bloodstains for all the killing she had done. What was she but a tool in the Agency's hands? A bloody knife, an arrow, an axe. Kill, kill, kill—that's all she'd done, make other people's lives miserable just to salvage her own world.

"Michelle? Michelle! Can you hear me?"

Isabel. Another person swept up in Michelle's duty; another tool to be used, like Gwyn. Like Diego, like Meric. And if they were misplaced, traumatised or killed, then that was the cost—but it weighed heavily on Michelle's mind.

"Michelle!" Isabel sounded frantic. Michelle struggled to form words, to tell her that she was alright, she was just having a rest, but the effort to produce coherent sound was insurmountable. A strange wheeze escaped her. She tried again and it turned into an incoherent honk. She fluttered her fingers to wave Isabel away—she just needed another few moments.

Then she was lying on her back, staring at the dirty ceiling. Isabel pressed a damp cloth to her forehead.

"What happened?" Michelle asked. "Did I faint?" *Surely not.*

"You did," Isabel replied tentatively. "You paled and didn't answer. Then you rolled over and your eyes were open but you couldn't seem to see me."

"Oh." *How embarrassing.*

"Are you feeling better now? Normally when people faint it is because they have suffered an injury. I could see no mark upon you."

Michelle sat up slowly. She felt only residual dizziness but her limbs were weak. "I… I think I had a panic attack." She flushed at the thought. "I didn't think I was prone to those."

"You… panicked? Why? Are the king's men after you?"

"No, at least—not that I know of. Ferdinand was angry. I just felt overwhelmed." She forced herself to be analytical. "A panic attack can be triggered by lots of things. I think I've been suppressing how anxious I am about this turning point—all the turning points, really."

Isabel bit her lip, clearly thinking. "Perhaps you need one of Gwyn's counsellors. She said they help people work through strong feelings rather than pretending it's not there. I am only a healer of the body, not a healer of the mind, but I will listen if you need to talk."

Michelle looked at Isabel's thoughtful expression, and felt a small smile form on her face. Some of the tension left her shoulders and jaw. *Thanks, but I'm fine,* she wanted to say. Instead she spoke of how hard it was knowing there was no backup, no second chances if she broke the timeline. Isabel listened and nodded, and didn't try to pretend she understood everything that was at stake. She understood that Michelle was frightened and angry and felt guilty about everything that had happened. "I've kept myself detached from all the people whose lives I've ruined because I know the future will be better. But even if we do save the future, what will I be at the end of all this?" The horrible realisation hit Michelle. "I've been an Agent for so long. War is coming but I don't know how to be a soldier. I'm a killer, a fixer."

Isabel nodded slowly, taking a deep breath. She opened her mouth but a loud hammering at the door interrupted her. Both women looked up, startled. It was near sunset, and while the streets of Segovia came alive again after the heat of the day, most of Isabel's customers visited in the morning before siesta time.

The hammering came again. A deep voice barked, "We are here for Michel! He is ordered to the presence of the king!"

Isabel paled. Michelle swallowed and stood, putting out a hand to steady herself. She faced the door and squared her shoulders.

"What are you doing?" Isabel hissed.

Michelle cocked her head quizzically as the hammering came again. "I'm going with them."

"They might be taking you to prison! Or to be executed!"

Michelle nodded speculatively. "They might. But it might be my only chance to see this through."

"What about me?"

Michelle paused. "If I'm not back in three days, go to Valladolid and find Gwyn and Diego."

"What?"

Michelle opened the door, forestalling the soldier's fist raised to hammer once more. "I'm Michel," she said, deepening her voice. "Isabel, pass me my cloak."

The soldier leant to see past Michelle, taking in the herbs hanging in little bundles above the bench with mortar and pestle stowed neatly to the side. Several roots lay half chopped next to a knife, and little jars of powders and liquids lined the small shelf behind. "This an apothecary?" he rumbled.

"My mistress is a healer." Michelle accepted her cloak from Isabel's shaking hand and tucked it over her arm. The evening wasn't cold, but she didn't know when she might return.

If she returned.

* * *

Michelle was gone. Isabel stood at the door and watched the soldiers march her down the narrow street. Now the stars winked in the darkening sky and passersby greeted each other. Shopfronts re-opened, neighbours gossiped and children played.

Despite the balmy temperature, Isabel shivered when she realised she had been standing for some time, uncertain of what to do. She had grown used to Michelle's comings and goings, but always with the expectation that the other woman would return.

What to do? "Eat something," she told herself, stepping back into the shop and shutting the door. She cooked, ate and tidied, checked on her medicines and supplies. No customers came, no soldiers arrived for her. The smell of cooking drifted in through the open window; laughter and music punctuated the night. It was dark outside; people gathered inside for meals and bedtimes, and still Isabel didn't know what to do.

"Three days?" She looked about the small room, lit by a single candle. "I'm to wait three days then go to find Gwyn?" Had Michelle forgotten that respectable women didn't travel alone, didn't ride horses astride like they had taught her? Apart from the brief journey as part of King Ferdinand's entourage to meet Juana and Philip they had stayed in Segovia, and even then Michelle had taken care of the hiring and stabling of any mounts they'd required. Isabel didn't know if she had it in her to attempt the journey to Valladolid, as much as she wanted to. She wasn't brave enough. Not like Michelle. Not like Gwyn.

Thinking of Gwyn was a stab to her heart. Surely if she felt something for Gwyn, she would be prepared to risk everything to ride to find her? But what if Gwyn didn't feel the same? They hadn't known each other for long.

Isabel rummaged in a drawer and pulled out the lovely, leather-bound parchment book she used to record notes of medicines and people's ailments. Her father had taught her to write in Hebrew as well as Latin. She didn't dare use the former, not when the Inquisition hunted for evidence of lapsed conversos, slavering to burn heretics at the stake.

Isabel opened to the back and smoothed her hand over the page, feeling the bumps of the parchment, inhaling its crisp, fresh smell before sharpening a quill and dipping it in ink.

My Dearest Gwyn, she wrote. She set the quill down. "What am I doing?" she muttered. The blank space below held the promise of hope and despair at the same time. Isabel forged ahead.

My Dearest Gwyn,

You'll never read this—likely I'll never see you again. Michelle has been taken by King Ferdinand's men, and my greatest fear has come true; that I'll be left alone.

How pathetic I must sound. I'm not brave like you, not bold like Michelle. You came into my life so unexpectedly, asleep under that tree like a violet quietly blooming in the shade. You saved my life and opened my eyes to a new world, and I fell in love, though I didn't realise it.

But if I see you again, I will try to have the courage to tell you. Likely you will laugh, or be ashamed—despite what Michelle tells me I find it incredible to believe that a love such as mine should be returned.

Perhaps that is my true fear? Not that I shall be left alone—after all Michelle has left me money, I am establishing myself as a healer here in Segovia, the shop is owned in my name—but that I shall be left alone without you, before I truly had a chance to know you.

I will pray for that chance.

Love, Isabel.

Twenty-Four

1506 AD

Valladolid. Juana's moods swung wildly as her court established itself in the city of her youth, and Gwyn didn't blame her.

"We must celebrate your victory, my darling!" Philip exclaimed. "Juana, Queen of Castile, triumphantly returned with her handsome and devoted husband." He smiled charmingly, and Juana softened, but Gwyn sensed she was still on edge.

"He doesn't understand," Juana muttered in Latin. "This place is a crypt. Mother's ghost is everywhere—she never stops frowning at me." She dismissed her ladies, leaving only Gwyn hovering uncomfortably, twisting her hands in heavy linen skirts. She had seen a tailor in A Coruña and ordered a new dress to appear presentable at court. It was cream and pale blue, without elaborate embroidery because there hadn't been time, but a thin line of Italian lace edged the square-cut neck. Gwyn wore a matching blue ribbon around her neck for adornment, wondering who she was trying to impress. Certainly not Juana, who pouted at Gwyn and beckoned her closer.

Gwyn curtsied. "How may I serve you, majesty?"

Juana considered Gwyn. "I don't know what to do with you, Gwynia. Should I send you back to Don Juan Manuel, or whoever his spymaster is? I could use a spy, but how could I ever trust *you*? You are a snake in the grass of my court."

Ouch. Gwyn tried not to be wounded. She had hoped to have proved her worth by now. She needed to stay close enough to Philip until

Michelle got there, to report on his movements and how it would be best for an assassin to poison him. *Why isn't Michelle here yet?* It had been six weeks since the meeting on the plain, and while Gwyn had skipped days here and there to reduce the wait, she worried that somehow she'd missed the Time-Space Agent, or worse, something had gone wrong and Michelle wasn't coming. The turning point was meant to happen in three days, and Gwyn didn't know when or how Philip would be poisoned.

"Please don't send me away, majesty," Gwyn begged. If Michelle didn't come, Gwyn would have to act alone. She dreaded it—the last assassination she had orchestrated had been at the hands of another, but she had borne witness and it had been awful.

Juana spun a gold ring round and round her forefinger. "You may stay for now. Listen for plots, and report to me, not my husband. Stay away from him."

"Yes, your majesty." Gwyn's curtsey wobbled as a strident voice came from outside the doors.

"She will see me!" a woman declared. "I am the closest thing left to her dear mother, so announce me, you buffoon!"

Gwyn froze, trying to place the voice. It was elderly and somewhat familiar, pitched at a volume that suggested deafness had set in.

"Speak up!" the voice demanded. "I am Lady—"

"Valentina," Juana finished, skin paling. "Ugh, just what I need, that old crone fussing about me and reminding me how mother would have done things." She spoke in Dutch, then switched to Spanish as she ordered Gwyn, "Leave—use the side door."

Gwyn happily complied, fleeing the moody queen as Lady Valentina hobbled through the doors with the aid of a cane. "Majesty, my dear Juana—I knew you would need the comfort and advice of a loyal friend so I came as fast as the litter bearers could carry me. Horribly slow, despite the fine weather. Anyone would think a little heat was the end of days! Now, tell me..." Her voice faded as Gwyn shut the door behind her and made good her escape.

Great, now I have to avoid that old biddy. How am I meant to spy on Philip if Juana has ordered me away from him? Kind of don't blame her—I've seen him eyeing up the ladies of the court already. How can he be so supportive to her as a queen yet a jerk of a husband?

She reached her room on the servants' level. The door was ajar. Gwyn paused, then crept forward. She relaxed when she heard Diego's familiar rumble with Michelle's low tone. "Michelle!" She burst in. Michelle leant against the mantle—no fire was burning on such a warm day. Diego stood by the little table, face expressionless.

Michelle smiled. "Ah, there you are, Gwyn." She tensed as Gwyn hugged her, then relaxed.

"Where's Isabel?" Anxiety struck Gwyn. Had something happened?

"In the town; we took a room at an inn—the Bough of Grapes, near the market. How are you getting on?"

"Do you need me?" Diego interrupted. Michelle shook her head—he bowed and left. Gwyn supposed he felt unneeded as a protector now Michelle was here. She filled Michelle in on all their doings since they had separated. In return, Michelle outlined the progress they had made with Ferdinand.

"I thought I had ruined everything," Michelle confessed. "Isabel was convinced they had taken me away to execute me—poor thing was terrified."

"Oh, how awful." Gwyn's heart panged for the fear her friend must have felt. She knew what it was like to feel alone.

"She would have managed." Michelle shrugged. "I left her money, and she was set up in her healing business."

Gwyn found herself irritated by Michelle's callousness, though she wasn't surprised. *We picked her up and carried her along; it's not fair just to dump someone when you're done with them!*

"Well, I might go and see her now, if that's alright? You don't need me."

Michelle yawned. "No—I might have a rest here then re-familiarise myself with the castle. Ferdinand has sent me to do the deed, with orders to be as discreet as possible, but I want to gain enough notice for people to link me back to Ferdinand so the suspicion and blame falls on him."

"That'll be a fun balance." Gwyn pulled a face, then fussed briefly with her hair, wishing she had a mirror.

"You look fine," Michelle said quietly. "She'll be thrilled to see you."

Gwyn blushed. "I'll be happy to see her. I like having her as a friend."

As she walked from the castle into the town of Valladolid, she wondered if Isabel had said something. *Surely not. Get a grip or you'll embarrass yourself!*

When she reached the Bough of Grapes, she paused for a drink of water with sliced lemon. She mopped the sweat from her face and neck then flapped her handkerchief to cool herself. "A friend of mine is staying here," she told the barmaid. "She has red hair, a few years older than me—is she here?" If Isabel had gone out Gwyn would wait.

"Upstairs, last room on the right," the barmaid replied, wiping a table. "She might've gone a-walking with her soldier friend—I was out the back awhile. Didn't see all the comings and a-goings."

Soldier friend? She must mean Diego—why didn't he say he was coming here? He could have waited for me. Gwyn finished her drink and paid, heading up the stairs to see if Isabel and Diego were there.

They weren't. Gwyn tried the door and found it unlocked, so went in. *Where have they gone?* She glanced about at the small amount of luggage sitting on the bed. A square of parchment peaked from one saddlebag, the flap not tied down. Gwyn ignored it at first, but after ten minutes of waiting the parchment caught her eye again. It was badly creased and, looking more carefully, Gwyn realised the Latin she saw written there said *Love Isabel.*

She forced herself to look away. Who Isabel wrote to was none of Gwyn's business. She waited another five minutes before curiosity overcame her and she carefully slid the parchment from the bag.

What she read left her floored.

* * *

Diego shuffled. Isabel gave a smile of encouragement. Reserved as he usually was, she was unused to seeing him this hesitant. Was he nervous? Why had he come down from the castle without the others? *Maybe Gwyn doesn't care to see me…*

She and Diego stood under a large tree in the plaza. Stallholders were beginning to close for siesta and crowds dispersed as people sought shade, lunch and rest.

"What is it you wished to ask me, Diego?" Isabel wished he would hurry up. There was no breeze; the tree provided only the barest of respites from the heat.

Diego took a deep breath. "I wish to… I wish to ask you something important, señorita."

"Yes?" *Did Gwyn even miss me?* The uncertainty of it all distracted her and she missed what Diego said.

"I'm sorry?"

He coughed and turned red. "I said, I offer you my hand. In marriage. Gwyn and Michelle will be moving on from Spain soon. Since you have no family, I would marry you and give you my name."

Isabel's stomach turned inside out. Surely she had heard wrong?

Diego gave a small smile. He reached out and took her hand. "I will be a good husband to you. We will have many children, and I will build you a good home."

She felt cold. Her hand was listless in his, and her voice was a squeak when she spoke. "*Marry* you? I don't want to marry you!"

Diego dropped her hand. "I don't expect a love match, but you have no prospects. You work as a healer and you're little better than a whore!"

Eyes widened, Isabel wanted to slap him. The worst of it was, he was right. With no family, no name, no connections, she had little chance of establishing a life for herself. It would be a precarious existence, and worst of all, there would be no Gwyn.

"I… I have to think," she said breathlessly, turning and fleeing Diego and his ridiculous, sensible proposal as quickly as she could.

Twenty-Five

1506 AD

The door opened. Gwyn's heart beat faster when she saw who it was "Isabel!" she exclaimed. She shoved the letter behind her and stood. Her friend burst into tears.

"What's wrong?" Gwyn held out her arms and Isabel threw herself into them, sobbing. A tumult of emotion coursed through Gwyn. "It's alright, it's okay. Tell me what's wrong." She walked backwards and seated them on the bed.

Isabel clung to Gwyn. "I'm sorry," she sniffed. "I thought it was you before, but it was Diego, and he wanted to talk to me and insisted we walk to the plaza."

"Talk to you?" *About the mission?*

Isabel sat back and blushed, two spots of red colouring her olive skin. Gwyn found herself fascinated by the slightest dusting of freckles across Isabel's nose—had she acquired them during the weeks with Michelle in sunny Segovia? Her stomach somersaulted, wondering how to address the attraction that she had suppressed, which now burst to life at the knowledge Isabel felt strongly about her…

"He asked me to marry him."

"What?" Illogical fury rose in Gwyn—she shoved it down. "Why?" She was aware she sounded incredulous—would Isabel be offended and think Gwyn believed her undesirable? *Argh, this is getting complicated!* Gwyn didn't know what she felt, didn't know what to think, wanted to find a horse and ride fast so she didn't have to think or feel, but Isabel was here, obviously distressed and Gwyn wanted to comfort her. "I mean, he hasn't known you that long—not that you can't fall in love with someone in a short amount of time!" *Oh, god, you're making it worse.*

Isabel wiped her face on her sleeve and shrugged. "I don't think love has anything to do with it. He thinks he's doing me a favour."

"A favour?" *What are you, a parrot? Stop repeating everything she says or she'll think you're an idiot!*

"He thinks I have no prospects." Isabel wiped her eyes again. "He doesn't know Michelle bought the shop in Segovia and put it in my name. If she hadn't returned I would have been able to continue as a healer there—I already had people coming to see me. But she came back and we left there. I could have stayed."

Gwyn stilled. "Why didn't you stay?"

Isabel took a deep, shuddery breath. She blushed furiously and looked at her lap. Gwyn was fascinated by the way Isabel's auburn hair fell in curls to frame her face. She reached out, her breath coming short, and brushed one curl back, tucking it behind an ear. Isabel looked up, startled. Gwyn leant forward and brushed her lips against Isabel's.

Their eyes met. The same, intense look that Gwyn felt she must be wearing was mirrored in Isabel's eyes. She bit her lip hesitantly, then carefully kissed her again. Isabel closed her eyes.

"I, uh, read your letter," Gwyn confessed.

Isabel's eyes flew open. "My letter?"

They were holding hands. Gwyn squeezed, feeling guilty. "I wasn't going through your stuff. I was just waiting, and I got bored—the barmaid told me you'd gone out with Diego and I was going to wait until you got back."

Isabel squeezed back. "I'm glad you waited. And I'm glad you read it. I know it is a sin, but I cannot change how I feel and I… I know you will be leaving soon. I wanted to tell you before you went." She looked as if she would cry again.

Gwyn wrapped Isabel in a hug, delighting in the scent of Isabel's hair—sunshine with a hint of cinnamon and cloves. "It's not a sin." It was as if daylight danced in her heart. It felt right to hold this woman in her arms. A world of possibilities opened up to her even as the raincloud of caution darkened any potential future. "We… we should talk about this. But for now, let's just be."

* * *

Diego paced the empty plaza, brooding. His proposal had not gone to plan. He was confident that Isabel would come around—he would persist—but it was the other issue on his mind that occupied him now.

I gave an oath to obey. But he was allowed to ask questions, they said. Well, he would ask.

Back at the castle, he tried to rest—it was siesta, after all. Once the heat had lost the worst of its bite, he made his way up to Gwyn's room, hoping to find Michelle still there. No luck.

He didn't find her until the evening meal was served—a banquet in the great hall; nobles one end, king and queen on the dais, servants, guardsmen and commoners crowded onto the lower tables. She sat with Gwyn and Isabel—Diego frowned when his intended didn't acknowledge him and concentrated on her meal of spiced vegetables instead.

"Michel." He used the masculine version of her name—she was still dressed as a man. "I would speak with you."

Isabel stiffened. Gwyn put a hand over hers and squeezed. *No doubt she told Gwyn—does she think I should ask Michelle's permission?* He considered that—perhaps it would speed up her acceptance. But he had more important things to discuss right now.

"Can it wait until I've eaten?" Michelle helped herself to more roast eggplant. It was dusted with that new spice Diego liked—paprika, he had heard it called. His mouth watered. Perhaps he should eat before this confrontation.

"It is important," he stated.

Gwyn muttered something to Michelle, using a tongue Diego didn't understand. Michelle raised her eyebrows and stopped chewing. She swallowed, sighed, and stood. "Alright—I suppose you want some privacy?"

Diego led the way past servants pouring wine and toting platters of beef, fowl and fish. He didn't stop in the corridor, nor on the stairs to outside. He took a torch from a bracket and lit their way into a small kitchen courtyard—empty at this time of night except for a pair of lovers kissing by the cucumber frame. They giggled and fled, leaving Diego irritable. He offered Isabel a respectable future, not a grope in the garden—how dare she refuse that?

"What can I do for you, Diego?" Michelle stopped and put her hands on her hips, seemingly relaxed, but he observed that her dagger was in easy reach. Did she suspect what he might have to do? He reminded himself not to underestimate her.

"You said I could ask questions."

She gestured widely. "Ask away. What do you want to know?"

This was it. "You planned to warn Queen Juana and King Philip that her father would attempt to steal Castile from her. You have done this."

"Correct."

Deep breath. "Why, then, must you add murder to your conscience? Castile is safe, Philip seems a good man. He will protect his wife and lands."

It was hard to discern Michelle's expression in the flickering light. She broke a spray of parsley from a bush and crushed it in her fingers, the acrid smell mixing with the smoke from the torch. She sounded tired as she replied, "I need to discredit Ferdinand so badly he will never stand a chance at ruling Castile. He won't stop wanting it, and if anything should happen to Philip and Juana before their son Charles is old enough, he'll be in a position to swoop in and take over."

"You cannot know that."

Michelle cocked her head. "I know more than you. There's really no need for you to worry about it. If you wish to part ways with us, I release you from your oath."

Diego's heart lifted. His chest swelled as he declared quietly. "Thank you." He stepped forward and hit Michelle. She slumped, unconscious. He lifted her over his shoulder and stole away.

Twenty-Six

1506 AD

Michelle didn't return after the feast. "Well, you can't walk back to the inn by yourself in the dark," Gwyn ventured.

Isabel smiled shyly. "Can I stay with you?"

Gwyn blushed. "I'd love that."

They walked arm in arm—no different any other pair of maids or noble ladies in a tête-à-tête. Michelle wasn't there, so Gwyn and Isabel cosied up on the bed, talking.

"It was nice, earlier today, when you were telling me about your childhood," Gwyn said, twining their fingers and lifting Isabel's hand to kiss. "It sounds like your parents really loved each other for your father to leave his family and religion to be with your mother. It must have been hard for them, though."

"It was. He was never fully accepted by the village, even though people came from miles around to see him for healing. When mother died, he travelled up and down the river, taking me with him."

"I suppose that's why you were more curious about the outside world than the people around you. You knew there was more out there."

Isabel's eyes lit. "And now I know there is even more." She turned to face Gwyn, kneeling. "Gwyn, I want to go with you when you leave. Don't leave me behind. I could scratch a living as a healer, until the Inquisition comes for me again. I want to learn to be a doctor like your parents. I want to be with you, in a time where people will accept us."

Gwyn gazed at the beautiful woman before her. She reached up and cupped Isabel's cheek, then kissed her. "I don't want to leave you." The kiss deepened, and slowly Gwyn drew Isabel down to lie beside her. She had been tentative earlier in the day—at the inn they had kissed, then lain quietly and talked of things other than the revelation of feelings that had just taken place. They had spoken of Isabel's childhood, and Gwyn had elaborated more on her own journey through time, finishing with her desire to get back home once history was set to rights.

Their feelings made clear, Gwyn didn't hold back. Slowly but deliberately, she moved her hand down Isabel's back, over the curve of her buttocks and legs. Isabel tensed, and she halted.

"Please don't stop," Isabel said breathlessly. Gwyn kissed her again and continued her exploration, pushing Isabel's skirt up and venturing caresses higher and higher.

Isabel moaned. "This should feel wrong, but it doesn't," she breathed, her heartbeat thumping hard against Gwyn's chest. Her back arched as Gwyn pressed her face into Isabel's neck.

No one disturbed them, and they fell asleep in each other's arms, waking quietly as sunlight reflected off the shutters of the window Gwyn had forgotten to close.

They dozed on and off as the sounds of the waking palace drifted in. Gwyn's stomach grumbled, and Isabel laughed.

"Yeah, yeah." Gwyn gave a lopsided grin.

After breakfast, they walked through the gardens. "Strange that Michelle hasn't come to find us," Isabel remarked. She stopped to smell the budding gardenias. "She usually left a note when we were in Segovia."

Gwyn shrugged. "She can look after herself. She'll turn up. I'm surprised Diego isn't lurking."

Isabel looked up and winced. "Oh no, there he is!"

Diego strode towards them. "Good morning, Señoritas." He gave a stiff bow. "I apologise for not escorting you back to the inn last night. Thank you, Mistress Gwyn, for chaperoning Mistress Isabel."

Isabel looked as if she might vomit; Gwyn raised an eyebrow and coughed. "Uh, no problem."

"A woman's reputation is more precious than gold," Diego intoned, evidently in a philosophical mood.

"It sure is," Gwyn cut in. "Have you seen Michelle?"

It was Diego's turn to cough. "No. I believe she returned to the inn last night." He reddened, looking at Isabel, and Gwyn fought the urge to growl at him.

"I guess we'll have to go find her," she said, reluctantly. "We're running out of time for this turning point."

"No!" Diego burst out. "She said to wait in the castle, that she, uh, would find you with instructions. She said do not leave."

Gwyn and Isabel looked at each other. Gwyn shrugged. "I'm sure she has it in hand." She linked her arm with Isabel's and walked them away from Diego. "He's got a nerve talking about bloody reputations," she said, feeling Isabel quiver with what she assumed was anger. They rounded a high hedge and Isabel burst out laughing.

"Oh my… oh my goodness!" she giggled hysterically.

"What?" Gwyn frowned, baffled.

Isabel looked at her, trying to suppress her laughter and failing. "Can you imagine?" she asked. "If he knew what… what we…?"

Gwyn started to giggle too. "Oh my god, his brain would explode. A woman's reputation, indeed!"

They spent the day in cheerful company, walking, talking, or sometimes just sitting in silence and being together. Towards evening, Gwyn became anxious.

"This is weird—she's not like this. Well, not anymore."

"What do you mean?" Isabel asked. They stood on the battlements, gazing down at Valladolid, watching for a lone figure making its way up the road to the castle. None came, and the growing shadows stretched until the gate closed for the night.

"Well, before she met me, she was a lone ranger—operating solo, or sometimes with other Time-Space Agents, I guess. I think she really felt threatened that I could do what I did without any training—use the timepiece, influence people, see the timeline and the turning points. She was a bit of a bitch about it, honestly."

"But she trusts you now."

"Yeah, I think she does, mostly." Gwyn leant between the merlons and tried to glimpse any late traveller that might be on the road below. She sighed and straightened. "We haven't seen Diego all day either and typically he looms nearby in bodyguard mode. I appreciate he's following orders, but I survived just fine before. And you'd think he'd be trying to charm you, but he's nowhere in sight."

Isabel touched Gwyn's elbow. "Michelle said she could concentrate and sense where you are because of your chrono… chrono…"

"I just say timepiece," Gwyn interrupted. "Chronokinetor is too wordy."

"Timepiece, then. Can you do the same for her?"

Gwyn slapped her head. "Brilliant idea. Let's go back to the room and I'll try that."

After several minutes' meditation, Gwyn opened her eyes, frowning. "She's nearby. Definitely in the castle. Was there a note when we came in? I didn't see one."

"No." Isabel paced. "I think you are right, Gwyn. Something is not right. Did you not say the turning point is tomorrow?"

Gwyn closed her eyes and concentrated again. "Yeah. But I have no idea what poison she was intending on using, or how she planned on giving it to him. She was sussing all that out yesterday, and we couldn't exactly talk about it at dinner last night. If Philip doesn't fall ill by midday tomorrow, we might miss our chance."

They looked at each other apprehensively. "Let us try to find her first. Where should we look?"

Their search took them down past cellars, into the bedrock upon which the castle was built. "I don't like this," Gwyn whispered, brandishing a torch in front of her to dispel the darkness. Isabel squeezed her other hand, encouragingly.

They came to a locked and bolted door. Sweat ran down Gwyn's back despite the coolness of the air.

"Gwyn, are you unwell?" Isabel felt her forehead.

Gwyn nodded, feeling sick. "Last time I was underground in a place like this, a psychopath was murdering women for their blood."

Isabel paled despite the orange torchlight, but her voice remained steady. "You can do this."

Gwyn nodded and tapped the door. "Michelle?" she called. "Michelle!" There was no reply. "She's in there, I can feel her," Gwyn muttered. "We need to get past this door."

"An axe," Isabel suggested. "Where can we find an axe? The smithy?"

Gwyn swore. "I hate leaving her here. How the hell did someone get the jump on her? And why?"

They looked at each other, the same thought crossing their minds. "Come on," Isabel urged. "Let us find an axe and get her out of there. And if we see Diego, hide."

* * *

"Urhh." Michelle's mouth tasted vile. *Must see a dental hygienist. It's been a while.* Her eyes flew open to utter blackness, and for a second panic gripped her heart tight. She forced herself to breathe, concentrating on counting each breath. *Don't have a panic attack. Don't have a panic attack.* Where was she? Her head ached, the air was cool but stale—she smelt her own sweat and… a man's odour?

Diego. That bastard! Irritation crawled up her skin—or was that something else? The panic rose again and she spent what felt like an eternity quelling it. She sought anger instead; fury comforted her even as she berated herself for letting him surprise her like that. *Obviously, loyalty to his king and queen overrode his oath… oh, shit, I released him from his bloody oath! Argh!*

Stop. Be calm. She had been in worse situations than this—why was she losing her grip? *Because the stakes are so high, you fool!*

Assess. Tied with rope at wrists and ankles. Test. There was no give in her bonds and her dagger was gone from her belt. She couldn't see a thing; not her hands in front of her face, not an outline of a door. She had no idea how large or small the room was and didn't fancy struggling to her feet only to hop around and crash to the floor when the wall greeted her without warning.

Where is Gwyn? Michelle concentrated. The girl was somewhere in the vicinity. *She's higher than me. I must be underground—a dungeon, I suppose.* She wished the chronokinetor had the capacity to transmit communication.

You would think with all its other features the Shanista would have included that!

Bitterness didn't help, but it was hard to avoid with the foul taste on her tongue. The biggest problem she had, even more so than the pressing urge to go to the toilet, was that she didn't know what to do next.

Twenty-Seven

1506 AD

"It's locked," whispered Gwyn, creeping back from the smithy door. "I might be able to squeeze through the gap between the wall and the roof, but there's a bloody great dog sleeping inside. I like dogs, but I'm not stupid enough to jump on top of one I don't know."

Isabel cursed quietly. "What do we do now?"

Gwyn rubbed her face in her hands. "I don't know. Where else might there be an axe?"

"The stables?"

They ventured to the stables. A groom chased them away before Gwyn had a chance to try to persuade him. They huddled in a corridor near the kitchens, having lifted bread from a basket destined for the banquet hall.

"We're running out of time and I'm out of ideas." Gwyn nibbled on her loaf, not tasting it.

"We'll have to try again in the morning."

Despite their anxiety, or perhaps because of it, a comforting embrace turned into a passionate one, and they both slept. Up with the dawn, Gwyn laid out men's clothes and tried to decide what to do.

"She would want us to complete the mission," she said reluctantly.

"She might be injured and cold," Isabel pointed out. "We can't leave her there any longer—what if we get to her too late?"

"I know!" Gwyn burst out, her expression torn with fear and worry. "And this isn't the last turning point. I need her for the next ones. But if we muck up this one, there's no point worrying about the others, because it'll be too late!"

Isabel hugged her. "I don't know what poison Michelle planned to use, but I know something that might work. If I can find it at an apothecary…"

Gwyn looked at her. "That's risky. What if someone wants to know why you're buying it? You don't have the timepiece to help influence people."

Isabel gave a false smile. "Help me dress and arrange my hair. I'll charm my way past any grouchy guard."

Gwyn started. "Wait, you're not thinking of actually poisoning Philip? You don't have to do that! It's dangerous, and… I don't want it on your conscience."

Isabel stroked Gwyn's cheek. "You don't think my hands aren't as dirty as yours, helping with this business? I know it gives you nightmares, what you have had to do. I won't have you shoulder that burden alone. Besides, you must rescue Michelle."

"I'll be back in time," Gwyn promised. "I'll get her out as quick as I can and we'll be back here in the room before you even find an apothecary that's open."

"You said the queen ordered you to stay away from the king. She will not suspect me."

Gwyn bit her lip. "You won't have to do it. I'll be back."

Isabel's smile was genuine now. "Then I will see you soon."

* * *

Dark. It was still dark. Her legs were numb. Was that the scuttle of cockroaches she could hear, or rats? Surely Diego didn't mean for her to rot? Any time Michelle had been imprisoned before her jailer usually visited to interrogate, gloat or at least feed her. It had been over twenty-four hours, she guessed.

He means for me to miss the turning point. He obviously listened more than he let on. Damn, I'm a fool! She wondered what Gwyn was doing, whether she was trying to find her. *I hope she concentrates on the turning point first. Damn, she'll have to work something out with Philip.* Would the girl cope? Michelle dozed, awash with guilt over using Gwyn as another tool to achieve her necessary ends. *I hope she doesn't end up as broken as me…*

A thud jarred her from her somnolence. Another thud, then another. Michelle squinted and made out a thin glimmer of light opposite. The bottom of the door?

More thuds, then a different thump that made the door rattle. *Thud, thud, thud!* "Argh!" came the muffled exclamation.

"Gwyn?" Michelle croaked, her voice dry from disuse. The sound stopped. Michelle licked her dry lips and tried again. "Gwyn!"

"Michelle? Are you alright?"

"What do you think?"

"What? Just hold on, I'm getting you out of there!"

"No, you're not," a deeper voice said. Michelle heard a scream and a scuffle. The door opened momentarily, blinding her with torchlight, as a dark shape was thrust towards her. The door slammed shut and a bolt slid home before the click of the lock sounded.

"Bastard!" Gwyn screeched, sounding infuriated. Michelle agreed but was too exhausted to chime in. She heard Gwyn scrabble around and bump up against her legs. "Michelle?"

"I'm here," Michelle muttered. Thirst clawed at her throat. "Don't suppose you have any water?"

Gwyn patted Michelle's legs gently, finding the rope that bound her. "No. I'm sorry—I thought I'd just break you out and get you back to the room for Isabel to look after. Are you hurt?"

Michelle sighed. "Headache. Legs numb. No real injuries." She felt Gwyn move and there was a quiet sawing noise. Something tugged at her legs then they sprang free. She groaned, trying to wiggle her toes.

Gwyn carefully cut Michelle's wrist bonds as well and, once pins and needles replaced numbness, Michelle activated her light.

"Oh shit, you look terrible." Gwyn winced in the light.

"Thanks. Does Isabel know we're here?" She touched her head tentatively. Her hair felt matted, but the wound where Diego had hit her wasn't bleeding.

"Um, yes, but…"

"But what?" Michelle extracted her tiny first aid kit from inside her shirt. She cracked a capsule and jabbed herself with it, wincing as the hyper-concentrated hydrator hit her system. She breathed easier, feeling moisture bead on her tongue.

"She's gone to buy poison to kill Philip. I was meant to rescue you and meet her back in the room. We knew we had to act soon or we'd be out of time."

Michelle controlled her anger. "Why didn't you just help her? The turning point is more important than me!"

"We didn't know what condition you were in! You didn't answer when we came down here last night. We couldn't find a way to break down the door." Gwyn took a breath, then spoke more slowly. "I'm sorry. I stuffed up. Again. We were trying to do the right thing."

Michelle let her fists unclench. She reached out stiffly and pulled Gwyn into a hug. "You did do the right thing. It's what makes you a better person than me." When she let go, Gwyn sat back with a stunned expression. Michelle frowned. "What? Can't I pay a compliment? Now help me think of a way to get us out of here before the turning point passes, so poor Isabel isn't left all on her own."

* * *

Hellebore had been hard to find—Isabel had asked at three apothecaries before one shifty-eyed old man sold her some. She wrapped it carefully in a handkerchief, not wishing to incur the rash that came from over-handling the roots, and stuffed the bundle into her bag, hurrying back to the castle.

Gwyn wasn't in the room. No one had been there, not even a maid, judging by the rumpled state of the bed. Isabel straightened it absent-mindedly, wondering how long she should wait. Impatience got the better of her after an hour. *Something has happened to her.*

She ventured down past the kitchens, to the lower cellars. At the stairway leading to the cell where Michelle was locked, Isabel hesitated. She withdrew, and lingered in a doorway, chewing her thumb. Closing her eyes, she breathed deep, then marched towards the sunlight… and promptly ducked into a storeroom when she heard Diego's voice. "I was sent to collect small beer for the men in the armoury."

"You don't look like an errand-runner, m'boy," a woman cackled.

"Help an old dear back up the stairs, would you?"

Isabel listened to her heart thump as Diego's footsteps faded, giving thanks to God that she had heard him before he had seen her. Steeling herself, she found a different route that brought her out near the stables.

"Have you seen my axe?" she heard a man ask a lad as she hastened past. *How am I going to do this?* She returned to the room. On her trip to the town earlier, she had retrieved her medicine box from the inn. Now she withdrew the tiny mortar and pestle that lived within. She carefully chopped and ground the hellebore root, pulverising it as best she could. *Will it be enough?*

Scraping it back into the handkerchief, she folded the sheet from the bed and carried it in her arms with the poison hidden beneath. As she made her way towards the royal apartments, several guards asked her business; she deflected them saying, "Just sheets for the king's rooms," batting her eyelashes and smiling. The guards nodded knowingly. "The king is not present now, is he?" Isabel asked.

"Out on the lawn, playin' ball, with the queen and her ladies watchin'," one guard replied. "Y'might be waitin' awhile," he added suggestively.

"Thank you!" Isabel didn't even try to reach the innermost chambers, leaving by a different door and asking a maid for directions for the lawn. She remembered walking that way with Gwyn the day before. Finally, she found it.

I'm no Gwyn, nor Michelle. They will throw me out in a heartbeat if I try to walk out there. Richly dressed ladies fluttered fans and Flemish noblemen posed elegantly. Isabel glanced down at her brown and red dress—finer than anything she had ever owned, but drab compared to the silks and lace that swirled before her. Her heart faltered.

Shamefaced, she retreated to the king's apartments, earning the winks of the guards. *Should I rub the hellebore over his sheets and pillows? What if someone else touches it?* She believed in healing people, not making them sick. This wasn't her.

Exiting past the guards, one of them caught her arm. "Impatient missy, aren't ye? Y'need some company, y'only have t'ask."

Isabel gave him a brittle smile. "No, thank you." She clutched her skirt where the hellebore lay in her pocket.

The guard held on. "Got somethin' there?"

Isabel's hand sprang from the fabric. "No!"

"Search her," the other guard chimed in. Isabel was subjected to a most indignant groping before they turned out her pockets and found the bundle.

"Don't touch it!" she warned. The guard looked at his partner and shrugged, then started to unfold the handkerchief. Isabel took the opportunity and ran.

Twenty-Eight

1506 AD

Isabel heard their shouts but the wind was in her feet as she bolted. *They will search. I must hide or flee.* Other cries joined the guards' and Isabel made for the only place she could think of that she might go unfound.

She slammed into a broad chest. "Señorita!" Diego balanced her when she would have fallen. "What are you doing?"

"Hide, I must hide," Isabel babbled. "They will think I tried to poison the king. I did not, but they have the poison. I must hide."

"You… tried to poison the king?"

"No! I had hellebore. I thought to help Gwyn and Michelle, but I could not do it. They will think I tried, though. Please—take me to the room where you have them locked. Throw me in with them."

"I… I can hide you…" The uncertainty in Diego's voice added to Isabel's panic.

"No! Please! Take me to Gwyn and Michelle!"

Diego said no more as he put a controlling arm around Isabel and steered her into the depths of the castle. They descended the stairway but he stopped them part-way down.

"So the king is alive."

"Yes!" Isabel replied. "I didn't touch him! I couldn't get close enough."

"But you tried."

She took a sharp breath. "Yes." Diego let her go. The orange light from the torch in the stair bracket flickered over his face. Despite the shadows, she could tell an expression of distaste when she saw one. "You don't want to marry me," she said quietly. "I am not what you want. I never will be."

"I should put you in there to rot with them," he muttered.

Isabel sighed. "Go on. At least I'll be where I belong.

* * *

"Help me sit near the door," Michelle said. "If you hear someone coming, crack this open and jab me with it." She lifted another tiny capsule from her first aid kit.

"What is it?"

"Adrenaline, amongst other things. I don't think Diego will leave us here to die, so when he shows up I will need an edge over him. Give me your knife."

"Hmph." Gwyn took the capsule and assisted Michelle, refraining from commenting on the smell of urine. "Are you going to kill him?"

"I'll try not to." They waited, Michelle dimming the light to a faint glow with a tap to her computer. It was enough to dispel the utter blackness of the cell without highlighting the disturbing stains on the floor, but it made time pass in a surreal way.

The scrape of the bolt drew Gwyn from her stupor. "Are you going to send for the palace guard?" she heard Isabel ask loudly, and the bolt stopped.

"I should," grunted Diego.

"Michelle!" Gwyn hissed, snapping the adrenaline capsule open and stabbing Michelle's arm with it. Michelle jerked as if she had been electrocuted then flicked off her light. The cell fell into darkness as the lock tumblers clunked, and it was only because Gwyn knew where to look that she saw Michelle's dark shape snake past Isabel's skirts and strike upwards at the hulking figure behind, framed by torchlight. Isabel screamed. Diego grunted and crashed to the ground as Michelle tackled his knees.

"Isabel! Are you alright?" Gwyn found her friend and hugged her. A wave of nausea went through her. Isabel held her as she swayed.

"Gwyn!"

Michelle and Diego scuffled on the ground then Michelle slammed the hilt of Gwyn's dagger against his temple and he went limp.

"Is he dead?" Isabel gasped.

Michelle checked his pulse. "No. Help me put him in the cell. We've got to hurry."

"Michelle," Gwyn said, unsure.

"You want light? Here." Michelle turned her computer light on, illuminating the doorway and the room beyond. She grabbed Diego's legs and started dragging him.

"Michelle… we missed it."

"Gwyn, help me—what?"

Gwyn sank to the ground. Isabel patted her frantically, searching for a wound. "We missed the turning point—I just felt it pass. Philip is still alive." She braced herself for the outburst that would surely follow.

Michelle stopped. Her eyes were strangely bright, whether from the adrenaline or tears, Gwyn couldn't tell. "Help me get Diego in here," she said gruffly.

"But… the turning point."

"This is my fault," Isabel whispered. "I bought hellebore to try to poison the king, but I didn't know how to get close to him. I could have left it in his chambers but it might have hurt someone else. Then the guards became suspicious and found it on me and I ran. I'm so sorry."

Gwyn and Michelle looked at her. "I should have been the one to do it," Gwyn said.

"Maybe I shouldn't have let this lug-head overpower me and lock me in a cell!" Michelle interrupted. Silence hung between them. "None of us are perfect. This is a nasty, imperfect mission that ruins lives. I'm sorry you two have to be involved but… I couldn't have made it this far without you both. Especially Gwyn." She reached down and placed a hand on Gwyn's shoulder. "We tried."

Gwyn stood slowly, Isabel supporting her. "We're not done yet. We got history back on track in Italy—we can do it here."

"We don't have long until the next turning point," Michelle said doubtfully. "We have to be in Navarre in a few weeks to…"

Gwyn looked at her. "To what?"

Michelle glanced at Isabel, who lifted her chin. Michelle sighed. "To ensure the death of… of Cesare Borgia."

Gwyn stiffened. Her jaw worked. *When were you planning on telling me this?* Instead she said, "Then we'd better sort this timeline quickly. She grabbed one of Diego's ankles and looked at Michelle expectantly. Together they dragged Diego into the cell and locked it, leaving the key on the outside.

"Alright," said Michelle. "What's the plan?"

"They'll be looking for me," Isabel said. She hugged herself, rocking anxiously.

"Michelle, can you get Isabel out of the castle and somewhere safe?" Gwyn asked.

Michelle raised her eyebrows and nodded. "And what are you going to do?"

"I'm going to look at the timeline and work out what needs to happen to get it back on track. Give me a minute." She sat back down and closed her eyes.

Some turning points were more significant than others. When Queen Isabella had arranged marriages for her children with the Habsburgs of Austria, the effects rippled throughout European history. Gwyn wanted to know what would happen if Philip were to live.

The timeline was stretched out before her, extending from the nexus it had just passed. Juana having more children, despite Philip's affairs. Philip directing Spanish foreign policy while Juana managed Castilian affairs. Their son and heir, Charles, didn't take the throne until he was much older, didn't marry a Portuguese princess, didn't have a son called Philip.

The son they did have would successfully invade England, conquering Elizabeth I and extending the Habsburg Empire to the British Isles.

"Well, shit," Gwyn muttered, opening her eyes.

"Yes?" Michelle shifted impatiently, blinking at a rapid rate.

"We've got to try," Gwyn said. "If we kill Philip as soon as possible, we might have a chance at correcting history."

"If you try, they'll kill you!" Isabel pleaded.

Gwyn stood. "Get Isabel to safety, and I… I'll kill Philip."

"Oh, don't try to be a hero." Michelle twitched. "You're not a killer, not like me."

"You're not in a state to do anything!" Gwyn exclaimed. "You're jerking around like a bloody marionette."

Michelle glared. She reached a shaky hand into her pocket and drew a tiny, red capsule from her first aid kit. "If you can jab him with this, without anyone noticing, they'll never know it was you. It's painless and doesn't act until the brainwaves hit deep sleep. It's what we use for euthanasia in my time."

Gwyn mouth opened in surprise. "You planned to use this all along?"

"Of course. I was going to tell you both after dinner the other night, but Diego got the jump on me."

Gwyn ground her teeth, then held out her hand. "Give it here." She looked at Isabel. "I'll find you soon." Isabel nodded, seemingly bashful.

They climbed the stairs and stopped in a kitchen where they disguised Isabel with flour and ground chickpea paste to make her look spotty and ill. "Cover your hair really well." Gwyn hovered worriedly.

"Get out of here, Gwyn," Michelle ordered. "I'll take care of her." Michelle still seemed jittery to Gwyn, but with one last squeeze of Isabel's hand, she left and hurried towards the royal apartments.

A guard eyed Gwyn as she neared. He barred her way with a spear. "What do you want?"

"I have news for the queen," Gwyn declared breathlessly. "You know an attempt was made on the king's life? I saw the woman who did it. I must report to the queen at once!"

"You'll report to the king." Pieter, the king's advisor, appeared from a side corridor, a grim expression on his face. "Let us pass," he ordered. The guard stood back and rapped on the heavy carved wooden door. Pieter hustled Gwyn through, past anxious, whispering courtiers. In an inner chamber Philip sat on the traditional backless chair, while Juana paced, a flurry of skirts and bad temper.

"You!" Juana whirled and advanced on Gwyn. "You were supposed to prevent this sort of thing!"

"I know, your majesty!" Gwyn fell to her knees and shuffled forward. "The woman! The redhead! She came from King Ferdinand. I pretended to befriend her. She discovered me searching her things and had her servant attack me and lock me in a cell beneath the castle. My guard, Diego, rescued me, but was injured and lies down there still!" She bent her head and clasped her hands, begging. "Please forgive me, majesty, I tried." *Bloody hell, moving on your knees in skirts is awkward!*

Philip sprang to his feet. "Speak gently to the wench, my dearest— she has served us well, thus far."

Oh, Philip. I'm so sorry. Gwyn turned to him and shuffled towards his feet, bowing as if to kiss them. "I am sorry, your majesty." Sincerity etched every word. She slipped the killer capsule from the notch in her sleeve, snapped it and stabbed through the top of Philip's stockinged foot.

"Ow!" He leapt, slipper kicking Gwyn in the face. "Oh my!"

"What is the matter, my lord?" Juana rushed to her husband's side.

"Forgive me!" Gwyn exclaimed, reeling. "I clutched his majesty's foot too tightly."

"Get out of here!" Juana snarled. "They are searching for the assassin. I have no more need of you."

Gwyn clambered to her feet, and, hands shaking, bowed. She remembered herself and curtsied. Juana rolled her eyes in disgust. Gwyn backed from the room and fled.

When the bells tolled that night, she vomited and cried, knowing she was a murderer.

Twenty-Nine

1506 AD

"Go away." Juana's voice was choked. She sniffed behind the curtain of hair that shielded her face, her head bowed as she leaned over her deceased husband.

"Your majesty…" Gwyn braced herself for an onslaught of abuse. She hated intruding on Juana's grief, as much as she disliked the woman herself. The servants had been easy to talk her way past—they were distressed and uncertain. Gwyn had sent them from the room so she could approach Juana alone. "Majesty, your father will try to take control again. You must nominate a different regent for your son."

Juana sniffed again and raised her head. Puffy eyes stared hatred at Gwyn, tear-tracks glistened on pale cheeks. "How can you even say such a thing to me? I am Queen. My husband has died, but my duty is to rule." Fresh tears poured down her face, and she flung herself back onto Philip's dead shoulder. "Oh, my love! Why did you have to leave me?" she wailed. "I would have tolerated a hundred mistresses, a thousand, just to have you by my side."

Gwyn fought the urge to cry herself—Juana's grief was awful to watch. She took several deliberate breaths, inhaling through her nose, breathing out through her mouth to bring herself under control. "I am… truly sorry, your majesty. They will not let you rule—they will call you mad, and say you are incapable. Ferdinand has already spread the word that you are distraught with grief."

"I *am* distraught with grief, you stupid, interfering bitch!" Juana shrieked and threw herself at Gwyn. Gwyn fell backwards, fending off the wild blows. She caught Juana's fists, dragged her up to a sit, then pinned the queen in a bear hug, while Juana cried great, hiccoughing sobs. Gwyn rocked the Juana gently, making shushing noises until the queen grew still except for the occasional hiccough and shaky breath.

"I am so sorry," Gwyn whispered. "I am so, so sorry." Knowing she had helped orchestrate this death fed guilt into her heart. After a while she loosened her grip. Juana continued to sob silently on her shoulder. Gwyn heard the door creak and glanced up to see Valentina and Pieter peer around it. "Who is she?" Valentina stage-whispered. "I don't know any of these new ladies at court. None of them are as respectful as they should be! Young people these days!"

Gwyn caught Pieter's eye and gave a helpless shrug. When Valentina started forward, Pieter stopped her. He drew her back and closed the door despite her protestations.

Gwyn took another deep breath. The movement prompted Juana to straighten, sniffing and wiping her nose with the back of her hand. Gwyn found a handkerchief in her pocket and offered it. The queen accepted and blew her nose. She looked utterly exhausted and made no motion to get up. They sat in a sea of elegant skirts, billowing around them like a deflated cloud.

"What do you want?" Juana asked tonelessly.

Gwyn thought, then replied, "It's more, what do you want? Do you wish to rule?"

Juana gave a humourless chuckle. "It is my duty. I am the daughter of a great queen, sister to queens."

Gwyn wondered if Juana would understand Gwyn's own desire not to follow in her parents' profession, then decided the comparison wouldn't translate. "You will always be Queen, your majesty." Gwyn looked at her solemnly. "But you do not have to rule—many conspire to bring you down unjustly and…" A fist of injustice gripped her heart. "It's not fair."

Juana's forehead crinkled as she frowned at Gwyn. "Why are *you* upset? It is the way of the world—pretenders and usurpers conspire to take power from rightful rulers. They will be punished."

"No, your majesty, *listen* to me." Gwyn's eyes widened as she spoke intently. "They will not let you rule. They are going to send you to a convent and tell everyone you are insane. They will spread stories about how you clung to your husband's body and refused to abandon him."

"But… but that is true." Juana looked over at Philip's body on the bed and tears trickled down her face.

"Yes, but they will twist it in such a way that makes it seem as though you are incapable of making rational decisions. They will not allow that your grief is normal. They will use it against you. Do you wish to fight them?"

Juana straightened. Gwyn could see the steely determination in her eyes. "I could," she whispered. "I am the daughter of a great queen…"

Gwyn was torn. Should she use the power of the chronokinetor to influence Juana into abandoning her claim to the throne? *Why couldn't it be that Juana rules? It's bullshit that she gets labelled mad and locked away.*

"I don't want to."

Gwyn fixed Juana with a sharp look. "What? I mean, pardon, your majesty?"

Juana shook her head. "I don't want to be queen," she said simply. "I was happy with Philip. Yes, he betrayed me, and I could have gouged his eyes out for that, but I loved him. We had a life together."

Gwyn ground her teeth. It was what needed to happen, but she hated it. She didn't like Juana but still didn't want to see her diminished in this way. "And your father? Do you wish him to be regent for your son, Charles, knowing he'll try to take power for himself? If he has a son by Germaine de Foix, he'll name him heir and bring war to Spain again."

Juana's eyes took on a faraway look. "No," she said finally. "My people do not deserve that. I will name another regent for my son." She focussed on Gwyn. "Will that make you happy? Will you let me be alone in my grief now?"

Gwyn steeled herself. "Once the new regent is named and accepted, yes."

"No doubt my mother looks down from Heaven and is disappointed," Juana said bitterly. "I don't care. I could never be what she wanted. I thought I had escaped her when I married but in death, she will always haunt me. Perhaps in a convent, she will let me be."

Gwyn stood, pity and guilt churning her stomach. "I hope you will find peace there, your majesty." She held out a hand to the queen. Juana looked at it, sniffed and rose unassisted, back straight.

"I will do this one last duty," she declared quietly. "For my son. For Castile. Then I want to be alone."

* * *

When Gwyn had gathered her things and ordered her horse to be readied, she remembered Diego. "Oh, shit," she muttered. Had anyone followed up Gwyn's story to free him? *I am a terrible person.* The thought made her even more miserable. "Excuse me," she said to the groom who brought her horse. He glanced up and Gwyn's jaw dropped. Ten years older and still handsome, it was Matias.

"Señorita?" he asked, puzzled.

"Ah, I borrowed an axe from the stables yesterday," she said. "You'll find it at the bottom of the stairs that run behind the kitchens."

Matias' expression cleared. "*That's* where the bloody thing went! Pardon me, I thought one of the lads had pinched it." He collected himself and cupped his hands as a stirrup. She mounted, arranging her skirts, and kneed the horse into a trot before he could say anything else. She glanced back to see him scratching his head, no doubt remembering another young woman who rode astride. She wondered if he had tried to forget, or if the tale made an impressive story for him to tell and cadge drinks from agog listeners. Her heart lifted.

Michelle and Isabel were waiting at the inn. Together they rode east from Valladolid. "We've at least a week's ride ahead of us," Michelle said.

"Plenty of time for you to fill us in with *everything* we need to know," Gwyn replied. Michelle sighed and nodded.

She obliged Gwyn and Isabel that night when they camped. "Cesare was sold out to the Spanish by the current Pope, an enemy of his. He was imprisoned for some years, but recently escaped and fled to Pamplona, the capital of Navarre, where his brother-in-law Juan is king."

Gwyn's lip curled. "Who was the poor woman who married him?"

"A French noblewoman, Charlotte de Albret. A political alliance."

Gwyn stared into the campfire. "I feel sorry for her." Isabel's hand crept over and gripped hers. Gwyn smiled, and despite wanting to lift Isabel's hand to kiss it, she made no move to do so. She had noticed Isabel's reticence to show affection in front of anyone, even Michelle.

"Well, she hasn't been graced with his presence for some years now—it is his sister Lucretia who beseeches the Pope and any monarch who will listen to free him, or to at least send him his ducal income from France now that he is free. France studiously ignores her. Cesare is holed up in Navarre, acting as a military commander for King Juan as he puts down rebellions and fends off Ferdinand's attempts to absorb his little kingdom into Aragon."

Gwyn sighed. "And we have to kill him?"

Michelle hesitated. "No, actually, some rebels do that. But we have to incite him into riding after them without support during a battle. It's going to be… quite dangerous."

Gwyn's chest tightened. "Let's sleep on it." Isabel suggested. "We can talk about it tomorrow."

But Gwyn sank into a melancholy mood the next day, exhausted by nightmares and wary of any traveller they passed. Isabel stayed close, taking charge of Gwyn like she would a patient. Gwyn appreciated it but couldn't shake her glumness. "Sorry I'm so miserable," she told Isabel when they were over halfway to Navarre. "Are you having second thoughts about wanting to come with me?" They sat by their campfire, set well back from the road in a sheltered copse. Michelle checked the perimeter and Gwyn and Isabel had only the horses for company.

"Do you wish for me to pity you?" Isabel asked. "Because I don't."

Gwyn shot her a startled look.

Isabel shook her head. "My heart aches for your pain, but you are stronger than me. Look at what you have already overcome."

Gwyn was suddenly angry. "I'm a mess, Isabel! I'm so sick with fear at the thought of going anywhere near Cesare Borgia again I can't sleep. I killed Philip. I've been the cause of the death of hundreds, if not thousands, of people! That fact won't change once I'm back in my own time."

"No. It won't." Michelle appeared out of the darkness. "Nor will it change for me, nor for Isabel who has aided us. I hope you don't become as inured to it as me."

Gwyn flushed with shame. "You've had training," she retorted, knowing she was being unfair.

"Michelle is not immune to the distress that comes with death, much as she may pretend." Isabel levelled her gaze as the older woman. Michelle's face tightened and she raised a warning finger. "Do not shush me, Michelle," Isabel said. "Yes, you frighten me sometimes, but you are not without feeling."

"Isabel," Michelle started condescendingly, then stopped.

"What's she talking about?" Gwyn wanted to know.

Michelle's face went impassive, though her jaw worked. She leant stiffly against a tree, crossing her arms. "I... may have had a panic attack while Isabel and I were in Segovia. I found myself overwhelmed when I thought I had pushed Ferdinand too far."

"Oh." Comments about not being a robot floated through Gwyn's mind, but she refrained. "That's pretty understandable. I don't know how you compartmentalise it all."

Michelle flashed a humourless smile. "Obviously, sometimes I don't."

"Perhaps you should both try to find one of your 'counsellors' once you are back in your own times to help you through these feelings," Isabel mused.

Gwyn's mouth quirked at Isabel's serious tone. She caught Michelle's eye, who appeared to be suppressing a smile. This made Gwyn snort a laugh.

"I didn't mean it in jest." Isabel frowned.

Gwyn laughed, "I know, you just look so serious. You're too good, Isabel."

Her friend looked perplexed. "You are the one who saved me, Gwyn. And you, Michelle."

Gwyn leant across and pecked Isabel on the cheek. "Alright. This situation is all pretty messed up, and we're only human. Doesn't make it any easier, but..." She pulled a face. "I wish I could forget Cesare Borgia. But if we've got to deal with him, then I should be the one to do it." She closed her eyes.

"Why?" Isabel asked.

Gwyn's eyes flicked open, disgruntled. "What do you mean, why?"

Michelle straightened off the tree and moved closer to the fire, fighting a small smile. "Gwyn, you don't need to be a hero. I'll deal with Cesare."

Gwyn raised her eyebrows defiantly. "I'm a better horsewoman than you. If we need to entice him out onto a battlefield, I'll be able to stay ahead of him."

"You can't fight—I can disguise myself as a soldier and ride with him. I will need you to pretend to be a scout and make sure the rebels know he's alone and vulnerable." She looked at Gwyn seriously. "I also can't afford for you to freeze. I know you're brave, Gwyn, you're resourceful and capable and talented, but what he did to you was awful, and it would be completely understandable if you hesitated in some small way. You're not cold, like me."

"Michelle," Isabel said warningly.

"Alright, I'm not completely cold," Michelle huffed. "I have a lot of issues that I obviously repress because I haven't had the same kind of psychological support that I normally get in a mission."

Gwyn rolled her eyes. "We could have some awesome group therapy." Then she had to explain the concept to Isabel and didn't notice Michelle slip off into the night. The other woman returned some time later. Isabel had fallen asleep already, and Gwyn was ready to turn in.

"Everything alright?" Gwyn asked.

Michelle nodded, turning slowly to examine their surroundings. "Maybe we should take watches. It could just be an animal, but I feel like something is out there."

Thirty

1506 AD

A chill prickled down Gwyn's spine. Wolves and bears were always a risk, but human predators were more of a danger.

"It could be nothing," Michelle shrugged, wrapping herself in her cloak and making a pillow with her pack. She lay with her feet towards the fire, short sword and crossbow within reach.

"Times like this I wish we had a dog. Or three," Gwyn muttered, kicking dirt over most of the fire, leaving only one log crackling into ashy oblivion. Snuggling down next to Isabel, she breathed in the cinnamon-clove scent of her friend—her lover? Preoccupied with the thought of danger in the woods, Gwyn couldn't sleep. A pair of frogs croaked back and forth, then went silent at the hoot of an owl. *There's no point lying awake worrying,* she scolded herself. Still, she couldn't sleep, so she thought about Isabel instead. They had only been intimate those two nights, but the memory kept Gwyn warm. Patient, brave, caring, and most of all interested in all the new things she encountered, Gwyn found her sexy as hell. Since discovering that Isabel loved her, Gwyn had looked at the woman in a whole new light. She longed to touch her olive skin, stroke her auburn hair, but noticed quickly how Isabel stiffened when other people were present. Gwyn could understand. So in the dark of the night, inhaling Isabel's aroma, she let her imagination roam free.

Isabel stirred. Gwyn stopped nuzzling her neck. "Sorry," she whispered.

Isabel half-rolled and smiled. "I feel the same," she whispered. "If we were alone, perhaps."

"Of course!" Gwyn raised her head to see Michelle's apparently sleeping form. "An audience isn't a turn on for me." She lay back down and put her arm over Isabel, content to drift off imagining all the places and things she wanted to show Isabel in her own time.

Morning came without incident. They travelled on, buying bread and vegetables from the river town of Logroño where they stopped to water the horses. They rode out of the river valley through shallow ravines, emerging onto a plain. A small castle lay in the distance, the only landmark interrupting the wind that shivered its way across the vastness from the Bay of Biscay. The seasons had changed quickly as they left Castile. On a small hillock, Michelle called a halt for their midday meal. Gwyn unsaddled the horses and let them graze.

"The battle will take place not far from here, at a town called Viana," Michelle said. "That's the castle you can see from here."

They considered Viana. It perched on the highest piece of land for miles around, commanding a view of what Gwyn had initially thought a flat plain, but was gouged sporadically with dips and gullies. "Lots of places to hide soldiers," she observed. It made sense. When she observed the turning point through the timepiece, she had seen Cesare galloping alone through a ravine, before being ambushed by men hiding behind rocks. The alternative future showed him advancing more cautiously, soldiers riding with him to overwhelm the men who tried to ambush them.

"You said the Count de Beaumont's son holds the castle," Isabel said. "And Cesare Borgia besieges him."

"Correct," Michelle replied. "In the next few weeks Cesare will ride with King Juan from Pamplona to besiege the castle. Beaumont bows to Castile and Aragon—Ferdinand has been funding him to ferment rebellion."

"Because Ferdinand wants Navarre." Isabel shielded her gaze from the sun. Fat, fluffy clouds billowed on the horizon, but the brightness belied the potential storm.

"Correct. Ferdinand was instrumental in imprisoning Cesare as a favour to the current Pope. He's a military strategist—he knows how dangerous Cesare can be."

"The plan is to take up residence in the town so we can be on hand when the siege takes place," Gwyn stated, thinking they should look for shelter sooner rather than later. She hadn't forgotten the lightning strike that had almost killed Juana. "Well, let's get going then—I don't fancy being out in the open if it's going to storm." The plain was sparse of trees. *Best to make for the town.*

Michelle glanced up. "Good point. Isabel, pass me those things to pack up."

"I'll ready the horses," Gwyn said.

The first rumble of thunder sounded when they were halfway to their goal. "You were right about the storm, Gwyn!" Michelle called as the wind picked up. She rode at the rear of their small column as the road narrowed and dipped into a gully.

The sky darkened as the storm drew closer. "That last one sounded like hoofbeats," Isabel declared, riding in the middle.

"Just thunder," Gwyn replied, urging her mount into a trot. The animal snorted and tossed its head. Gwyn patted its neck, trying to calm it. She hoped none of the horses would panic and bolt.

Another rumble came, echoing off the rocks as the gully got deeper.

"Gwyn…" Isabel called warningly.

Gwyn pulled up. Her horse whinnied in protest as Isabel's mount bumped it from behind.

"What's wrong?" Michelle asked, reaching them a moment later, hand already on her crossbow.

A horse whinnied in response. "Shit, it was hoofbeats. Sorry, Isabel!" Gwyn reached over and grabbed her friend's wrist, ready to jump in time if required.

"Hold," Michelle ordered. "Twenty-four hours if need be."

"Got it," Gwyn replied. "Isabel, hang onto your reins."

Half a dozen soldiers trotted into sight, bearing spears pointing upright. Gwyn glanced back and saw the same number appear behind them—they were boxed in.

A man rode to the front. "This is no place for travellers to be caught in a storm. Let us escort you to shelter."

Gwyn frowned and turned to Michelle, seeking guidance. Wind whipped the women's hair as the horses shifted nervously as thunder boomed again. Michelle's face was inscrutable. "Who are you?" Gwyn asked bluntly.

The man's eyebrows rose. "Antonio Gonzalez at your service. My lord is the Count de Beaumont." He bowed in the saddle. "I would ask what brings three fair ladies out on the road with no escort in such weather, but the weather becomes too inclement for such conversation. Fear not, my men will protect you from molestation."

The soldiers to the rear pressed forward. Gwyn and her companions had no choice but to advance or be pushed. She nudged her horse to follow Gonzalez.

"Do you not wish to leave?" Isabel spoke in a low voice.

"Just stay close," Gwyn murmured. "This guy might be useful."

Antonio Gonzalez led them to a large cave partway up the sloped wall of the ravine. He ordered the horses to be cared for and a place made at the fire for his guests. He didn't seem perturbed that Michelle and Gwyn were dressed in breeches and tunic, though he had plainly identified them as women. Outside the cave, a downpour began.

"It will last well into the night." Gonzalez nodded at the rain sheeting across the cave mouth. "Please, my men will prepare a meal. There is grotto on this side of the cave if you wish privacy to repose."

The crisp air rushing in pushed the smoke from the fire away from them. Gwyn sat and huddled close to Isabel, glancing around at the grotto.

"That's an excellent make of crossbow," Gonzalez commented to Michelle, who still held her weapon and stood. "You will have no need for it here. Not a man here will disturb you, or I will kill him myself. Now, what brings you on the road to Viana?"

"Thanks, but I'll hang onto it," Michelle replied. She sat carefully by the fire, opposite their host. The firelight flickered and danced; soldiers busied themselves with camp chores—everyone had to speak loudly to be heard over the storm.

Gwyn found herself liking his directness, even if she didn't trust him. "Do you normally ambush travellers on the road like that?" she asked.

"We heard you coming," Isabel declared.

"Ambush?" Gonzalez looked astonished. "I have scouts, and when one reported a party of women trying to outride the storm, I knew it was my duty to find you. At this time of year, rain can cause flash-flooding."

Gwyn exchanged a glance with Michelle and Isabel. The former nodded slowly, the latter gave a tiny shrug. Gwyn wasn't sure why Michelle was letting her take the lead in the conversation, but in the absence of any other signal she continued. "Well, thank you."

Gonzalez bowed his head in acknowledgement. He made polite conversation while they ate a meaty stew served to them by a young squire, discussing the weather and the crops in a way only a seasoned soldier would. The same squire placed their saddlebags in the small grotto hidden behind an outcrop of rock. Michelle took Isabel to set up bedrolls while Gwyn went to check on their horses. The beasts were picketed further back in the main cave where the sound of thunder was deadened. They shifted nervously, and a soldier went from horse to horse, stroking and soothing them. He nodded to Gwyn as she approached. "Yer bridle is close to breaking," he said. "I can stitch it up aways, but ye'll need a new piece afore long."

A torch had been wedged into a rocky crevice nearby, so Gwyn could see the soldier was about her age, perhaps a few years older. "Um, thanks?" she replied, holding out her hand. "I can fix it."

"Eh," the soldier shrugged. "I 'ave other leatherwork to mend. Cap'n says we is to treat you ladies well. I is just settlin' the 'orses first."

"Oh, okay." Gwyn patted her horse over. The gelding snuffled at her, searching for a treat. She fished out several apples from her belt bag and checked the other mounts too.

"Do all women ride astride where you come from?" The soldier sounded genuinely interested, not critical or salacious.

"Uh, yes," Gwyn decided to shut down the conversation rather than explain why she and her companions were such an exception to side-saddle.

"And where is that? Portugal? Granada?"

Gwyn had to smile. She supposed those places were far enough away from Navarre to seem exotic to the man. "Italy," she replied.

He shook his head in wonderment as she finished her inspection.

"You've a nice 'and with the 'orses," he said. "I'll 'ave your bridle stitched by mornin'."

"Thanks." She smiled at him before returning to her companions. Other soldiers bowed or nodded respectfully as she walked past them, and if a few were bold enough to run their eyes up and down her, it felt habitual, rather than overtly lecherous. *Doesn't make it that much better, but guess Gonzalez really does keep his men in order.*

Michelle and Isabel were in quiet discussion. Gwyn joined them. "What are you thinking?" she asked Michelle.

"Isabel and I were just talking about it—these guys might be useful killing Cesare," Michelle said.

Gwyn sat next to Isabel. "How're you going to make them do that?"

Isabel looked pleased with herself. "Captain Gonzalez mentioned a scout saw us. We simply encourage him to be vigilant for any lone soldiers who are not known to him, as they are likely spies of King Juan. You will be able to convince him of that, with your powers?"

Gwyn nodded thoughtfully. "Is that why you didn't get us to jump away when they caught us?"

"That and we can't afford to lose time—we need to beat Cesare's army into Viana. I'll pose as a camp follower if I must, but I'm not having you two do it. I'd rather we pose as respectable citizens of the town caught in the siege."

"Also, we don't appear to be in immediate danger here," Isabel chimed in. "Captain Gonzalez seems quite decent."

Gwyn agreed. "You don't look convinced, Michelle," she commented.

Michelle got up and peered out the opening of the grotto, then returned. "I don't entirely buy his story of rescuing us. And he hasn't made a single comment about how we're dressed." She gestured at her breeches, shirt and tunic. Gwyn wore the same, though Isabel preferred a more conservative outfit of breeches under a skirt split for riding.

Gwyn paused. Was the captain too polite to mention their outlandish attire, compared to the soldier with the horses? "What's his agenda then?"

Michelle paced. "I don't know. Isabel's right, we don't seem to be in danger for now. We've been fed, we're dry and sheltered, so get some rest. You two sleep nearer the wall, I'll lie on the outside."

Lulled by the sound of the rain hammering down outside, Gwyn cuddled up to Isabel and they slept.

* * *

The morning saw Gwyn venture outside in search of privacy to relieve herself. She ran into the friendly horse soldier on her way back into the cave. "Bridle's all mended." He held it out for her inspection.

"Thank you." Gwyn smiled her thanks and accepted it. The soldier bowed and returned to leading horses from the cave, bringing them out into the weak sunlight and taking them to graze on the tussocky grass that grew at the top of a side gully.

"What did he want?" Isabel appeared at Gwyn's side, a tinge of annoyance in her voice.

"Mended my bridle," Gwyn replied, still smiling as she turned to face Isabel. "Strap was about to break." Her smile dropped as she saw Isabel's expression. "What's wrong?"

A smatter of emotions played over Isabel's face. "He was very friendly," she said stiffly.

Realisation struck Gwyn. "Hey, you're not jealous, are you?"

Isabel's expression cleared. "No, sorry. I didn't sleep well, and you were gone when I woke. I was worried."

Gwyn hugged her. "You don't need to apologise. I'm sorry, I really had to pee. I thought you'd be fine left with Michelle."

Isabel rested her head on Gwyn's shoulder. "Perhaps I am too protective of you. I had a bad dream, that you had left me and gone back to your own time."

"Oh, Isabel." Gwyn wanted to kiss her, but was conscious of other soldiers emerging from the cave, carrying out various camp chores and making use of their own 'facilities' a short distance away. "I'm so glad you want to come back with me. I get... I get scared that it won't be as wonderful as you think it will be. I worry that you'll find it all too strange and you'll miss this time and I won't be enough for you," she confessed.

Isabel straightened and gazed at Gwyn, her hazel eyes intense. "My

198

heart tells me I should follow you. I trust it. Everything I have seen since leaving my village has been strange and wonderful, yet how quickly some of it becomes normal. It shall be the same in your time."

Joy and fear overwhelmed Gwyn and she hugged Isabel again. "Come on," she said. "Let's see if our nice captain is providing breakfast." By the smell of cooking coming from the fire at the cave entrance, she suspected they would be in luck.

She didn't expect Michelle to be standing there, arms folded and lips taut.

"What's wrong?" Isabel asked.

Michelle flicked her eyes over Gonzalez, who was inspecting some of his men's weapons. "Rust!" he declared, pointing to a sword. "Clean it, and don't let me catch a spot of it again!" The shamefaced soldier nodded and hastened away to burnish his blade.

Michelle nodded to Gonzalez. "He won't let us leave," she said.

Thirty-One

1506 AD

"Why not?" Isabel asked. The captain was friendly and his soldiers quite proper. Not like the horrible Rafael or even honourable but zealous Diego. She had faith that Michelle and Gwyn would see them out of this.

Michelle ground her teeth. "Says he and his men aren't ready to move out, and he wouldn't dream of letting us continue to Viana without an escort."

"It's not that bloody far!" Gwyn exploded. Isabel wondered if she, too, was cursing herself for being lulled into a false sense of security by Gonzalez and his men.

"Let us eat, then discuss," Isabel took Gwyn's arm and guided her to the fire. Gwyn and Michelle hid their irate expressions and thanked the squire politely for the breakfast porridge.

"What's his game?" Gwyn wanted to know. "Should we just grab the horses and go?"

"I don't think we'll get out without a fuss." Michelle ate mechanically. "I want to keep a low profile, and that means no tricks."

"So we pretend we're happy for the assistance and wait." Isabel fetched her spice box from her bag—it matched the medicine kit she had bought in Segovia. Little carved compartments and a hidden section for coins. She sprinkled a pinch of cinnamon on their porridge to make it palatable.

"I worry we're going to lose time," Michelle said. "Gwyn, when is Cesare meant to arrive with his army?"

Gwyn stopped chewing, closed her eyes and was still. After a minute or so she blinked and said, "In the next few days. We should make it."

They waited several hours before the purpose of Captain Gonzalez' delay became clear. A tall, bearded man galloped up the ravine accompanied by a score of soldiers. Gonzalez' squad stood at attention and the captain himself bowed deeply to the newcomer. "My lord de Beaumont," he said.

Isabel exchanged glances with Gwyn. Michelle was stony-faced but had put her crossbow away. They rose from their place by the fire as the Count de Beaumont approached, yanking his gloves off a fingertip at a time and thrusting them in his belt, which was dirty like the rest of his clothes, but appeared to be of excellent quality.

"Señoritas." He bowed. Gwyn and Michelle mirrored the gesture. Isabel curtsied.

Gwyn took her cue from Michelle's silence. "Captain Gonzalez has been most gallant in his hospitality, my lord. He rescued us from last night's storm and has offered us an escort to Viana. We are most keen to proceed if you can spare a few soldiers?"

The count hesitated, then smiled. "Forgive me, señoritas, may we speak a moment? Please, sit." He turned to the lad standing behind him. "Ricardo, some wine."

Isabel caught Gwyn biting her lips, trying not to smile. "What is it?" she whispered.

"Wine before lunch," Gwyn whispered back. "I know it's normal here but it still makes me laugh."

All trace of laughter disappeared once they were seated and the count began his interrogation. "Why do you travel to Viana?" he asked bluntly.

Gwyn appeared unfazed. "We are seeking a distant cousin of mine. We heard he had travelled to Navarre and married."

"Why do you seek him?"

Gwyn opened her eyes wide. "He is family. We have news from home for him."

Beaumont took a swig of wine. He sat on a rock with knees wide, back straight and fists resting on his legs. Isabel thought he was the kind of man who lived his life in discipline, and it was clear his soldiers followed his example, even if Captain Gonzalez—standing at ease behind the count—had a much more relaxed manner. "Three women, travelling alone, to give news to a distant cousin who may or may not have married in Viana." His scepticism was clear.

Gwyn opened her hands wide. "But we are not alone—there are three of us."

The count rubbed his hand over his beard. "I think you are lying to me."

Isabel hid a smile at Gwyn's expression of hurt. "My lord? Whatever do you mean?"

Beaumont jabbed a thick finger at Gwyn. "You have elements of the truth in your tale, but you are lying. Captain Gonzalez here says his scout followed you from Castile, and you spoke of the Duke of Valentinois, Cesare Borgia. Another of his men said you told him you were from Italy. I think you are seeking him for the price on his head, though why anyone would send three women is beyond me."

Gwyn continued to protest until Michelle interrupted. "Forget it, Gwyn, the count is too savvy. He's found us out."

Gwyn raised a disgruntled eyebrow. "Fine—you tell him the truth then." Isabel detected a relaxation in Gwyn's shoulders and wondered why Michelle hadn't discussed this plan ahead of time. Or were they both making it up as they went along?

Michelle squared her shoulders and met the count's eye. "We are seeking Cesare Borgia. He has enemies in Italy who would like to see him imprisoned again for good. We know he fled to King Juan's court in Pamplona, and that he will lead the king's army against those he deems rebels."

Beaumont chuffed a laugh. "And how on earth do you intend to accomplish his capture? He is an erstwhile soldier. You cannot hope to overpower him, even if you could get him alone."

Michelle smiled dangerously. Isabel shivered, reminding herself never to get on the wrong side of this woman. "People underestimate us. You were too clever to, or your captain was. And we have something that will draw Cesare Borgia out."

"What is that?"

Michelle looked sidelong at Gwyn. "Her." Gwyn stiffened.

Beaumont looked Gwyn over. "No offence, señorita, but who are you to the Duke of Valentinois?"

Gwyn paled—with anger or shock, Isabel couldn't tell. She took her friend's hand, glaring at Michelle, who answered. "In Italy, the Duke kidnapped Gwyn, but she escaped. He is not a man to be thwarted, even over the smallest thing. You know his motto? 'Cesare, or nothing.' Her presence will taunt him and distract his focus."

Beaumont snorted, but his eyes never left Gwyn's face. "He is a feared soldier and brilliant tactician—he won't become distracted over a… over any woman."

Michelle shrugged. "He's proud. Insult him enough, say he was outwitted by a girl—that'll infuriate him. We have had dealings with him before. We know how he will react."

The count considered. Isabel squeezed Gwyn's hand tighter, feeling her friend tremble. "Perhaps we could come to some arrangement," he declared. "You know Borgia's face. If you were to draw him out, my men could capture him, and we might split the bounty. The price on his head is high—there's enough to satisfy us both."

"We can identify him for you," Michelle agreed.

"Safer than you three trying to capture him alone." Beaumont shook his head. "You must be hell-bent on revenge. I don't blame you," he said to Gwyn. "Not enough is done to punish rapists. At least he didn't get you with a bastard." He rose and bowed. "My son currently holds Viana. I don't intend to be trapped in there with him, which is why I'm out here riding about. Gonzalez will bring you to my main camp, and we will await the Duke of Valentinois there."

"I need to be in Viana if I am to get close to him," Michelle objected, walking with him back towards his horse.

She and the count haggled over details as Isabel turned to Gwyn. "Are you alright?" she whispered.

Gwyn gave a bitter laugh. "I'm fine. Typical Michelle, using whatever she can to get her way."

Isabel's heart sank. "She should have spoken to us earlier if she planned to speak thus."

Gwyn shrugged. "She probably thought of it on the spot. This tends to be a 'think on your feet' occupation. Bloody hell, I'll be glad when it's over."

Isabel agreed.

* * *

While Michelle went to Viana, Gwyn and Isabel waited the next few days in Count de Beaumont's camp. It lay in a shallow basin on the plain, surrounded by hills that concealed their numbers from any who passed by on their way to the city. Captain Gonzalez saw to it that Gwyn and Isabel had a tent and several of his men slept nearby at night for protection.

Isabel wondered whether Michelle would try to assassinate Cesare before it ever came to a battle. She hated him already, for what he had done to Gwyn, but was also curious to know what the monster looked like. Gwyn told her, in stumbling detail, what had transpired in Italy, tears rolling down her face as they lay quietly in their tent, bundled in blankets. Isabel burned with fury, holding Gwyn and rocking her gently, wishing she had a dagger to stab the Borgia bastard in the heart. She would overcome her calling as a healer for that.

Gwyn slept better that night however, and Isabel was glad her lover trusted her to share such a horrible trauma. She lay awake for some time, wondering how this quest would transpire, and what it would do to Gwyn to have to face her abuser again.

From a rise above the camp the next day they watched the incursion of Cesare Borgia's forces. The army rode down from the north with King Juan's complicated royal banner on display. Cesare's own red bull quartered with his wife's fleur-de-lis flying taut in the stiff wind.

"Do you think Michelle is alright?" Isabel asked, clutching her cloak around her.

Gwyn's mouth twisted in a humourless smile. "She'll be fine. Anyone who gets in her way had better watch out."

Three more days and Gwyn's mood deteriorated. Even Isabel found herself irritated and asked Captain Gonzalez if they might take the horses and ride so Gwyn could burn off some of her restless energy. He refused at first, saying he couldn't spare the men to escort them, until

Isabel reminded him she had treated several of his soldiers for various ailments then pressed him to return the favour.

"Just send one man with her," Isabel begged. "Please. Even your soldiers grow restless, but you can keep them busy with drills."

Gonzalez sighed. "I will take her myself. The count would hang me if anything were to happen to her. He takes his honour very seriously, as do I, and you are both under my protection."

Isabel appreciated it, and told him so. A weight lifted from her as she watched Gwyn ride off onto the plain, the captain vainly trying to keep up. Isabel laughed before she returned her attention to camp, discovering a gathering of bashful soldiers seeking ministrations from the healer for various acquired wounds, coughs and rashes.

By the time she had finished tending to them, Gwyn returned, flushed despite the chilly wind. "Better?" Isabel asked.

Gwyn blushed. "Yeah, thanks." She hugged Isabel. "Not sure I deserve you."

Isabel shook her head. "You are the wondrous one, Gwyn." Despite her apprehension about the confrontation ahead of them, Isabel was glad.

* * *

Michelle was edgy. Her tension merged with the atmosphere of fear pervading the besieged city. After three days, Cesare breached the walls of Viana but the castle itself held strong. Citizens stayed in their homes, venturing out only for the most desperate of errands. Covert markets sprang up in tiny plazas, trading vegetables and freshly slaughtered animals as people tried to consume what they could not hide from the invading army.

The night before the turning point, Michelle didn't sleep. Under the cover of rain, she flitted from doorway to doorway, lurking near the southern gate. With silent ruthlessness, she dispatched two guards and pushed open the gate. Captain Gonzalez, soaking wet and grim, led a convoy of soldiers and mules carrying provisions for the soldiers holding the castle. They moved as silently as possible, the mules' hooves muffled with rags.

After Beaumont's men had passed, Michelle stripped the helmet and spear from one of the dead guards and waited.

The hours blurred. Michelle passed some of the time meditating, but struggled to maintain the equanimity she usually possessed during a mission. When Beaumont's men led the mules back through the gate she wanted to punch the stone wall at the time it took them to clop quietly out of town. The rain eased as dawn passed with no lightening of the sky, until only a persistent drip twanged on a fallen shield. Michelle kicked the shield aside and thrust the stolen helmet onto her head. Bearing the spear, she marched towards the house she knew Cesare Borgia had commandeered for his quarters.

At the stable adjoining the house, she woke a groom and demanded a horse. "Ready the Duke's horse too!" she ordered.

Mounted, she rode into the courtyard. "Alert the Duke!" she hollered. "The Count de Beaumont was in the city! He is escaping! Quickly!"

The reaction gave her a keen sense of satisfaction, but it was hollowed by the jaded déjà vu she felt. So many missions, so many deaths. That Cesare Borgia deserved it didn't compensate for the guilt of the Navarrese guards she had killed.

She shoved that aside and projected her most masculine, soldierly attitude as Cesare Borgia burst through the doors. "Where is that little count?" he roared.

"This way, your grace!" Michelle wheeled her horse and pointed the spear.

"Tell the king where I have gone!" Cesare bellowed. "To me!"

Soldiers scrambled to follow. Michelle didn't wait for them to catch up. "Hurry, your grace!" she urged, praying the horse wouldn't slip on the wet cobbles as they galloped to the south gate.

Through the gate and out onto the plain. Slipping and jolting, Michelle wished she had Gwyn's ability in the saddle, but she clung on doggedly. A mile out they slowed to a juddering walk.

"Where did they go? Where is that bastard count?" Cesare's head whipped back and forth.

"Over there!" Michelle pointed to where the ground roughened and broke into large rocks. Should she attack him now? He might not expect it, but he was a fighter—should she fail to kill him, he would be alerted and on guard. And should she succeed but be severely injured, that would jeopardise her ability to fix the next turning point. *Gwyn could do it alone…* her mind whispered. *Since when have you been afraid of death and injury? Or is it just that you feel too important to risk yourself?*

Cesare glared. Michelle saw his face clearly for the first time and was glad the helmet hid her own. She couldn't afford him to doubt her for a second. "Hurry, your grace!" she repeated, forcing her will onto his. "Reinforcements are coming," she told him. "We mustn't delay or we will lose him! He was riding alone!"

That cinched it for him. He spurred his stallion and it reared. Michelle kicked her horse after him and gripped her spear. She would strike him from behind before he had a chance to even realise. This far from the city no one would see it happen—it would be back to the camp, collect Gwyn and Isabel and on to the next turning point.

Then her horse stumbled.

Thirty-Two

1506 AD

Gwyn persuaded the horse tending soldier to let her ride that morning, saying she had orders to meet Captain Gonzalez and the count on their return from the city.

"How did you get him to prepare two horses?" Isabel asked softly, passing up saddlebags. The mist clinging to the ground hid their movements from the main camp.

"Told him another soldier was escorting me. Are you okay to tie these rags around the hooves?"

Pulling hoods down low to both shelter them from the drizzle and disguise their faces, Gwyn and Isabel clopped quietly out of camp.

They avoided the returning mules and their escort, then made for the ravine where Michelle had said she would meet them. *This would be impossible if we both didn't know exactly when the turning point was. She knows what she has to do, and I'll know when it's passed.*

"Let's wait here," Gwyn said, looking around. The ravine walls angled up steeply, rocks pressed in diagonal layers and interspersed with scraggly bushes. The floor of the gulch was pitted but wide enough for two carts side-by-side, narrowing as it curved away behind them.

"How long?" Isabel asked after a while.

"Turning point's almost upon us." Gwyn gripped the pommel tightly, nausea building. "Either he's dead already, or Michelle will get him soon."

Hoofbeats from behind distracted Gwyn from her sick feeling. "Oh, shit," she muttered. "Isabel, I need you to talk, I feel too sick."

Isabel blinked, then turned and understood. "Captain Gonzalez! What are you doing here?"

The captain's genial face was creased in a frown. "The question, rather, is what are you doing here? You ladies are not to leave camp without the count or my express permission!"

"Bite me," Gwyn whispered.

Isabel made an impression of being confused. "We were told you wanted to meet us out here. One of the count's soldiers said a man was injured and needed a healer—we have been looking for you."

The two men accompanying Gonzalez looked at each other and shrugged. The captain rubbed his face with a gloved hand, plainly wanting sleep. "I gave no such order. You will identify this man and I will have him flogged. Don't you know how dangerous it is out here? Valentinois' forces could sally out at any moment!"

"Oh! How strange," Isabel exclaimed. "Um, give me one moment. Gwyn does not look well." She shot an anxious glance at Gwyn.

Gwyn almost missed the next set of hoofbeats echoing down the ravine. A rider burst into view and wheeled at the sight of them. Gwyn paled as she realised who it was, though his face was different from the handsome young cardinal she had known in Italy. Ten years and the pox had left Cesare scarred and aged. The cruel lips held no charm, the hateful eyes no mystery.

"Stop!" Captain Gonzalez yelled, drawing his sword. "Who are you, and what is your business?" His men aimed their spears like lances. "Señoritas, get behind me!" Gonzalez ordered.

Cesare's glare fixed on the captain. "You're not Beaumont," he snarled.

Gwyn watched Gonzalez take in Cesare's bearing, armour and insignia. Fighting sickness, she spat, "It's not him, captain, it's not Valentinois." She kneed her horse towards Cesare.

His eyes widened. As he swung his sword at the perceived attack Gwyn threw herself off to the side. She hit the ground hard and rolled to see the blade chop into the saddle, wrenching the weapon loose from Cesare's grip.

"Help!" she shrieked. Gonzalez and his men charged. Gwyn felt someone grab her and screamed again, this time for real, before realising it was Isabel.

"Come away! Come away!" Her friend yanked Gwyn back from the fight, gasping in panic. "What were you thinking?" She hugged Gwyn tightly.

Gwyn watched as one of Gonzalez' soldiers smashed into Cesare with his spear, thrusting the man from his horse. The captain raised his sword and hacked, spraying blood. Cesare's stallion screamed and bolted past Isabel and Gwyn, its thunderous hooves counterpoint to the wet thwack and gurgle that graced the dying duke.

The turning point washed over Gwyn and she reeled. She would have fallen if Isabel hadn't held her up. Instead she vomited, helpless as each convulsion brought up food, water and finally, acidic bile. Tears streamed down her face as hopelessness engulfed her. She sobbed, Isabel rocking her, until she regained control and heaved a sigh, her soul empty.

Captain Gonzalez stood over her. "Are you alright, señorita?" He seemed not to have noticed the blood spattered across his face. "You are lucky to be alive!"

"Lost control of my horse," Gwyn muttered, struggling to her feet. She looked over to see one of the captain's men resting a spear point on the mail between the chest plate and underarm guards.

"Wait!" Gonzalez ordered. He shot Gwyn a shrewd look. "It's definitely not Valentinois? The count wants to ransom him if it is. He is worth much to us alive."

She felt Isabel squeeze her hand. Gwyn squeezed back, then let go and walked slowly to the man who had tormented her. He was mortally wounded, but a livid eye fixed on Gwyn's face as she approached. There was no flash of recognition. She smelt the tang of blood and it was as if the breeze died in that moment.

"It's not him," Gwyn said.

The fury in Cesare's eyes blazed before a swift spear thrust extinguished it. Gwyn watched the bloom of blood spread from between the sectioned metal and blossom onto the dirt beneath him.

Captain Gonzalez sighed. "What a waste," he muttered. "Strip his armour and weapons. I don't want to know where they end up," he ordered his men, rubbing his face again. "You ladies must return to camp with me."

"Need my horse first," Gwyn objected.

"You can ride behind me," he responded, swinging into his saddle and reaching his hand down to Gwyn.

A whinny interrupted. *Another bloody horse?* Gonzalez drew his sword; his men stopped pillaging Cesare's body and grabbed their spears. A single rider came into view, on Gwyn's horse. They stopped and pulled off their helmet. It was Michelle. She bore a massive bruise on her chin, and cradled her arm.

"What happened?" Gwyn ran past the corpse and grabbed the reins, shushing the animal. "Did he attack you? Are you alright?" She stroked the horse's neck anxiously while examining Michelle for sign of further injury.

Michelle grunted. "Bloody horse threw me. Did Cesare come this way?"

Gwyn turned back. Isabel stood with her hand over her mouth, Gonzalez' men looked sideways at their captain, who glared at Gwyn. "It wasn't him," Gwyn insisted. "Just some random soldier—you must have mistaken him for the Duke."

Michelle cast her eyes over the scene. "Ah," she said. "I failed then. We should go. There may be other soldiers heading our way."

Gwyn climbed up behind Michelle, while Isabel mounted her own horse. The soldiers finished stripping the body and they trotted away swiftly. Gwyn reached around Michelle to grip the reins.

"Gonzalez is pissed," Gwyn murmured to Michelle. "He knows I'm lying, but is in damage control so he doesn't get in trouble with the count."

"I deduced as much," Michelle replied. "How did you get them to kill him?"

Gwyn grit her teeth. "I rode at him, made him attack me. They rode to my aid, then I insisted it wasn't him."

"Ah. Clever. Dangerous but clever. You're lucky to be alive."

"So are you!" Gwyn was irritated. "Falling off your horse like that. I told you I should be the one to draw him out."

Michelle patted Gwyn's hand. "I know. It was a hard choice. I'm sorry."

Mollified, Gwyn relaxed. "Now what? Beaumont is not going to be happy."

Michelle glanced at Isabel, riding just ahead of them. "I see you two packed all your gear. I think we might farewell the good captain and go, say, ten years from now? Can you check that far ahead Gwyn?"

Gwyn closed her eyes for several moments, connecting to the timepiece, then nodded. "Isabel!" she called. "I'll need you to look at Michelle's arm—she might have broken it."

Isabel reined in her horse. "Not now!" barked the captain, but it was enough for Gwyn and Michelle to catch up to their travelling companion.

"You handle it, Gwyn." Michelle half-turned her head and gave a wry smile. "I trust you."

Gwyn rolled her eyes and grabbed Isabel's wrist. "Thanks for having us, captain. All the best."

He shouted something but the rushing sound of time-travel rose around Gwyn with the blue haze and drowned him out.

Flick.

Thirty-Three

1516 AD

"You know I never thought we'd get this far," Michelle said as they rode into Viana—now ruled by the kingdom of Aragon—seeking an inn in which to stay, rest and plan their next move.

"Well, that's a vote of confidence," Gwyn drawled.

"What is next?" Isabel asked.

"Wait—that place looks alright." Gwyn pointed at the inn they were passing. She slid off from behind Michelle and strode through the archway to the taproom. She returned ten minutes later, saying, "Looks clean, beds aren't flea-ridden, and—best of all—they have a small bathhouse on the ground floor. Thank god Spain is more civilised when it comes to bathing than other parts of Europe in this century. I've said we'll pay for an hour if they get water boiling right away."

After handing the horses over to the groom and throwing their bags into a spacious room on the upper story, the three women converged on the bathhouse, eager to be clean after weeks of rough living.

"I'm filthy thanks to that stupid horse dumping me in the mud," Michelle said. "You two go first. I'm still dressed as a man, so I'll wait outside and make sure no one disturbs you."

She pretended not to see the heated look Gwyn gave Isabel and sat on the bench outside the bathhouse door, her legs stretched out in front, crossed them at the ankle. She dozed, hearing nothing untoward from the other two while they bathed, but couldn't resist saying, "Water was hot then?" as a dig at Gwyn and Isabel's rosy cheeks when they emerged, clean and looking quite pleased with themselves.

"I should examine your arm," Isabel said hurriedly, blush creeping into her dark red hair.

"I'll go organise food." Gwyn grinned and sauntered back into the main inn building.

Michelle let Isabel check her over, but insisted she was more than capable of bathing herself. As she sank into the warm tub, she sighed. *Be nice to have a lover to fuss over me.* The thought came out of nowhere and surprised her.

She lay there, letting the water ease her aches, wondering if Brrrys would be interested in a more permanent arrangement when she returned to her time. *I suppose I can think about that now—we're so close. And if we succeed, if we actually fix all the turning points, then it's no more time travel. I'll be out of a job. A relationship wouldn't be such a bad thing while I work out what I'm going to do.*

She chuckled, then attacked herself with the lye soap that had been provided along with towels. When she emerged, dressed in fresh breeches and shirt, she handed her dirty clothes to the maid outside their room and went to find the others in the common room.

Michelle tucked into the venison stew Gwyn had ordered. "Right, Isabel—you wanted to know what's next."

"I also want to know why," Isabel said. "You've told me you have to make events happen a certain way, that it determines the future, but you never explained why it all happened in the first place? Something shifted?"

"It's a natural phenomenon, you said," Gwyn eyed Michelle. "At least, that's what you first told me. But then you talked about enemies of the Allied Planets and the war to come. I thought you meant those Earth First nutters, but you also mentioned the engineers of the Shift."

Michelle sighed. "Engineers. That's as good a name as any. Before I came back and found Gwyn in Italy, I learnt that the Shift has come to Earth before." She thought, then pulled out a handkerchief from her pocket and draped it over her wine cup. "The cup is Earth." She pointed. "The handkerchief is the Shift—it's an incredibly complex time-space energy wave." She dragged it slowly over the cup.

"I'm sorry, I still don't understand." Isabel sounded unhappy.

"Yeah, even I'm a bit lost," said Gwyn. "You said that once the Shift is here, we can't travel backwards in time, only forwards."

Michelle nodded, thinking of how to rephrase. She placed the handkerchief on the edge of the table. "Somewhere, on the far side of the galaxy, is an alien race with incredible technology. They evidently see us as a threat, but rather than engage us directly, they seek to weaken us first by changing history so that humans never join the Allied Planets."

Isabel pondered. "Like… a general spying another army from afar, and… and… poisoning the water so it flows downstream to make them sick before the battle?"

"Not exactly, but close enough." Michelle dragged the handkerchief half onto the wine cup. "When my people first investigated this technology, they could only see into the past, not travel there. They could chart the timelines, and by extrapolating, they could predict what might happen in the future. That's how we knew we faced attack sometime in the not too distant future."

"You could see the poison coming towards you, and guess that meant they would attack once you were weakened."

Gwyn beamed proudly at Isabel. Michelle laughed and nodded. "Very well. The poison is part of it—something about the Shift makes humans particularly violent on a large scale. It came in the twentieth century, and there were some terrible wars that encompassed the whole world."

Gwyn went quiet. "There sure were," she murmured.

Isabel looked at her, concerned. "Did you live through them? I thought you said your home was relatively peaceful."

"It is," Gwyn replied. "But it's still recent history, even if it was before I was born. Some really awful stuff went on that affected millions."

Isabel shook her head. "Millions of people. I can't fathom it."

"Well, it's the fate of billions now," Michelle said. She dragged the handkerchief further across the cup. "The energy ahead of the Shift, the water ahead of the poison, let us see and travel back in time. Now that the poison has reached certain parts of the stream, you can't go back and change its course. You have to jump ahead and control the water's flow where you can. The turning points are places where the stream might divert."

"Wouldn't diverting the poison be a good thing?" Isabel asked.

"Ah, that's where the analogy fails. The stream still needs to flow, your army still needs to drink. The poison will eventually flow past and come clean again, but if you divert the stream, parts of your army might not be able to reach it, so will be weakened when the inevitable attack comes." She looked at Gwyn, who raised a sardonic eyebrow.

"Yeah, I think we've reached the limit of our metaphor. It was good while it lasted." She covered Isabel's hand with her own and smiled.

Michelle whipped the handkerchief off her cup and took a drink. "Well, you wanted to know. And," she added quickly when she caught Gwyn's eye, "you do an amazing job of understanding these concepts, Isabel. I never expected to meet someone so bright and curious in this time."

Isabel blushed. "There is much to learn. It's overwhelming sometimes. At least I have some time to learn before I go to Gwyn's time."

"You're determined?" Michelle asked.

Gwyn and Isabel looked at each other. While holding hands they shared a look of such affection that Michelle felt a pang of bittersweet pleasure. *I helped bring them together—I should be satisfied, not envious.*

"I am determined," Isabel said softly. Gwyn's face was a picture of joy.

"Well, you don't have that much longer to wait." Michelle drained her cup. "We have one turning point left to go."

* * *

With the knowledge Michelle possessed from her computer, and Gwyn's examination of the timeline and the turning point, they determined that letters to the king would have the most significant effect. They rode to Madrid and skipped ahead to 1580 AD, where Juana's grandson Philip—named for her husband—ruled an empire that stretched from Austria to Portugal. The biggest thorn in his side was Elizabeth of England funding the Protestant rebellion in the Netherlands.

They chose spring for the warmer weather, though accommodation was at first difficult to find. Madrid's population had multiplied in recent years. On the north-west reaches of the great hill that housed the city, the palace-fortress overlooked the river below. Finding somewhere close had been challenging until Michelle made it clear they were happy to pay.

"Why did they think we wouldn't pay?" Gwyn whispered after their now-enthusiastic host had welcomed them in and shown them to the second story of his home, promising to send up hot food and wine shortly.

"Since Philip made Madrid the capital in 1560, the royal court is here much of the time," Michelle told them, crossing to the window and opening the shutters. "There wasn't enough space for all the nobles and their hangers-on at the palace, so he passed a law that private houses must accommodate members of the court."

"How rude," Gwyn commented, joining Michelle and peering down into the street. Fashionable men in ruffs and short ballooned breeches sauntered alongside well-dressed noblewomen in large farthingales.

"And I suppose those nobles are not obliged to pay." Isabel nudged Gwyn aside and took a look at the scene below them too. "Look at how everyone is wearing black—they must be very wealthy. What a shame to waste such money on clothes and not recompense the people who are forced to open their homes to you."

After dinner, they discussed the royal situation more. "Philip hates to delegate," Michelle told them. "The historical records of him complain that his attention to detail is 'a subject for regret'—he spends hours and hours working and insists that every report goes through him."

"So he's a micro-manager," Gwyn chimed in.

Isabel look perplexed. "Surely a king decrees what is to be done? You make him sound like a clerk."

Michelle smirked. "Maybe fewer people would want to be king or queen if they knew the work it entailed. Different monarchs rule differently. The best ones pay attention to what is going on in their kingdom. There are no days off, and while Philip had extensive training, there is hardly anyone in the world who will tell a king he is doing it wrong."

"What extensive training?" Gwyn asked.

"From the age of twelve his father had him sit in on councils, and as he grew older, Charles delegated more and more responsibility for different parts of the empire to Philip. It's an ideal upbringing for a king, but Philip's personality makes him obsessed with controlling the details."

"If King Philip wants to read every letter," Isabel said slowly, "How will we make sure our letters get read in time? They will be lost amongst the scores of others. And from whom are these letters meant to come?" She couldn't quite bring herself to speak of a monarch by his first name only.

"We can write and send ours ahead of time," Gwyn said excitedly. "We know some of what is going to happen, so ours will get in first."

Michelle nodded. "More importantly, I know the area we need to focus on—the Spanish Netherlands. We need to sow confusion and mistrust between generals and the king, forcing Philip to agonise over decisions and slow down the chain of command. This will be critical when he orders an armada to invade England."

"*That* armada?" Gwyn's eyes went wide.

"What is an armada?" Isabel wanted to know.

"Yes, *that* armada," Michelle replied. "It's a fleet of ships, a navy—Philip sends several over the years but the one that we're talking about, the 1588, is famous because it ended in disarray. Fireship attacks by the English, terrible storms. Through our letters, we have to ensure Philip appoints the Duke of Parma to lead the armada—Parma is a noble without naval experience."

"Plus he'll be hamstrung by needing to run everything back through Philip?" Gwyn nodded approvingly.

"Correct. I have a list of different possible correspondents—let's start drafting some letters."

With that, they spent several days outlining the known relationships between different members of the Spanish court and determined who might criticise or undermine each other. The actual sending of the forged letters proved the most exciting part of what was really a dull mission: Michelle and Gwyn disguised themselves as couriers and, under the colours of various nobles, handed over letters meant for the king at intervals between 1580 and 1588. Sometimes they delivered as many as three letters in what was only a few hours for them, but months apart in actual time. Michelle insisted on no more than three jumps in a day, then a day's break between, which left a considerable amount of time for Gwyn and Isabel to plan for their future.

"We'll need to get you a passport somehow," Gwyn worried one night. "Everyone needs proof of identity to travel between countries in my time, though we could probably get away with it in Europe for a while."

"I can help out with that," Michelle interjected, looking up. She had her wrist computer in front of her, projecting a tiny display of text and images as she continued to read up on everything she could find about the Spanish Armada.

"How?" Gwyn tapped her quill on the parchment in front of her. Various English words littered the page—she was teaching Isabel to read and speak it.

"Can you ple-ah-seh say that again?" Isabel read from a different page.

"Oh, those two letters together make an 'ee' sound," Gwyn correct. "Please, not ple-ah-seh."

"English is so inconsistent," Isabel muttered.

"Yeah, I know," Gwyn replied. "How can you help, Michelle?"

"The Agency carefully seeded resources wherever possible throughout history to provide a safety net for Agents," Michelle told her. "Particularly as we could only make time jumps, missions took months to complete and often required rest time, so some of the first missions were simply prep work to open bank accounts, hide portable assets and plant our own technology that could mimic current documentation. These were always backup measures—Agents got sent with whatever resources they could carry—but they did get used when things went wrong. I'm sure I'll be able to program something to work for Isabel."

"Oh." Gwyn sat open-mouthed. "That's... handy."

Michelle half-smiled. "It reinforces how well you've done, with no resources and no support. No wonder I was jealous of your ability."

Gwyn remembered to close her mouth after several more moments of gaping. She looked at Isabel, wondering if the other woman had heard. Isabel winked and mouthed, "I told you so."

When the turning point came, it was anti-climactic. Between the letters they had forged, the inexperience of the Duke of Parma, and Philip's own indecisiveness and obsession with controlling every detail, the Spanish Armada failed to invade England. When Gwyn sank into the timepiece to check the timeline ahead, the way was clear.

"No more turning points," she told the others when she opened her eyes. "I can see clearly through to my time, and yours after that, Michelle. Anything after where I've actually been is blurry."

"Yes, you can't travel past your own present by yourself. Only someone from the future can bring you into it, hence why we've been able to take Isabel with us." Michelle looked at Isabel. "You're a hundred years ahead of your own time, but you're about to go a lot further than that."

"I'm not afraid." Isabel smiled lovingly at Gwyn. "It is daunting, but I'm not alone." Gwyn grabbed her hand and kissed it.

Michelle grinned. It made her look years younger, and Gwyn realised how much Michelle had changed from the cocky, self-assured Agent she had met back at Masada.

"Hey, if you want to stay with us for a bit in our time, you know— after you've helped us with the passport stuff—you're more than welcome to," Gwyn offered. "Have a break before heading back to your time. Sounds like some serious shit is going to go down there. Though I guess you have people you want to see."

Michelle's grin faded, replaced by a strange look. "That would be nice," she said quietly.

Is that a tear in her eye? Gwyn had never seen Michelle cry.

The older woman cleared her throat. "Pack your things, only what you can carry—we'll worry about new outfits when we hit Gwyn's time. I'll go and settle the bill for the inn. Meet you back here in an hour. Then we go."

Thirty-Four

2011 AD

Gwyn had discussed it with Michelle and Isabel, and they agreed that two weeks before she had last left her time was ideal.

"You may feel queasy," Michelle advised, "because you already exist in this time. But you're over a thousand kilometres away and I have anti-nausea medication still. I was saving it for the Armada—in case we had to be on a ship."

"Thank god we didn't," Gwyn muttered. Then she thought about it. "Though it would have been cool to land at Tilbury and hear Elizabeth's speech. She's one queen I would have liked to meet.

A few hours later, in a quiet back street, the three women linked arms and made the jump.

Instead of a chorus of birds that usually met them when they jumped to the dawn, Gwyn heard a car beep in the distance. At the end of the street, a moped putted past, startling Isabel. "What was that?" she exclaimed, head snapping around.

"One of those motorised vehicles I told you about." Gwyn let go of Michelle. Isabel still clung tight. "It's early, but you'll see a lot of them soon."

"Come on." Michelle's tension was controlled, but visible all the same. "Let's source some clothes and locate the bank we need before it opens."

Isabel's jaw stayed dropped most of the day, and Gwyn could sympathise with every twitch and wide-eyed stare of astonishment. Even a slow morning in a major Spanish city was overwhelming—so many tall buildings, cars, motorbikes, scooters, mobile phones, radios, music, television screens.

"How… how do they not crash?" she said breathlessly. "How can they even concentrate?"

"Yeah, it's giving me a bloody headache," Gwyn muttered. She pulled at her jeans, feeling exposed with a t-shirt rather than a tunic. Isabel had blushed and muttered how indecent it felt to be wearing such a thin skirt when they had broken into a clothing store to acquire appropriate outfits. Michelle had casually left the last of her travelling stash of gold rings.

"Saves me pawning them for cash," she had said, ripping the store-tags off the clothes and placing them next to the rings on the counter. "Come on, let's jump a few days to throw any law enforcement off our trail."

The bank had been next, where Michelle had accessed an anonymous lock-box containing cash and cards that could be programmed to mimic identification and hack into electronic banking. Afterwards, they found a hotel with quiet rooms and Gwyn was delighted at the prospect of introducing Isabel to the wonders of modern plumbing.

"I'll be next door working on your passport," Michelle smiled at the excitement of the other two. "Restaurant is downstairs if you're hungry, charge it to the room; otherwise we can wander out later for dinner." She closed the door and left Gwyn and Isabel alone.

"This is wondrous," Isabel gushed. "Surely this is for kings and queens?"

Aware of how private they were, Gwyn pulled Isabel close and kissed her. "Come on—let me show you the shower."

* * *

Isabel woke in the night. She lay there, revelling in the softness of the bed, then glanced over at Gwyn, expecting to see her lover fast asleep. The moonlight that peeked in through the window showed Gwyn's eyes open, staring at the ceiling.

"Can you not sleep?" Isabel whispered.

Gwyn smiled, rolling to face Isabel. "Bed's too soft."

"And you are anxious about seeing your family again." Isabel could tell Gwyn's mind was far away. "They will be overjoyed to see you again."

"But it will only have been a few minutes for them. It's been… maybe a year for me. I've lost track. I don't even know how old I am now—twenty, maybe twenty-one?"

"You told me they are intelligent people. They will be able to tell you have been on a long journey, and they will welcome you home." Isabel prayed she was right. She also hoped Gwyn's family would accept her, a stranger, who barely spoke their language, who was overwhelmed with the newness and loudness of their world.

Gwyn stroked Isabel's face. "I've got you. Means I won't feel alone."

The rest of the week was spent familiarising Isabel with some basic survival skills in the modern world. A phone, paper money, how to cross the road without getting killed. Gwyn's favourite part was taking both Michelle and Isabel to get gelato every day. Isabel's eyes had widened like a child's when she tasted ice cream for the first time, and they enjoyed trying different flavours. Isabel grew confident practising her modern Spanish on the shopkeepers.

"We never worked out how to get this out of me," Gwyn mentioned to Michelle as they sat at an outdoor table in a plaza, waiting for Isabel to bring back dessert.

"The chronokinetor? Yes—I am sorry about that. But if I take you forward to my time, you'll never be able to get back to now. At least, until the Shift is over, and I don't know when that'll be." Michelle fanned herself with a table coaster, watching people amble past.

"It's okay." Gwyn shrugged. "I like the translation aspect of it. I guess I'll just have to make sure I don't abuse the whole persuasion thing."

Michelle gazed at Gwyn solemnly. "You have a better moral compass than me, Gwyn. You will be fine."

Gwyn blushed as Isabel returned triumphantly. "They didn't ask me to repeat myself at all! I have iced lemon, vanilla coconut and something called English Soup." She offered a tiny plastic spoon to Gwyn, who tasted it.

"Tastes like… trifle, I think?" They enjoyed the gelato and talked. Despite the anxiety of seeing her family again soon, Gwyn had never felt such a degree of contented companionship between them all. Michelle caught her eye and smiled sadly.

"I might even miss you two," the older woman said.

Gwyn rolled her eyes. "Don't get all soppy on us." She beamed at Michelle, feeling a warm glow that wasn't just from the afternoon sun hitting their table. Isabel smiled knowingly before stealing the last of Gwyn's gelato.

Two days later they flew to Rome. Isabel's hand never left Gwyn's, who reassured her that plenty of people were scared of flying and no one would question it. She was grateful to have Isabel to comfort—it distracted her from the sense of queasiness that grew every moment they drew closer to Italy.

"Shall we go straight there?" Michelle asked, eyeing Gwyn as they landed. "You said you arrive in Rome with your family tomorrow—we might as well jump to just after you left, spare you any more proximity sickness."

Gwyn nodded, swallowing hard. "Will you… jump straight on?"

Michelle hesitated. "I can if you want. I… I'd like to meet them, though." They disembarked the plane and made their way to the taxi rank. Michelle kept talking. "You know how we suspect there's a genetic link between us? Well, suppose there is—that makes you my only known family."

"Oh!" It hadn't occurred to Gwyn that Michelle might want to explore that connection.

They negotiated a fare with a driver and piled into the back of a dented hatchback.

"I'd like you to stay," Isabel declared, gripping the handle above the passenger door as they hurtled around corners, their driver beeping and gesticulating while loud pop music played. "I know you need to return to your own time, but perhaps you can help convince Gwyn's family to believe her." She smiled at Gwyn. "Though I imagine you are far more experienced at convincing people of things than you were when you first told them."

A year ago, Gwyn would have insisted she could manage herself.

Now she nodded. "I would like that."

When they reached the Colosseum, they took the time to visit the ruin. "It's a dull shell compared to when it was freshly built," Gwyn told them, describing what she remembered from walking past the amphitheatre in ancient Rome. "It was white and shiny and seemed lot larger," she said. Turning away from it, Gwyn faced the path up onto the Palatine Hill. "Up there," she pointed. "Three days from now."

Isabel took one hand, and Michelle the other. Together the women climbed the hill. Gwyn's mind tried to piece together the halls and columns from memory. "It was so clean and colourful," she murmured. Then she remembered the colour of Emperor Domitian's blood and lurched. Her friends steadied her. Gwyn straightened her shoulders. "Let's do this."

They found a secluded corner of the palace ruins, away from other tourists, and joined hands again. Gwyn closed her eyes and concentrated, feeling along the timeline for the moment she had left, then choosing a minute after that, just to be safe. They jumped.

Flick.

* * *

Her mother's voice was the first thing Gwyn heard. She sounded panicked, yelling—Gwyn could hear her father shouting about calling the police. *How weird—mum and dad are pretty calm types, normally. Guess me disappearing in front of their eyes, rattled them.*

She glanced at Michelle and Isabel. The former gave a solemn nod, while the latter smiled nervously. Refusing to let go of either of them, Gwyn walked out to meet her parents.

Her sister Naomi saw her first. "Gwyn!" She hurtled forward, arms outstretched. The next few moments were a collision of hugs, exclamations and confused questions from Maria, the tour guide.

"She is not missing? No police?"

"She's fine," Gwyn heard Michelle say in Italian. "We might end the tour here if that's alright—here's a tip."

Gwyn was too busy being smothered by her parents to apologise to the guide. "I'm fine, Mum. Dad, I'm fine. Calm down, I'm here, I'm fine." She was crying, and laughed, hugging her brother and sister. "God, I've missed you guys."

"Missed us?" Her brother Justin sounded confused.

"She did the thing!" Naomi bounced excitedly. "She did the time-travel thing! It's true—you saw her disappear!"

Gwyn's parents drew back and exchanged a look. Gwyn used the breathing space to locate Isabel and Michelle. "Mum, Dad, Naomi, Justin—this is Michelle and Isabel. I think we should find somewhere to sit down and have a chat—I've got a lot to tell you."

Thirty-Five

2011 AD

Tell them she did, with some details omitted. Isabel watched, fascinated, as they crowded into Gwyn's parents' hotel room and Stephen and Danielle Turner reacted incredulously to the tale.

"Surely it's impossible," Stephen said for what seemed like the tenth time. Isabel caught the irritated glances Gwyn's brother and sister shot their father. *They believe her. Why don't her parents? Gwyn said her time was more open-minded than my own.*

Gwyn flushed and Isabel wondered if her lover was about to lose her temper. "What would you rather, Dad? That I've been taking drugs and this is all a hallucination? Michelle and Isabel are pretty real figments of my imagination. Or are they drug addicts too?"

Her father flushed and his wife looked alarmed. Michelle stood. "Stephen, Danielle, may I interject?" Everyone looked at her. "I know this is a lot to take in. I propose conducting a scientific demonstration to help you understand, because Gwyn has been through some majorly traumatic events in the last year. Your scepticism, while extremely natural, is not particularly useful in supporting Gwyn to return to normal life in this time."

Gwyn's lips went tight, then she sighed. "Thanks, Michelle," she said in a low voice.

Gwyn's mother placed a hand on her husband's arm. "Let's hear them out, Stephen. You know Gwyn's not the wild type."

"You're the one who suggested she see a psychologist," he grumbled. "Alright, what's this demonstration?"

Michelle smiled. "Thank you. Stephen, may I borrow your watch? And would someone else keep time?"

Baffled, Stephen removed the band from his wrist and handed it to Michelle. Danielle fished a slim, rectangular device from her pocket. "I have a timer on my phone. Will that do?"

"Excellent." Michelle showed everyone the face of the circle. Isabel saw numbers. *A watch, she called it. It must tell the time!* "It has just turned 11:53am. I'm going to time-jump one minute into the future. Danielle, please time sixty seconds." Isabel saw the familiar blue haze rise around Michelle. When it faded, she had vanished.

"Cool!" Gwyn's younger siblings chorused. Isabel smiled. Gwyn sat back on her small armchair and crossed her arms, raising an eyebrow. Perched on the chair's padded arm, Isabel squeezed Gwyn's shoulder in support. A curious look came over Danielle Turner's face, and Isabel blushed. She must remember that people in this time would be far quicker to assume she and Gwyn were lovers if they showed physical affection. *But that is alright. They are more accepting, Gwyn said. Mostly.* Isabel dropped her hand, conflicted.

The minute dragged. Stephen Turner waved his hand in the spot Michelle had been, an intent look on his face. "Incredible," he muttered.

"Honey, maybe move back," Danielle warned. The corners of Gwyn's lips turned up. Justin and Naomi watched with eagerness, leaning forward from their spot against the bathroom door.

The blue cloud appeared, and Michelle in it. Unflustered, she handed the watch to Stephen and said, "11:53am still, and will be for another fifty seconds."

Gwyn's father stared at the device. He mouthed the numbers as he counted.

"Now, I could have adjusted the time on your watch; obviously this is not a controlled experiment, but I hope it goes some way to convincing you that Gwyn is, indeed, telling the truth." Michelle resumed her seat in the matching armchair next to Isabel.

When Gwyn's father looked up, his eyes were alight with the kind of fever that reminded Isabel of the priest who had tried to burn her. Her stomach clenched. "This is incredible," Stephen declared. "This will change the face of science for–"

"You also understand," Michelle overrode him, "why this information will not leave this room. I will soon return to my time. Gwyn will be left with the chronokinetor, but should you try to advise the wider scientific community they will treat her as an experiment, and she will never have peace. Isabel has come forward to this time, and I have arranged certain documentation so she may start a life here, but again, if you try to tell people, they will either disbelieve you, or conduct experiments on her."

Isabel squirmed at the thought of being locked in a room for people to poke and prod. Scientist or priest, a fanatic was a fanatic. Gwyn noticed her stir and reached for Isabel's hand. "I won't let that happen to us," she promised.

"Why are you leaving the chronokinetor with Gwyn," Danielle Turner asked. Unlike most people, she pronounced the name of the device perfectly. Her troubled eyes gathered in the sight of her daughter, not missing the way she leaned towards Isabel. She gave Isabel a small, sad smile.

"Yeah, why?" Gwyn's sister wanted to know. "If you just took it back to your time, there will be no proof."

Michelle nodded, acknowledging their questions. "Somehow it fused to her. It was originally tuned to me, but we think we share a genetic link. When Gwyn did a thing that no one else has done, jump in time *and* space, it bonded with her physically, and I can't take her forward to my time to try to remove it, because as we explained before, time-travel into the past is now impossible. She would have no way of getting back."

"When did I do that?" Gwyn sounded puzzled.

Michelle smiled. "On Vivaldis, when we were trapped in that cell. You jumped back to the Agency and got Brrrys."

"Oh!" Gwyn looked at the timepiece in her hand then grinned at her siblings. "Wait till I tell you about the aliens."

"Aliens!" Justin and Naomi exclaimed.

"Genetic link?" Stephen Turner asked.

Danielle rose from the edge of the bed where she had been sitting and crossed to stand in front of Michelle, examining her intently. "I can see it. You look just like a photo of my grandmother. Incredible. How many generations must it be?"

Michelle shrugged. "Six hundred years' worth. I was raised by the state, so I never knew my parents."

Danielle leaned down and hugged Michelle. "Thank you for bringing my girl home." She straightened and looked at Isabel. "And you have come from the past to be with my daughter."

Isabel blushed. "She is very special to me."

Danielle smiled and hugged Isabel too. "Then you're welcome to our family too."

Comprehension dawned on Stephen Turner's face and he grinned goofily. "Alright. But can I ask questions in the meantime? Just for our own satisfaction?"

"Please?" Danielle added, seemingly satisfied that her daughter's state-of-mind was no longer in danger. "It isn't our area of speciality, so there's not much danger of us influencing the field."

"Of course." Michelle stood. "How about we do it over lunch?"

"Oh, thank God!" Gwyn practically leapt out of her chair, dragging Isabel with her. "I'm starving."

* * *

Several days later, Michelle farewelled Isabel and the Turners on the Palatine Hill as the sun set over Rome. Gwyn struggled to not cry, and Michelle found herself hugging the younger woman tightly, speaking in a gruff voice. "Can't thank you enough for everything you did. You've given my world a fighting chance."

"It's so hard not knowing what's going to happen to you," Gwyn sniffed. Her tears shone gold on her face as other tourists snapped photos of the city before the light died.

Michelle patted her back. "I'll be fine—I'm a survivor, just like you." She looked at Isabel. "And you. Good luck. It'll be hard for you sometimes, but I'm sure it'll be worth it."

The rest of the Turners stood back awkwardly. Despite her best attempts to be congenial, Michelle recognised that she didn't have the genuine openness that Isabel possessed—an openness that won Gwyn's family's affections quite quickly. Michelle bowed to them formally, already assuming the social behaviour of her own time and abandoning the past.

"Remember to look for our letters," Gwyn said. "I hope they last."

"I will." The final rays of sunlight threw themselves into the pink sky. "Take care of yourself." There was nothing more to be said. Michelle jumped.

Flick. Flick. Flick. Fli-fli-fli…

Thirty-Six

2623 AD

Thunder boomed and Michelle was soaked in a deluge of rain. She jerked at the cold, then laughed. *Never count on the weather.* She would have to buy another all-weather, temperature controlled, adjustable jacket—her last one had been lost on her mission to rescue Owen.

Owen. Was he still in the past, where the Earth First fanatics had kidnapped him to study astronomical patterns of the nineteenth century? The Shift had come before, in that time, and Earth had almost wiped itself out because of it. Every turning point she knew of was fixed now, but she still had to contend with Earth First now that she had foiled their plans to change history.

She needed to contact Dirk Tokoyashi. She hoped he and Hanli had escaped the attack on their ship—Michelle had jumped back in time to Renaissance Italy, so didn't know if they were dead or under arrest. She wanted to contact Brrrys. She missed his support and comradery. She would ask if he wanted a more formal relationship when she saw him next.

She picked her way carefully down through the garden that covered the Palatine Hill. A handful of ruins existed still, not nearly as many as in Gwyn's time. Climate change had not been kind to them. At an all-night coms-café she slouched into a private booth. Keying an interstellar address, she wiped her hands through her hair, aware she must resemble a bedraggled Mayash that had been rolling in a puddle.

The centre circle of the com's holo-projector lit up. A creature that looked like a bipedal dragonfly clicked and chittered as it faced Michelle. "Agent Michelle," the Shanista scientist said. "Have you been away long?"

"Citizen Colsa," Michelle bowed, even though holo-communication etiquette didn't typically include such a formal expression of greeting. "I have been away… for quite some time. I think I succeeded. How are things here?"

"Troubled. There have been many attacks and arrests on Earth—the rest of the Allied Planets watches with interest."

"Attacks?"

"Extremists of the Earth First movement have staged violent acts towards non-human citizens. There have been several deaths, and while the perpetrators have been arrested and charged with hate crimes, they continue to speak out with apocalyptic rhetoric. We have been hoping for your return to make a public announcement."

"About what, exactly?" Michelle's trust in the Shanista had been shaken, despite being told they hadn't known the Shift was engineered until recently. What did they intend to tell the worlds?

Colsa clicked, points of light from the holo-projector peeking through its image as it cocked its head. "The truth. However, we need one more citizen to bear witness."

"Owen."

Colsa clicked in the affirmative. "He is in this time, on Earth. Thanks to the terrorist attacks by Earth First and evidence you collected linking the Fitz family to the extremists, the Earth government has frozen their assets and is seizing evidence all over the planet. But they cannot find Owen. We can, but have been reticent to interfere because of the turmoil that still exists over the investigation into the Agency. I will transmit you Owen's co-ordinates. You will need to get in where the Earth law-enforcers cannot, and retrieve Owen."

Michelle remembered her 'rescue' of Owen in nineteenth-century Argentina. "He didn't want to come last time. Are you telling me to kidnap him?"

"No." The click that accompanied it was emphatic. "That would be unethical. Persuade him."

Anger surged through Michelle. "Almost everything I've done in all my missions has been unethical. I've murdered people, lied to people, stolen from them—why is our time any different? Those humans in the past were still people. 'The end justifies the means' has been used to excuse some of the worst crimes in history—you just don't want to look bad in front of the Allied Planets!' The accusation hung in the air.

Colsa couldn't sigh, not like a human could, but its wings drooped. "This is true. You know why, though. We need to be united if we are to survive the war to come. Earth First's actions will cause the other members of the Allied Planets to doubt humans. You must show them differently."

Michelle ground her teeth. "Send me the co-ordinates."

Colsa bowed its insectile head. "Transmitting. Take him to Berlin once you have found him. Oh, and, Agent Michelle…"

"Yes?" Michelle's hand already hovered over the key to disconnect the com.

"We discovered something from the blood sample we had taken from young Gwyn when she was in our time."

"There's a genetic link? We guessed that." In that moment Michelle was uninterested, but Colsa's next words shook her.

"She is your mother's mother. There are only two generations between you."

* * *

How would it be possible? The question buzzed in Michelle's head despite her efforts to shove it aside and focus on her mission. Distraction could be fatal. Every time she had gone up against Earth First, she had been severely injured or almost killed. What did Colsa think she could achieve alone?

I wish Gwyn were here. She had to laugh at that. She was a far cry from the angry, single-minded Agent of months past, carrying the weight of the worlds on her shoulders. She wanted help and was not upset by that fact.

Michelle gazed out the com-café window at a rain-swept Rome. Lights outlined several buildings nearby; several hover-cars navigated the sky despite the weather. She inhaled the steam from her tea, glad to be in a time where alcohol wasn't the primary choice of beverage.

"You need a dry shirt, Citizen?" A man emerged from a booth, looking at Michelle's bedraggled state.

"Thanks, I'm fine."

The man shrugged and pulled his own coat on, activating the water-repelling field on it as he stepped towards the café door.

"Wait!" Michelle turned on her stool. The man paused. Michelle drummed her fingers on the table. "I need you to call the police to arrest me. Please."

* * *

"I have been following the furore regarding time-travel, of course," Commissioner Singh said, gazing at Michelle as she sat across from her in the police hover-car. "You are telling me you breached the ban to travel into the past, and that is how you obtained knowledge relating to the whereabouts of one Owen Chang."

"Correct," Michelle replied.

"We have raided the Fitz' Paris mansion, and found nothing and no one of note. Already they are claiming to have been duped into financing terrorist activities." Singh sounded exasperated. "They'll be prosecuted, of course, but without sufficient evidence against them only lesser charges will stick."

"Trust me," Michelle looked at the Commissioner seriously. "Find Owen Chang, and you'll have all the evidence you need."

She had used every ounce of persuasiveness she possessed to talk the arresting police into contacting the officer in charge of the investigation. She would have called on Dirk Tokoyashi but until she had spoken to the Commissioner she hadn't even known if the director was alive.

They flew through the night, Michelle watching Singh surreptitiously. The Commissioner was a plump, dark woman with a commanding presence. She wore the dark blue uniform of the Earth police with a bright pink scarf embroidered with elephants, and spoke Hindi quietly into her com. Michelle could get by in Hindi, and her chronokinetor made fluency easy, so she switched to that language.

"Commissioner, it's possible I will be recognised if I don't disguise myself, and that may ruin any element of surprise."

Singh appraised Michelle—dry now but still unkempt. There was no way she could pass for a police officer. The Commissioner's eyes flared and she unwound her scarf. "Cover your face with this. I'll pretend you're my translator."

Michelle thought it unlikely that any police commissioner reached that rank without speaking all four major Earth languages, but didn't have a better plan. She hoped the element of surprise would allow them to enter the mansion and blitz past any opposition to find Owen, even if he was in a secret room.

It played out far more simply than that. A robot butler answered the door and its protests that the 'master' was not at home to visitors were overridden. Singh barked out law enforcement protocol that forced the robot to comply, and it led them through the ostentatious house— complete with restored historical tapestries and antique furniture—with a series of sad beeps as it whirred along on its wheels. Every time Singh questioned it as to the whereabouts of the listed owner of the mansion, Jaysen Fitz, it repeated, "The master is not home."

"Someone's done a good job programming it," muttered one of Singh's offsiders, striding alongside his superior while Michelle overtook the robot.

"This way," she said, consulting her wrist computer. "Downstairs and to our left."

They came to a room with a locked door. Singh ordered the robot butler to open it. "Only the master has the authorisation to enter," it said mechanically. "The master is not home."

"Enough!" Singh gestured to a fellow officer. He marched to the door and affixed a specialised computer to the lock, then loaded a crystal into it. The lock buzzed and released. Michelle sighed in relief—there were advantages to official law enforcement. They had the power to override any private security system, though it was only ever exercised under warrant. Singh nodded to Michelle, who pressed the button to slide the door open and strode into the dark room beyond… where she was almost brained by a stool swung at her by a panicky, and fortunately ineffective, assailant. She ducked, grabbed the stool and thrust her attacker back, then Singh's officers rushed forward. "Stop!" Michelle yelled as she activated her wrist light. "It's him, it's Owen Chang!"

The officers halted, each of them grasping one of Owen's arms firmly while the man himself, gasped and sobbed, hanging limply between them. "Please don't kill me," he begged, crying.

Singh moved into the room. "We're here to rescue you, Citizen Owen. Agent Michelle led us here—it appears Jaysen Fitz has fled."

Owen lifted bloodshot eyes and recognised Michelle. "You came back for me," he sobbed. "Thank you."

Thirty-Seven

2623 AD

Despite being unable to locate certain members of the Fitz family, the case proceeded swiftly once Owen's critical testimony was given. Michelle spent hours giving statements, footage of which appeared in the news releases issued throughout the Allied Planets. The motivation behind the Time-Space Agency was made clear to the public for the first time—that the correction of aberrant historical turning points was not just in reaction to a natural phenomenon, but that the Shift had been engineered by an alien species on the far side of the galaxy to weaken them.

Thanks to the careful broadcast and the inherent trust in the Shanista as the leaders of the Allied Planets, most worlds galvanised to face the looming threat, despite the alarm. Michelle found herself feted as a hero, Owen, a tortured survivor.

"It's strange," Michelle muttered to Brrrys as he accompanied her to one of the oldest still-operational banks in London. "I'm used to staying in the shadows, and now people know me wherever I go."

"You should be recognised for what you've done," he purred, wrapping a proud tail around her waist as they walked. He had shown his delight most imaginatively when Michelle had proposed an exclusive and more formal relationship, and it comforted her. She would be glad to return to Vivaldis, where strange looks at an inter-species relationship were far less likely than they were on Earth. She just had one last errand to complete.

Inside the bank, Brrrys took a com from Director Dirk Tokoyashi, who was to accompany them back to Vivaldis. Michelle waited impatiently to access a screen, then tapped out her request. A robotic voice told her to wait as a human clerk would need to attend to her.

Would anything have even survived this long? So many things could have gone wrong—what kind of bank carries letters for six hundred years?

"Citizen, sorry, Agent Michelle?" An orange-robed clerk appeared in a doorway. "Would you mind coming through to a private office? We have something that might fit your request but it will take some time to retrieve."

"Sure." Michelle signalled Brrrys, who nodded and carried on his conversation, indicating he would wait for her. She followed the clerk into a glass-walled room.

"Please," the clerk indicated a seat. The chair moulded itself to Michelle's body when she sat, making her feel trapped.

"I'm sorry," she said, getting up. "I'd prefer to stand."

The clerk raised his thin eyebrows and tapped at a screen on the table in the centre of the room. The glass walls turned cloudy, blocking the outside view. "I've sent someone to fetch the archive box. While we wait, I need to run some identification checks."

She frowned. She had identified herself already.

"What was the name of the Roman Emperor who was assassinated in 96 AD?"

Had she heard correctly? "Flavius Domitianus."

"Which Wallachian Prince was raised in the Ottoman Empire, but later fought against it?"

"Vlad Dracula."

"What is the name of the small mesa in the Negev Desert?"

"Masada."

The clerk nodded seriously. "You pass the identification test. How interesting—I've seen the use of secret questions before but they are an archaic form of security. Please wait here while we bring the archive box."

He left the room. The minutes stretched. Michelle paced. When the door reopened she whirled and hovered edgily as the clerk placed a slim, metal folder on the table. He tapped in a code and it opened, the sides folding up and over to reveal a sealed plastic sleeve.

"I'll give you some privacy," the clerk said. "Please use the com on the screen there if you need anything."

Alone, Michelle stared at the thick plastic. She examined the seal— some kind of glue—then applied gentle pressure. It cracked easily, no doubt weakened from the centuries it sat in the bank. The paper envelopes inside were soft and Michelle realised that, in removing them from their airtight home she might destroy them. Despite that, she drew the top one out. It was labelled: *Read this first.*

Opening it, she drew forth several sheets of paper, the typed words faded but still clear.

Dear Michelle,

If you're reading this, then our plan worked. I hope these last—I thought about recording video or audio but didn't know if you would have the technology to play something so old. So letters it is.

It's been three months since we returned to this time…

AUTHOR'S NOTE

Thus ends the Turning Points series, though it won't be the last I write about these characters. They are a part of my life—for the last six years I have travelled with them on adventures into the past, and I shall continue to do so in the future.

Spain is the only country where I haven't been to most of the places I write about, but fortunately I was able to call on a friend who lives in Bilbao, to give me information about the climate and geography of the city. The rest was a lot of research online and in books, to try to ensure the distances, the weather and the landscapes were accurate. Any mistakes are, of course, my own.

The history of this period is fascinating. Originally I wanted to write about Queen Isabella, a formidable monarch who ruled Castile in her own right and instigated the unification of Spain by marrying Ferdinand of Aragon. Together they drove out the Moors, sponsored Christopher Columbus, and married their children into royal houses all over Europe, spreading their reach and influence.

This empire building marked the start of extreme religious intolerance in Spain, and I didn't find Isabella so inspiring after all, despite her strength. Queen Isabella and King Ferdinand were named 'the most Catholic Kings'—they started the Spanish Inquisition to root out heresy and find Jews and Muslims who pretended to convert to Christianity in order to not be expelled from the country. The invasion of the Americas by Europeans led to the decimation of native peoples and the destruction of their cultures. I touch lightly on the Inquisition as a thematic background, but focus mostly on the dynastic elements of the

Queen and King's marriage, namely, Juana of Castile.

Juana, called "the Mad", was third in line for the throne of Castile, but due to the untimely deaths of her older brother and sister, she became queen upon the death of her mother Isabella. Despite the law that allowed women to inherit, there were many who did not feel Juana was suitable to rule, particularly her father. Considering how well it suited Ferdinand to have Juana declared unfit for the throne, it is entirely possible he put about the rumours of madness, and natural prejudice did the rest. I've taken the theory further, and questioned whether Juana wanted to live up to the illustrious reputation of her mother, though in reality it is more likely she was driven out by her own family. Certainly after Ferdinand died and her son Charles made no effort to restore his mother's rule.

A cruel tale, but one I have done my best to make accurate. I brought forward the siege of Viana by a number of months to put pressure on Gwyn and Michelle, and introduced willow bark tea several hundred years before recorded use in Europe, but apart from that, I have strived to keep times and places as close to recorded history as possible.

The title is a deliberate misquote of Elizabeth I's famous speech at Tilbury, because I believe it takes more courage to be a queen than a king, because you are fighting against greater odds.

Sometimes, such as in Juana's case, the odds are simply stacked too greatly, but this story is also commentary on a woman's right to choose.

I hope you enjoyed the tale! Please leave a review on Goodreads or Amazon, or you can get in touch with me via my website: www.jodielane.com or through my Facebook page: AuthorJodieLane.

If you have read this far you deserve a reward. I still get complaints about killing off Meric in Renaissance Woman, so if you want to find out what happens after A Soldier's Love, go to jodielane.com/product/soldierhonour/ and use the voucher SOLDIERHONOUR to receive the free short story featuring Meric and Mikhail.

ABOUT THE AUTHOR

Jodie Lane is an avid amateur historian, combining her love of travel and adventure with fascinating stories from the past. Brisbane based, she studied a variety of modern history at the University of Queensland, and loves to read a wide range of historical and science fiction.

Her travels have taken her all over the world: she has lived and taught English in China and Romania, backpacked through Europe and South America, and holidayed in the Middle East, Central and North America, South East Asia, New Zealand and South Africa. She speaks basic Spanish as a second language and is currently raising two small humans with her husband, Dan.

Heart and Stomach of a Queen is the fifth book in "Turning Points"—a time travel adventures series visiting pivotal historical events and exploring an exciting new future for humanity. *The Siege of Masada, Transylvanian Knight, To Kill An Emperor* and *Renaissance Woman* precede it. Turning Points short stories include "The Time Traveller's Date" (*Futurevision*), "Siege of the Heart", "A Soldier's Love" and "A Soldier's Honour".

Other short stories include "The Job", "Naughty Zombies" (*Obliquity*) and "The Voice" (*Evil Inside Us*).

You can find out more via www.jodielane.com or like her Facebook page www.facebook.com/authorjodielane.

BIBLIOGRAPHY

Camino de Santiago.
https://www.google.com/maps/d/u/0/viewer?ie=UTF8&t=h&oe=UTF8&msa=0
&mid=1lNtYJflLKyUQzwBIbBie6C8Ij2E&ll=42.78111641406656%2C-
7.4967103550920918&z=9

Camino de Santiago: Medieval Route.
https://en.wikipedia.org/wiki/Camino_de_Santiago#Medieval_route

Cavendish, Richard. **Death of Cesare Borgia.**
https://www.historytoday.com/archive/months-past/death-cesare-borgia

Hunt, Jocelyn. 2001. **Spain 1474-1598**. London: Routledge.

Kilsby, Jill. 1989. **Spain: Rise and Decline, 1474-1643**. London: Hodder &
Stoughton.

Moldoveanu, Dragoş. **The Downfall and Death of Cesare Borgia.**
https://www.elsborja.cat/blog/the-downfall-and-the-death-of-cesare-borgia/
2017

Native Language of Philip I of Castile.
http://www.theroyalforums.com/forums/f164/native-language-of-philip-i-of-
castile-philip-the-handsome-37484.html

Prescott, William H. 1962. **History of the Reign of Ferdinand and Isabella the
Catholic.** London: George Allen & Unwin Ltd.

Ridgway, Claire. **The Madness of Juana of Castile.**
https://www.tudorsociety.com/madness-juana-castile/ 2017

Spanish Currency History. https://www.donquijote.org/spanish-
culture/history/spanish-currency/

The Death of Cesare Borgia. https://theborgiabull.com/2013/03/12/the-death-
of-cesare-borgia/ 2013

The Complete Guide to Galicia.
https://www.independent.co.uk/travel/europe/the-complete-guide-to-galicia-
591181.html

Weissberger, Barbara F. 2008. **Queen Isabel I of Castile: Power, Patronage,
Persona**. Woodbridge: Tamesis.